The Retreat

Chris Ramsden

ISBN: 978-0-578-32388-6

Printed in the United States of America

Dedicated to Robert Ramsden

CHAPTER 1:

The Text

———

*D*ING. *DING. DING. DING.* A CELL-PHONE ALARM DISRUPTED THE QUIET morning and lit up the nearly pitch-black, curtain-drawn bedroom. *Ding. Ding. Ding. Ding.* Bill Foster let out a groan; he had never been an early riser. *Ding. Ding. Ding. Ding.* He slowly rolled over in bed and reached toward the nightstand. *Ding. Ding. Ding. Ding.* Bill fumbled around for several seconds before finding the correct button to silence the alarm. He lay facedown in the peace and quiet and dark, fighting to keep his eyelids from closing. It would be so easy to just go back to sleep, but Bill had school in an hour.

The senior rolled his body into a hunched over sitting position, his face only an inch or two from his knees, and ran his hands through his long, disheveled, dark-brown hair. He pulled his shoulder blades together, arched his back, let his neck hang backward and let out a grunt. The high school finish line was close; less than three months to go. Bill brought his head forward and was blinded by a small beam of sunlight that snuck through the gap where the curtains had been crudely taped to the wall. He reapplied the tape, pressing it down hard against the wall until his fingers hyperextended and began to hurt. The room plunged into heavenly darkness. After his eyes adjusted, he grabbed his phone and saw a text from his mother that read, 'Went to the hospital. Will call you later.' Bill's stomach turned over; the text had been sent almost four hours ago. Bill dropped his hand in his lap, and the phone slowly slid from his grasp onto the bed. He stared forward, now wide awake. He had been dreading this for weeks. Tears began to well up in his eyes before Bill summoned the courage to

1

pick the phone back up and call his mom. It rang a few times—the countdown to a conversation he didn't want to have.

"Hello," Bill's mom softly answered.

"Hey. How's he doing?"

CHAPTER 2:
Mourning

BILL STARED NUMBLY AT THE WATCH ON HIS LEFT WRIST AS HE SAT ON the side of his bed, feet resting on the floor. He had inherited the watch from his grandfather, who had inherited it from his father. Bill had never been interested in watches, but during the last week of his life, his grandpa had given him a brief rundown on the family heirloom and how to wind it. Bill wasn't exactly sure why he needed this lesson; he had figured the watch would end up around his eldest uncle's wrist, as he was the next male in line, and after all, Bill wasn't even a true male descendant in this family. Bill had been completely shocked when his grandpa offered the watch—such an important piece of family history—to him. He had tried to talk his grandpa out of it, but he insisted, and Bill accepted the watch.

Bill ran his hands over the dark-brown leather attached to the gold metallic trim that encircled a white face set with gold numbers in a gothic font. He watched the tiny seconds hand wind around the small face where the number six would normally be. It was a beautiful watch, and Bill was honored and terrified to possess it. He hadn't been able to bring himself to wear it. Instead, he kept it in a small drawer atop his dresser. This was the first time he had put it on.

His mom had just told him his grandpa had passed during the night—the disease that had ravaged him for over a year had finally taken him. Bill had known this was coming, and thought he had prepared himself, but it still hurt far more than he could imagine. His mom tried her best to console him over the phone, and Bill did the same for her.

Bill's mom and her siblings would be busy for the next few hours making the wake and funeral arrangements. She had already called the school and let them know he would not be in attendance that day. Bill wanted to make himself useful and asked if there was anything he could do. His mom said they had everything taken care of for now, but once they were done at the funeral home, the family would head over to Bill's grandparents for dinner. He would meet them over there.

Bill texted his oldest friend Matt about what had happened and let him know he couldn't drive him to school today. Matt's response came up on the screen. 'No problem. I'm really sorry. Let me know if you need anything.' *Just words*, Bill thought—the right words, but they didn't mean much or make him feel any better.

Bill passed the next few hours the best he could watching TV and playing video games, just trying to keep his mind occupied. When the time finally came, he put on some jeans and his favorite black zip-up hoodie and left his house. The sun shone brightly in the late afternoon sky, giving the impression it was warmer than it actually was. Bill immediately felt a chill upon closing the door. Spring wasn't quite there yet.

Even though Bill only lived four blocks from his grandparents, he always drove when he went over to mow the lawn or move something heavy or to accomplish whatever chore they had for him. He stared at the small, green sedan parked on the street next to the curb. It had been his grandfather's car until he upgraded to a new one and gifted the green sedan to Bill. It wasn't great by any means, but it made the five-mile trip back and forth to school, which was all he needed it to do. Today, however, Bill decided to walk.

The walk flew by, and Bill found himself standing at the door of his grandparents' house—the house he and his mother had lived in for the first nine years of his life. He didn't hear anything inside. He hesitated to knock, praying for the butterflies to leave his stomach. He hoped that he was all cried out, and he would be able to keep his emotions in check in front of his family. He knocked on the door and slowly pushed it open to see his family gathered in the living room. They all said hello, and his mom rose from the couch next to his grandmother to give him a hug. Bill walked over to the couch from which his grandmother was slowly lifting herself. Bill sniffled and held back tears as he hugged his grandmother. He hated seeing that pain in her eyes. His grandmother just kept asking if he was okay.

All of the arrangements had been made. The wake would be in two days with the funeral the following day. The rest of the evening was spent looking through old photos of his grandfather to add to the collages that would be on display at the funeral home. Bill picked out his favorite: He and his grandfather had just returned to the dock, and Bill stood in the boat, proud to show off his catch with his grandfather smiling in the background. There were plenty of stories and laughs, and the chosen pictures were glued to the boards. The aunts and uncles left one by one to go home and console their own families. Bill and his mom were the last to leave. Once in the car, Bill's mom turned to her son and asked, "Are you sure you're okay?"

Bill continued to look forward and nodded. "Yeah, I think so." He turned to his mom. "Are you okay?"

"Yeah."

Nothing else was said, and they drove the three minutes home.

"Can you check to see if your suit fits?" Bill's mom asked as they walked to the front door.

"I'm pretty sure it doesn't. I haven't worn it in a few years."

"Well, let's see."

Bill went to his bedroom closet and pulled the dangling light switch. He flipped through the various fancy shirts and trousers he never wore and finally came to the suit. It looked small as he pulled it out of the closet and held the pants to his legs.

He put it on and found his mom in the kitchen. "I don't think this is going to work."

Bill's mom turned to him and burst out in laughter. The suit was two inches short in both the arms and legs. "We'll go tomorrow after school."

Bill was happy he could make his mom laugh.

Bill decided to return to school the next day. His mom had given him the option with the blessing of the school to take the week off until after the funeral, but he hoped getting back to normal would make him feel a little better. Bill had forgotten to do laundry and thrashed through his hamper to find his school polos. He went with the red one—it was the least smelly of the four—and matched it with some tan khakis. He pulled the wrinkly shirt over his head. He had never used an iron before, and he wasn't going to start today. He rubbed a dryer sheet all over his shirt as if he were washing his body with a loofa. He left the shirt untucked, per usual, and he knew he would hear about it later.

He parked his green sedan in front of Matt's house and waited the typical five minutes for him to come stumbling out of the front door, backpack slung over one arm and a Pop-Tart in his hand. Bill and Matt had been friends since preschool. They had gone to the same grade school, played on the same teams, and generally hung out with the same people. That was until Bill stopped hanging out all together. The main reason Bill went to St. Zeno High School was to follow Matt. Bill wasn't the best at making friends, and four years at the school had undoubtedly proven that. But at least he still had Matt.

Matt sat down and dropped his backpack between his legs to the floor. "Hey, what's up?"

"Not much," said Bill, noticing Matt's new haircut—his black hair was shaved on the sides and back, and the medium-length top portion was combed over with what seemed like an entire bottle of gel. "Cute haircut."

"Thanks," said Matt. He reached to his hair and combed it over with his hand. "Rachel recommended it."

"Looks good," said Bill, steering the car into the middle of the street.

They sat in silence for a few seconds. Matt was sure Bill's comments were disingenuous, but he struggled with a comeback. He also wasn't sure how to handle the grandfather situation. He abruptly blurted out, "Sorry about your grandpa."

"Yeah, thanks." Bill didn't know what else to say, so he just turned the radio up. There was minimal talking the rest of the ride to school.

Bill's hopes of keeping his grandfather's death a secret were dashed when it was announced over the PA during the morning prayer. The notification asked to keep Bill and his family in everyone's thoughts and prayers. He stared down at the ground, pretending not to hear, but he felt everyone's eyes focused on him. There was nothing he hated more than attention. No one mentioned anything to him during first period, and he was relieved. He didn't want to be constantly reminded about it—his whole plan had been to go to school to forget.

The reminders continued later in the day, though, when he ran into his baseball coach in the hall. His coach expressed his condolences and let Bill know to take as much time as he needed. Bill had to get a new suit for the funeral after school that day but said he would be back at practice tomorrow. Throughout the day, not one authority figure told him to tuck his shirt in. He had a pretty good guess as to why.

The next day played out like the previous day, and the emotional roller coaster continued. Bill tried keeping his mind off his grandfather, but thoughts of him would trickle in every once in a while, and he would feel sad for a bit before they passed. Today, a few more students and faculty members had extended their condolences. He had accepted the kind words with a nod and a quick smile.

After school, on Bill's way to the locker room to prepare for baseball practice, he saw three members of the wrestling team down the hall at the water fountain in their singlets. As he came closer, he recognized the slim figure and square-shaped head of the student who was filling up a bottle. *Ugh,* Bill thought. It was Keith, his archnemesis since grade school. They hadn't attended the same school and they certainly had never hung out together but had played on the same baseball team at the local park. Bill chalked Keith's animosity up to jealousy, for he was far better than Keith at baseball, and Keith's father, the coach, knew this and wasn't shy about acknowledging it. He would have felt sympathy for Keith failing to live up to his father's expectations had Keith not acted out constantly like a bully. He had made fun of Bill numerous times over the years for being fatherless. Bill had always ignored the comments—he wasn't much of a fighter—until they had finally come to blows at football practice freshman year, where Bill came out victorious. Bill wasn't afraid of Keith. What was there to be afraid of? Keith was small and skinny and weak, but he acted tough. And then he always hid behind someone—anyone. Today he just happened to have two of his large wrestling buddies by his side. Bill put his head down and tried pass the group.

"I heard about your grandpa," said Keith over his shoulder.

Bill froze and bit his lip.

Keith finished filling the bottle and turned to face Bill. "So, first your dad bails on you and now your grandpa dies to get away from you? Jeez, how pathetic are you? No one wants anything to do with you."

Bill felt his entire body tense. He balled up his fists.

"What are you gonna do?" said Keith mockingly as his two cronies stood on each side of him.

Bill exhaled, relaxed his hands, and continued down the hall.

"What a pussy!" snickered Keith.

Bill could hear their laughs all the way down the hall. He was still steaming when he entered the locker room to several of his teammates saying they were sorry. Bill barely acknowledged them. Just a smile and a nod.

Bill was happy to be back on the baseball field. It had been his favorite sport ever since he started tee ball. And he was good at it—he'd been the best player at his park district and representative of the city all-stars every year. High school was a different beast though. Everyone was good, and each year they seemed to get better while Bill got worse. When he was younger, he had loved to hit, crushing balls over outfielders' heads onto adjacent fields. He wasn't sure exactly when or why it started, but he'd begun to struggle. The older he got, the more nervous he became each time he stepped into the batter's box. His concentration was no longer on the pitcher and the ball, but on all of the people watching him. No matter how much he tried to calm and center himself and focus only on the pitcher, the result was almost always the same: a strikeout. With each strikeout, his confidence eroded and was replaced with more and more anxiety, and he tumbled down the depth chart to the end of the bench, occasionally getting some playing time during a blowout.

Today there was an intrasquad scrimmage, and Bill found himself in left field. The first two innings went by, and luckily nothing came Bill's way as he was still too busy stewing about Keith to fully concentrate on the game. The next inning, it was his turn to bat. Now he had to focus, and since there were no fans in attendance, he wasn't racked with the fear that plagued him in actual games. He popped out weakly to the second baseman, but at least he didn't strike out.

The next inning, he found himself again stewing in left field. The more he stewed, the more Keith's words got to him. Was his grandfather ashamed of him? No, no way. It was just a hateful thing said by a terrible person who wanted to mess with him. It was clearly working. Bill's thoughts jumped to his estranged father who had abandoned him as a baby. That pain haunted Bill. If his own father didn't love him, how could anyone else? How could he love himself? There had to be something wrong with him, and his uncontrollable anxiety and contempt for himself grew exponentially. There was one solution—a quick way to end all of his suffering—and he thought about it often. Bill never noticed the ball sail over his head, the players racing around the bases, or any of his teammates yelling at him to get the ball. He didn't snap out of it until the center fielder came over, retrieved the ball, and threw it to the third baseman, holding the batter to a two-run triple.

"What the hell, dude?" yelled the center fielder with both of his arms extended and palms to the air.

Bill blushed from overwhelming shame and embarrassment. "Sorry," he quietly muttered to his teammate before turning and walking away with his head hung low.

The center fielder returned to his territory as another player came running from the dugout with his glove to meet Bill. "Coach said I'm in."

The coach stopped Bill before he made it to the dugout. "You okay?"

"Yeah. Sorry."

"Why don't you just go home? Take some time to yourself. All right?"

Bill eyes filled with tears. "I'm fine. I'd rather just—"

The coach put his hand on Bill's shoulder. "It's okay, Bill."

Bill, in his brand-new black suit, arrived with his mom at the funeral home where they met the rest of the family in the lobby. When it came time to go into the viewing room, Bill's heart raced. He had not been to a wake since his childhood, when he did not understand the concept of death. He'd never had anyone close to him pass, just great-grandparents and distant relatives he had barely known. He hadn't been sad, but he could tell that everyone else there was.

This, however, was different. This hit him like a sledgehammer—agony and sadness rippled through him. His grandmother and uncle went to the casket first while Bill waited with anticipation. Another uncle and his wife went next. As much as Bill did not want to go up to the casket, the waiting became even worse. He just wanted to get it over with. His aunt followed with her two children, reminding Bill of when he had to go up there as a child, not fully appreciating what was happening—just going up there because he was told to. He wished his cousins had had more time with their grandfather. He wished he had more time with his grandfather. Finally, it was Bill and his mom's turn.

They knelt down in front of the body, both making the sign of the cross. Bill observed his grandfather's face, which seemed like it was made of plastic, barely resembling the person he remembered. Thoughts rushed through Bill's head. *What am I supposed to think? What am I supposed to say? A prayer? That did nothing before; what's the point now?* Bill had prayed for bikes and baseball cards and other frivolous things throughout his childhood. He'd thought maybe praying about something important would make a difference. But those prayers, along with countless others from his family and his grandfather's parish had apparently gone unheard. God had not even granted his grandfather a simple respite from his pain or suffering. *What would a prayer do at this point?*

Bill thought about the good times and everything his grandfather did for him—picking him up from school, taking him to baseball practices, playing catch and video games, letting him watch *Robocop* and *Predator,* going fishing. Early in Bill's life he had been a happy kid, not knowing any better about his family life, and his grandfather and uncles filled the void of his missing biological father. He was rarely teased about it, but he knew something was off, and he couldn't help but feel awkward and different. Bill never realized what his grandpa meant to him or how much he did for him. It now hit him that the closest thing Bill had to a father was once again gone.

Bill's mom made the sign of the cross and stood up. Bill didn't want to leave, but he also didn't want to stay there alone. Bill quickly thought, *Thank you for everything you ever did for me. I love you. Goodbye.*

Bill spent most of the wake in the front row of chairs, watching the never-ending line of people pay their respects to his family. Some visited with Bill and told him about how proud his grandpa would say he was of him. Bill appreciated the kind words, but they were nothing more than a reminder that he would never see his grandpa again, and it made him crumble on the inside. Bill swallowed the sad feelings down and tried to keep his composure on the outside, wanting so hard to be a strong man.

Some of Bill's friends and teammates stopped by and gave him a few moments of levity, including the entirety of the baseball team. St. Zeno preached that all that attended the high school were family, and the baseball coach proved it. The line of thirty baseball players was a bit awkward, but no one said a whole lot, so it went by quickly. Another St. Zeno representative, Father Leo, the principal of the school, clad in black slacks and a black button-down shirt with a white clerical collar, also stopped in. He was an exceptionally large individual, and Bill always imagined the Kool-Aid man when he saw him, the red juice swishing back and forth in his enormous stomach as he rumbled from side to side with each step. The priest passed along his condolences and told Bill that if he needed anything, everyone on the staff was there for him.

Bill had never felt like part of a family at St. Zeno, but he blamed this solely on one person: himself. He only attended the school because it was the school that the most people he knew were attending, which meant he would have to meet the least amount of new people at St. Zeno, and that sounded great to him. Over the years, he hadn't really made any new friends, just a few acquaintances he could talk to during class or practice or lunch, and he barely held on to the few friends he had made in grade school. If it weren't for Matt, he probably wouldn't have any friends at all.

Matt tried to keep Bill close, but Bill would usually push away and keep to himself. He never went out, no matter how many people invited him. After a while, people stopped asking, and he found himself alone in his room most nights. He preferred that anyway—no anxiety, no stress, no fear. If he wasn't going to physically eliminate himself, Bill could at least eliminate himself socially and find some minimal peace and solace. Although they weren't as close as they once were, Matt still had Bill's back and Bill had his.

They talked sports, girls, classes… whatever to take Bill's mind off of his burden. At one point they laughed so loud, everyone in the funeral home looked at them, prompting a death stare from his mom. They kept it down from that point on. Before Bill knew it, twenty minutes had passed, and Matt had to leave. Bill found himself alone again. He kept an eye on his younger cousins, playing handheld video games, still numb to the situation. He wished that were him.

The priest arrived and everyone took a seat for a prayer. Most listened along and tried to find comfort in the words, but Bill paid no attention. No prayer saved his grandpa. No prayer eased his grandpa's pain. No prayer would bring his grandpa back. No prayer would fill the hole left in Bill's heart.

The next day, Bill felt awful. He had barely slept, and it felt like a grenade had gone off in his head. He thought about what lay ahead of him—it was the last day Bill would ever see his grandfather. Today, he had to say goodbye.

Bill put on his new suit for the second day in a row and tied a Windsor knot just like his grandfather had taught him. He patted his hair down and it fell just above his eyebrows. He and his mother said nothing on the way to the funeral home. The family hugged each other with tears in their eyes. The moment they had been dreading was upon them. Bill stuffed the feelings deep down inside him. *Have to stay strong. No crying.*

Bill and his mom knelt at the casket for the final time. His mom made the sign of the cross once again, but Bill didn't bother. He just stared at his grandfather's peaceful face in the casket, swallowed hard, and blinked as many times as it took to keep the tears from falling down his face. Bill wanted his mom to hurry. They sat down in the first row of seats, and Bill watched all of the people say their final goodbyes. He held it in as long as he could until he finally broke down and sobbed while his mother held him.

CHAPTER 3:

Walk on Water

BILL SLEPT WELL THAT NIGHT FOR THE FIRST TIME IN A WEEK. THE next morning, he felt refreshed and was happy to move on with his life—not forget, just move on. He finished up a bowl of cereal and grabbed his baseball bag, then shouted from the kitchen to his mom in the living room, "I'm going to the game. I'll see you later."

"Oh, you're going?" his mom called back, surprised.

"Yeah. Is that okay?"

"Yeah." She met him at the doorway of the living room and kitchen. "As long as you're feeling up to it."

Bill could see the concern on her face. He wanted her to stop worrying about him. "Yeah. I'm fine."

"All right," she said. A smile spread across her face. "Good luck! What time does it start?"

Bill opened the front door and paused. "First game is at one and the second should start around three-thirty."

"Do you think you'll play?"

"Nope."

"Well, maybe I'll bring grandma by for a bit."

"If you guys wanna watch me sit on the bench, it's your life."

Bill's baseball coach was shocked to see him so soon after the debacle at the last practice. Bill told him he was better and fully focused on the game. To Bill's surprise, coach told him he would start the second game at second base. He wondered whether to tell his mom or not. It would be his first time starting a game in high school. He didn't want to put the extra pressure on himself, but he felt guilty for discouraging his mom and grandma from having a potentially fun afternoon. Against his better judgment, Bill notified his mom, who excitedly responded and said she would be there with his grandma.

Bill spent the entire first game at the end of the bench, alone, trying to calm himself down. *It's just baseball. You've played it a million times.* The sky was grey and almost entirely covered in clouds. Light rain fell intermittently. Bill barely watched as his team easily won the first game. Then it was time to warm up for the matinee. He kept his nerves in check, and his arm felt strong as he played catch. He successfully made every play during infield practice and hit some balls off the tee in the batting cage just before the game started. He prepped himself as best he could, and he had a strange feeling of confidence. Until he saw his mom and grandma in the stands.

The field was uneventful, and three innings passed without Bill seeing any action at second base. In the bottom of the third, it was finally his turn to bat. After the leadoff man grounded out to the pitcher, he stepped to the plate. Bill could feel everyone's eyes on him, expecting him to fail. *He* expected himself to fail, and he struck out on three pitches. *Great start.*

Bill got some confidence back in the fourth inning when he caught a routine grounder and threw the batter out at first. The field never bothered him. Everything happened so fast, there was no time to get flustered. Hitting as usual was a different story. His next at bat in the fifth inning went slightly better, and he struck out on four pitches instead of three. *Progress,* was all he could tell himself.

In the sixth and seventh innings, Bill caught an easy pop-up and threw another runner out at first on a ground ball. The game went to the bottom of the seventh, locked in a 2-1 pitcher's duel with Bill's team trailing. He was due up fourth that inning. The opposing team had brought in one of the best relief pitchers in the state. Scouts from several professional teams were in attendance, as he was projected to be a first-round pick in the upcoming draft. They stood there with their radar guns extended, shocked and amazed that the lanky lefty could consistently hit triple digits.

As the clouds broke apart and the sun began to shine through, the pitcher made quick work of the first two St. Zeno batters, striking them out on six pitches combined. Bill wasn't sure if the next batter's fate was better or worse when he heard the one-hundred-mile-per-hour fastball whizz through the air and then thud directly into his teammate's back. The player grunted and crumpled to the ground like a sack of potatoes. After he had writhed around for a minute, the coach helped the player to his feet and walked him back to the dugout. A pinch runner took his place on first base. The coach gave Bill a simple nod and a pat on the shoulder as he passed.

Bill would have happily sacrificed his body for the game to keep going. He didn't care about being a hero; he just didn't want to be the goat. Bill's hands trembled around the bat as he walked to the plate to a tepid crowd reaction. They didn't expect much, and Bill didn't blame them. He settled in the box and waited for the pitch. He saw the pitcher lift his front leg and then his arm hurled forward. Bill heard something ripple through the air, and the next thing he knew the catcher was throwing the ball back to the pitcher.

"Strike!" the ump called out.

Bill kept his back foot planted in the box and turned the rest of his body to his coach at third base for the sign. The coach clenched both fists and said, "Let's go."

Bill put his front foot back in the box and waited for the pitcher's delivery. The ball came roaring at him like a missile, and he didn't swing until the ball was already in the catcher's glove.

"Strike two!"

Bill checked with his coach again and he simply replied, "You got this."

If you say so. Bill dug into the box and choked up on the bat. He squeezed it so tight his forearms began to knot. The pitcher lunged forward and hurled the ball. Bill never saw it, but he heard the sweet *ping* of the ball hitting the bat. The crowd roared, and Bill sprinted out of the box to first. He had no idea where the ball went. He just kept running as hard as he could. He dashed past first base and raced around second. He should have noticed the other team dejectedly walking off the field or the fans and teammates screaming at the tops of their lungs, but he was solely focused on running, as fast as he could, all the way to home plate where he was mobbed by all his teammates.

CHAPTER 4:
Morning

———

*D*ING. *DING. DING.* **BILL SHUT THE ALARM OFF BEFORE IT COULD** finish its first cycle. He had not slept much the night before and was awake for some time, playing games on his phone while counting the minutes until the alarm went off. Bill peeled the tape from the wall and slid one side of the curtain over. Blinding sunlight filled the room. It took a moment for his eyes to adjust. He sat up in his bed and looked at the packed bag on the floor—a reminder of the reason he had not slept, a reminder of the reason he did not want to go to school today—the retreat.

Everyone at St. Zeno was required to go on a retreat before they could graduate. There were two options: a one-day secular retreat at the school, or the four-day religious retreat held off campus. Roughly a quarter of the students at St. Zeno were a religious denomination other than Catholic, but their checks still cleared, so they were welcomed with open arms. Pretty much all of these students attended the one-day retreat. Bill had long thought about doing the same, but he had heard over the past year and a half at school that the four-day retreat was a great experience, and you could learn a lot about yourself and strengthen your faith there. Besides, the priests knew he had been raised Catholic and came from a Catholic grade school, so he would certainly have to explain why he was attending a secular retreat. He was better off just going through the motions at the religious retreat and staying under the radar.

The excitement and joy Bill received from his game-winning homer had left him, and he was back to his miserable depressed self, feeling sad and hopeless. He longed for something—*anything*—to make him feel better.

Perhaps this would be it. Perhaps the homerun was his grandfather calling to him from heaven for Bill to regain his faith. Maybe Bill could find a father in Almighty God. It seemed like the perfect opportunity to get his life back on track, so he'd signed up for the last four-day retreat offered to his class. All of those positive feelings had dissipated, and he had absolutely no desire to attend. His sole relief was that Matt would be attending as well, but that only soothed him so much.

"Ugh," he grunted as he dropped his head.

Bill sat at the kitchen table, eating a bowl of cereal, his head buried in his laptop like an old man with a newspaper. He checked the scores from last night's games—*yikes*… He owed Matt some money.

Bill's mom entered the room. "Let's go. We still have to pick up Matt."

He yawned and stretched. "All right, all right. I'm going as fast as I can." He looked at the watch on his left wrist. Since he had put it on the day his grandpa died, he had not taken it off except for baseball practice and to shower.

Bill carried his large duffle bag out to the car and dropped it in the trunk. The car sank under the weight. He probably had too many clothes for a four-day trip, but better safe than sorry. He tossed his backpack on top and finally the grocery bag full of brownies and cookies—his contribution to the retreat's communal snacks.

Bill buckled his seat belt, turned to his mom, and said, "Feel free to get into a major accident this morning."

His mom backed the car out of the driveway. "I'm late enough as it is."

CHAPTER 5:
School

————

BILL SAT IN HIS LAST CLASS BEFORE LUNCH. THE TEACHER GRADED THE history quizzes the students had just finished, leaving them free to talk amongst themselves for a few minutes. Bill and Matt used the time to play paper football.

Bill lined up the triangular "football" on his desk while Matt held his index fingers and thumbs up in the shape of a goalpost just below his chin.

"And it all comes down to this," said Matt, in his best imitation of a sports announcer.

Bill gently held the top of the football with his left index finger, positioned his right index finger and thumb behind it, and found the angle he liked.

"One kick," said Matt. "One chance for glory. One chance for immortality."

Bill flicked his finger and struck the football, forcefully sending it upward through Matt's fingers, directly into his eye.

Bill threw his arms up triumphantly as the piece of paper fell to the ground. "And he nails it!"

"Ow," said Matt, rubbing his eye. "You nailed my eye, too."

"Football's a tough sport," said Bill.

"My turn," said Matt. He picked the piece of paper up from the ground.

A student entered the classroom and held out a note to the teacher. The teacher thanked the student and read the note.

Bill placed his fingers in the goalpost position, turned his head and squeezed his eyes shut, afraid of the incoming revenge while Matt lined up the kick.

"Bill," announced the teacher.

Bill's eyes shot open, and he looked to the teacher just as the football drilled him in the cheek.

"Ow," said Bill, rubbing the point of impact. He glowered at Matt. "Nice kick." Bill turned back to the teacher, who was waving the note in the air.

"If you're not too busy, Father Andrew would like to see you."

"Oooooh," Bill's classmates chimed together as he stood up from his desk. Bill hated the attention this brought him. *I didn't do anything wrong.* He hurried to the teacher to grab the summons.

"Tuck your shirt in," muttered the teacher as Bill walked away.

About half of the faculty at Saint Zeno High School were priests— most were teachers of various subjects, and one held a guidance counselor position. The guidance counselors at the school were each given a different grade level and were known to do routine check-ins with the students where they would discuss how school was going, sports, clubs… life in general. But Bill did not believe this to be one of those random check-ins, for Father Andrew was no longer his counselor. He navigated through the hallways and knocked on Father Andrew's office door.

"Come in," the old priest said from inside.

Bill entered. "Hey, *Father.*" Calling priests that word always made him uncomfortable, and he hated having to use it. "You wanted to see me?"

"Hello, Bill my boy," he answered. "Yes." He slowly rose from his chair to greet Bill. His body was frail and wilted. The last remaining whiskers of grey hair wrapped around his head from ear to ear, but his mind was sharp and his passion for life was as strong as ever. He attended every school event, function, and game and was every student's biggest cheerleader. Bill liked Father Andrew… as much as he could like a priest; he could tell he genuinely cared about the students and their betterment. He did, however, have a tendency to talk a lot.

Bill reached across the desk and gently shook the priest's hand, afraid he might break it.

"Have a seat," said Father Andrew.

Bill plopped down in the chair. He had first met Father Andrew during his application process in eighth grade. When he entered St. Zeno as a freshman, Father Andrew became his guidance counselor; he counseled all incoming freshmen. During that time, Bill learned about all of the tales of the high school through the years and about most of Father Andrew's life. After freshman year, Bill hadn't had much interaction with Father Andrew except for a quick hello around the school grounds here and there. He liked it better that way. Father Andrew was the lone guidance counselor who was also a priest, so he was much more interested in the religious aspects of Bill's life, for obvious reasons. The other guidance counselors spoke more about life in broader terms, and his senior guidance counselor only talked about college.

"How are you?" asked Father Andrew.

"Good. How are you?" responded Bill, sitting upright and folding his hands in his lap.

"Good, thank you. Still buzzing from that big homer the other day?" Father Andrew mimicked the swing. "That was certainly something."

It had been a big day for Bill—one he'd sorely needed—but he never even saw the ball. "Oh, yeah, it was. Tell you the truth, I didn't even have my eyes open."

Father Andrew chuckled. "Oh, come on now!"

"No, no, I didn't see a thing. I just closed my eyes and swung. It must have been divine intervention."

Father Andrew laughed louder and waved his hand dismissively. "Oh, you're just teasing. I remember back when I was on the baseball team in high school. We had such good talent. We were the favorites to win the state championship. I remember…"

Bill started to drift off. *Ugh, here he goes again,* he said to himself. *Another wonderful, long, meandering story. I don't know if I'm gonna be able to make it through this one.*

Bill shook his head to snap out of it. *Stop being a jerk. He's just a nice old guy being friendly with you. Just keep smiling and nodding and eventually it will be over.*

Bill worked up a fake smile and nodded his head as Father Andrew continued his story.

After ten minutes of subtly rolling his wrist over to check his watch, Bill was starting to lose it. *For the love of God, end it. Maybe if I start banging my head against the desk, he'll get the idea.* He struggled to keep the smile on his face. *What is this, his life story? Great, I'll be here till graduation. I can't take anymore.*

Bill stood up. "Father, I'm sorry, but I have lunch now. Do you think we can pick this up another time?"

"Oh, sure. I'm sorry. You're a growing boy and you need your strength so you can keep smacking those dingers. We didn't get a chance to discuss why I called you down here, though. I do really want to talk with you and see how you're doing with the passing of your grandfather. Would you be able to stop by after school?"

For the first time today, Bill was happy he was going on the retreat. "Unfortunately, I can't. I'm off to the retreat today, so I'm going to have to take a raincheck." Bill inched toward the doorway.

"Oh, you're going today? Great! It will be so wonderful!" Father Andrew rose from his desk.

"I'm sure it will." *Two more steps. Almost there.*

The priest carefully walked over to Bill with several small steps. "I know you have to go, but just quickly, how are you doing in regard to your grandfather?"

"Oh, you know. It's tough." Bill's heels teetered on the border between the office's carpet and the hallway's tile.

Father Andrew nodded and put his hand on Bill's shoulder. Bill wasn't a fan of the contact, but he could see the concern in the priest's eyes. "Yes, yes it is. But you just have to keep in mind that he's with God now and, it's all part of His plan. It hurts now, but in time you will understand."

"Right." Bill never understood God's plan. He found it hard to believe that God's plan involved one of his devout followers contracting a horrific disease and suffering greatly. That sounded like a pretty crappy plan. What Bill did understand was that he was hungry, and he wanted to leave.

Father Andrew removed his hand. "Well, you'll have plenty of support on the retreat, so be open to the experience. You're going to have a great time!"

"I can't wait. Bye, Father. Thanks."

"Take care, Bill. And tuck in your shirt."

Bill entered the packed cafeteria and weaved through students and tables until he found his spot. He quietly took his seat at the end of the table next to Matt.

"Where were you?" asked Matt.

"I got caught up in a Father Andrew story," said Bill, unpacking his lunch.

"I'm surprised you got out of there alive," said Matt. "Or at least before graduation."

"No kidding," responded Bill. Directly across from him, Roy was reading a thick paperback. "How much you got left, Roy?" Bill asked.

"About two hundred pages, give or take." Roy's eyes darted through the words.

"And the quiz is next period? I don't think you're gonna make it," said Bill.

Roy paused and looked up. "Maybe all of the questions will be from the first twenty pages."

"Stay positive," said Bill with a smile and a nod. Roy lowered his head back down to the book.

Matt took a huge bite out of his sandwich and crumbs spilled all over the table. He barely managed to ask, "Where's my money?"

Bill reached for his wallet. It hadn't come up on the ride to school this morning. "I was hoping you'd forget."

"Not a chance," said Matt, finally swallowing the gigantic bite.

Bill flipped through the singles, found the lone twenty, and handed it to Matt. Matt happily snatched it and stuffed it into his wallet. "I can't believe you took the Bulls."

"I thought they were due," said Bill. "You know…"

Bill had lost Matt's attention to the other side of the table. He didn't hear what Matt said, but he did hear the laughter that erupted afterwards from his classmates. Bill just remained quietly in the corner like he always did and stuffed his face as fast as he could.

Across from Matt, Dan paused from his sandwich to ask, "You guys all packed up for the retreat?"

Bill muttered a yes.

"You excited?" Dan said mockingly. He knew the answer. Bill never denigrated anyone else for following any religion, but he openly didn't follow his own religion at school.

"Yeah," replied Bill with an eyeroll. "Four days without TV, internet, music, or sports."

"Don't worry, you'll have the Lord to keep you busy," said Dan, extending his hands like a priest offering a prayer.

"I don't know how I'm gonna make it," said Matt.

"My dad said they changed locations," said Dan. "You're the first group to check it out."

Dan's father was on the faculty at St. Zeno, so he would occasionally break extremely unimportant news.

"Awesome," replied Bill. "Where did you go?"

Dan shrugged. "Some place downstate. It was out in the woods."

21

Bill cleared his throat with a swig from his water bottle. "Where is it now?"

"I'm not sure," said Dan with a shake of his head.

"Why'd they move it?" Bill wanted any grain of information he could get.

Dan shrugged again with no answer.

"I thought you had connections."

"Sorry," Dan said sarcastically.

Matt leaned his head toward Bill to address him. "Coach O'Connell pissed you're missing games?"

Bill snorted. "Nah, it's not like it matters." Bill would be missing three games and two practices. He was the only student from the baseball team attending the retreat, as all of the other players had gone over the fall and winter when baseball was out of season.

"What are you talking about?" said Matt. "You're the big hero." Matt patted Bill on the back.

"I *was*. That was a week ago. Since then, I'm oh-for-seven with six strikeouts."

Matt tried to reassure him. "Everybody has slumps."

"Four years is a bit long to be called a slump."

Matt gave up and ate his food.

Bill looked back to Dan. "What happens on the retreat? You've already been on it."

Bill had asked a few students over the past couple weeks what happened on the retreat, but no one was willing to divulge any specific details. The only thing they ever said was it was a 'great experience' and 'a lot of fun.' They were sworn to secrecy, and surprisingly everyone stood by it. *It must be something important,* Bill thought. That worried him. But then again, most things did.

Dan mulled it over. "We're not supposed to talk about it. You're supposed to experience it yourself. I don't want to ruin anything."

"Please ruin it," said Bill, wanting any nugget of information that would ease his fear.

"You'll see," said Dan with a half-smirk. He knew full-well Bill would hate every moment of the retreat.

Bill exhaled dejectedly. "All I've heard is it's out in the middle of nowhere. No one will say where though."

"Out of cell phone range, I'm sure," said Matt.

"You can't even bring a phone," said Dan.

Matt crunched down on a potato chip. "I'll take my chances."

"It's probably outside of screaming range too. We're on our own out there," said Bill.

Matt channeled a movie-trailer narrator and said, "At the Lord's retreat… no one can hear you scream."

"Yeah, you better be careful," said Dan, joining in on the fun. "It could be some cult trying to mess with your head."

"So, just like here, then, huh?" replied Bill with a sardonic smile.

Dan smiled back and pointed at Bill. "Heyyyy."

The bell rang for the end of lunch.

"Aw, man, are you kidding?" said Bill. He looked down at the half-eaten sandwich, full bag of chips and brownie.

"I'll help you out," said Matt as he swiped the brownie.

"Thanks, pal."

Bill found himself in his final sanctuary before the retreat—Spanish class. He was supposed to be working on an exercise in his workbook, but he was unable to relax his mind. After each minute of blankly staring at his textbook, he would check his watch again.

I should have picked the one-day retreat, Bill thought. *Hell, I shouldn't have to pick any retreat. It should be optional… separation of church and state… Well, you probably shouldn't have gone to a Catholic school then, dummy. But everybody goes to Catholic School. I didn't even have a choice. Mom wasn't sending me to a public school.*

The teacher began calling on students to review their answers. Bill checked his watch again—one minute closer.

Come on. You wanted to do this. This is your chance to turn it around… to get back on the right track. This could be good for you. Make it good for you.

Bill didn't hear his name called until the fifth time. He snapped his head toward the teacher.

"Hey, Bill," she said. "Are you okay?"

"Yes," said Bill meekly. "Sorry."

"What did you have for number three?"

Bill looked at the blank space next to number three. "Uh." He briskly skimmed the directions. "Um, tengo… que ir…"

"Please pay attention, Bill," the teacher said disappointedly.

"Sorry," said Bill. He wasn't used to being reprimanded in public. He never got into trouble. Trouble meant attention, and he avoided it like the plague. His face burned with shame, and he felt sick to his stomach. Something as miniscule as this reprimand had brought on uncontrollable embarrassment, and he hated himself for that.

The teacher picked another student. As Bill cooled down and his heart-rate returned to normal, he finished the exercise. He was ready when the teacher came back to him for the final answer.

Bill was one of the last students still in the locker-lined hallway. He had ignored the first two PA announcements for retreaters to head to the south exit for the bus. Bill fidgeted with things in his locker, rearranging his books in the proper order for when he returned. As he once again pondered the penalty for missing the bus to the retreat, Mr. North, his English teacher, emerged from his classroom across the hall. "Hello, Bill," he said, in his usual calm, menacing tone.

Bill knew the voice. "Hey, Mr. North."

Bill thought it was silly to be scared of a teacher, but nonetheless Mr. North intimidated him. Maybe it was the slicked-back hair. Maybe it was the perfectly pressed, zero wrinkles, tucked-in shirt. Maybe it was the tie knotted so tightly to his neck, it seemed like his head might pop off. Maybe it was how hard he pushed his students and how he got the absolute best out of them. Bill liked the standard teacher policy of, 'if you know an answer, raise your hand and you will be called on.' Bill pretty much always knew the answers but refrained from answering anyway. It was nice and simple and peaceful. In contrast, no hands were ever raised in Mr. North's class. He would just pick randomly. It caused Bill great anxiety, and he hated being put on the spot, especially if he didn't have an answer.

Mr. North waved a paper around in the air. "I just graded your essay," he said playfully. "Want to take a look?"

"You know, my day has been pretty good," said Bill. "I don't want to ruin it."

"Well, you are right. Usually, you're spot on with your analysis, but this was not one of your better performances." Mr. North cracked a smile.

Bill shrugged. "Yeah, I guess fifteenth-century French poetry isn't really my forte. Now you want five pages on Matt Forte, I got you covered."

Mr. North let out a big laugh. "I'm sure you would."

An announcement came in over the PA, "All students leaving for the retreat must proceed to the parking lot at this time. The buses will be leaving shortly. This is the last and final call."

Bill closed the locker door. "That's me."

"Have fun. And why don't you take this along for some reading on the bus." Mr. North handed the paper to Bill.

Bill took the paper. "Thanks. Will do. See ya."

"Tuck in your shirt," said Mr. North.

"I'm not on the clock anymore," said Bill over his shoulder. "You don't have any power over me." He jogged off down the hall.

Mr. North cupped his hands over his mouth. "There's never a time to look like a slob!"

CHAPTER 6:

The Journey

BILL EXITED THE SCHOOL, BACKPACK SLUNG OVER ONE SHOULDER, HIS massive duffle bag slung around his other, nerves on a vicious roller coaster. But the sun shone brightly in the clear blue sky, and it was unusually warm for early April in Chicago. Perhaps God was smiling upon this retreat after all.

Bill waded through the groups of students, getting his first look at the rest of the participants. After four years of classes, sports, and activities, Bill would have thought he'd know most of the two hundred kids in his class—he was wrong. He recognized the faces but didn't know them at all on a personal level. You had some jocks, stoners, loners, and smarties.

Suddenly, someone bumped into his shoulder so hard it staggered him. The weight from his bag just about toppled him over. Bill turned back to see Keith's Lego-like block head staring at him. Keith had dipped his shoulder into Bill, and he now mouthed the word 'pussy' as he hid behind one of the same wrestlers that had guarded him the other day at the water fountain. Bill, disheartened, just shook his head and kept walking. *Of course he's on this retreat.*

He finally found the group of football players he would be hanging out with for the next four days. Bill knew these people well enough from his two years of football, though he had quit abruptly three days before the start of the season junior year. He had never told anyone the real reason he quit, and he never would. He remembered that day vividly. It was the closest he had ever come to taking his own life, but he'd lacked what he called 'the courage' to do it.

Bill, of course, stood next to Matt and dropped his bags down beside him. He had to squeeze next to Scott, a mountain of a young man—tall, solid, and one of the best offensive linemen in the city. The team had to order a special size helmet and gloves just for him. He was exceptionally strong for his age and often didn't realize it.

"Look what I got," said Pete, reaching into his bag and sliding out a full bottle of Jack Daniels.

"I don't think that's on the list of approved items," said Matt.

"You know they're gonna do room checks," said Scott.

"Whatever," scoffed Pete. He slid the bottle back in and zipped up the bag. "The worst thing that can happen is they take it. No big deal."

Pete was the stereotypical teen jock; his only reasons for living were football, booze, and girls. He played safety because he loved to hit people. Out of the people in this group, he was Bill's least favorite.

"If Father Stephen finds it, he might throw a few back with you," said Scott, nodding over to the bearded, pear-shaped, middle-aged priest. He stood with the two other faculty chaperones, Principal Father Leo—the bowling ball on stumpy legs who attended every retreat— and math teacher Mr. Linderman—a young, skinny man to whom Bill had never spoken a word. Bill always enjoyed the irony of overweight priests, the gluttonous bellies that hung over the waistbands. You couldn't see them if they wore their black cloaks, but when they wore button-down shirts like today, there they were, glorious and sinful.

"Or the whole bottle," said Matt. He nodded to Dee. "Remember the winter dance? Dude was hammered by nine o'clock."

Bill didn't remember. He hadn't attended the dance, or any dances for that matter. The conversation left Bill again looking around at the participants. Not far from the group, Bill saw Tom standing by himself. Bill could tell he felt alone and uncomfortable. He knew that feeling all too well.

"Yeah," said Dee. "We found him face first in the toilet, yacking his brains out. Then he gave us twenty each not to tell anyone."

"No kidding?!" said Scott.

"Whoops," said Matt with a raise of his eyebrows.

"Yeah," said Dee. "He was a mess."

Scott laughed. "That's great. What a lush."

Bill made eye contact with Tom and nodded for him to come over and join the rest of them. Tom was happy to accept the invitation. Tom was slight—shorter and skinnier than the rest of the group. He did not play sports, nor did he hang out with the "cool kids," but he liked to tag along with Bill and Matt at school when he could. Bill had battled with Tom and a couple others for the number one academic ranking in his class through sophomore year. Bill dropped to sixth after he passed on taking on a junior-year class that began before actual school started and slipped even further after multiple B's and even a C senior year. Thoughts other than academics had begun to cloud Bill's mind, and Tom now held the number one spot alone. The boys made fun of him, but no more than they would make fun of each other—except for Pete. Pete took every opportunity to drive Tom nuts.

Tom came over and set his bag down behind Bill.

"Tommyboy!" yelled Pete. He scratched at his military crew cut, leaving the short hairs on top pointing in every direction. "What's happening?"

"Hey," muttered Tom before he began a quiet conversation with Bill about their history quiz earlier in the day. Pete left him alone for now.

The boys were still waiting for the bus when they were approached by a middle-aged woman in black leggings and a pink pullover, carrying a brown paper bag.

Pete's eyes went wide. "Well, who's this?" he said, pulling his shoulders back and sticking his chest out. Each of the boys turned to look.

"That's my mom," answered Tom as he wriggled like a worm out of dirt and dug the brown tip of his loafer into the ground. He did not like it when she came by the school.

Her blonde hair was pulled back in a ponytail with a couple of loose strands framing her face on each side. Her makeup made her look at least ten years younger. The zipper on her pullover was down to her sports bra; her breasts bulged out of the top. The boys were unable to break the powerful force that, like gravity, kept their gaze locked on her. She knew it, and she didn't mind one bit.

"Hey, boys," she said with a smile. Tom's mom handed him the paper bag. "Here, honey. You forget your nasal congestion medicine."

"Thanks, Mom." Tom snatched the bag. "Bye," he said, shooing her with his hand.

Pete wasn't going to let him off that easy. He crossed the circle of people and extended his hand. "Hi, Mrs. Reedy. I'm Pete."

"Hi, Pete," she said. "It's nice to meet you. But it's Miss Reedy."

"You don't say?" said Pete, moving a step closer. "How could someone like you be single?"

"Oh, I don't know," she said. "I guess I just haven't found the right guy."

"I guess not," said Pete, smiling.

"You have everything else?" Miss Reedy asked her son.

"Yes, Mom! You can go now."

Matt casually stepped back to check out her butt in her skin-tight pants. It didn't disappoint, and he nodded approvingly.

"Okay, okay," said Miss Reedy. She was still enjoying soaking up all of the attention. "Love you." She used her hand to comb Tom's blond hair across his head.

Tom pawed at her hand to push it away. "Yeah, love you too," said Tom, barely getting the words out of his mouth, his face now hotter than the sun beating down on them.

"Bye, boys," she said. "Have fun!"

They all said bye together and stared at her as she walked away. She looked back to the boys and gave them a wink and a smile.

"Good god, almighty, how did that smoke show produce you?" asked Pete.

"Shut up," replied Tom.

"And single, she says," said Pete.

"Just shut up, man," pleaded Tom.

"Hey, Tom, you lookin' for a new dad?" asked Scott.

"Screw you guys," said Tom.

"Come here, son," said Pete, grabbing Tom's head.

Pete put Tom into a headlock and gave him a noogie. Tom's bony arms were unable to push him off. The boys smiled in amusement as Bill looked on with remorse. He was the one who had asked Tom to come over. Bill thought about intervening and breaking it up, but he couldn't find the courage.

"How was school today, son?" goaded Pete, his arm still securely locked around Tom's head. "Your mom and I made sweet, sweet love all day long. You're gonna have a little brother or sister soon. Aren't you excited?" Pete patted Tom on the head. By now, all of the students waiting for the bus were watching Tom's embarrassment. The longer it went, the worse Bill felt. But he still stood frozen, incapable of doing anything.

Pete's grasp loosened around Tom's neck, and he finally squirmed free. Tom backed away from his assailant, trying to fix his hair. "Get off me. What is wrong with you?"

Bill abruptly snapped, "Several psychiatrists have yet to figure that out."

Pete's smile faded from his face as he cast a glance at Bill. *Whoops,* Bill thought to himself. He hoped he wasn't the next one to be fitted for a headlock.

"Here comes the bus," said Matt.

Thank God, Bill thought.

The long ride had just become that much worse when the standard yellow school bus parked in front of the mass of attendees.

"At least we're riding in style," muttered Scott.

"Seriously? They couldn't even spring for a coach bus one time?" whined Dee. "I thought retreats were supposed to be relaxing."

"We can't even get a second bus?" questioned Matt. "How are we all gonna fit on that thing?"

They grabbed their bags and merged into the line for the door.

Father Stephen stood on the steps of the bus and addressed the retreaters. "Everyone put your bags in the designated seats and make sure you double-up. It's gonna be a tight squeeze."

Waves of angst pummeled Bill as he inched his way toward the bus. His hand shook when he grabbed the railing on the door for support. There was no turning back now.

"Mr. Foster, welcome." Father Stephen knelt in the first seat behind the driver, marking students' names off on a clipboard. "Phone?"

"No, sir. I left it at home." Bill adjusted the large bag on his shoulder, exposing his left hand and the watch.

"Good." The priest noticed the brown band around Bill's wrist. "You didn't leave your watch, I see."

Bill glanced down at his grandfather's watch. He had known he was supposed to leave it at home per the rules of the retreat, but he needed it like a comforting service dog, and then forgot to take it off for the bus ride. "Oh, yeah. I'm sorry, I forgot."

"I'll have to take that." Father Stephen extended an open hand. Rules were rules.

"Oh, please, don't," pleaded Bill. "I'll put it in my bag. I won't take it out. I promise."

Father Stephen mulled it over, frowning. "All right. Don't make me regret it," he said sternly, pointing his pen at Bill.

"I won't," Bill said immediately. "Thank you."

Bill wondered how big of a deal a watch could be as he dropped his massive duffel bag and snack bag off in the first few rows reserved for luggage. He swung his backpack around to his stomach, unclasped the watch, and shoved it in an outside pocket. Scott led the way down the aisle followed by Matt. The coveted back was already taken by students, so Scott took a spot on the left side in the middle of the bus. When Matt made the movement to sit down next to Scott, Bill's stomach dropped. Who would he have to sit with now?

"Oh, come on, man, I got the wheel here. Give me some space," said Scott, refusing to budge. There was hardly any room for him to move.

Bill took the seat across the aisle and slid his backpack under the seat in front of him as far as it would go. The wheel did make it a tight squeeze.

"Father Stephen said double-up," said Matt, standing in the aisle.

"Yeah, double with Bill," said Scott. "He's small. I deserve a one-seater if possible."

"Whatever," said Matt as he turned to Bill's seat.

Bill, relieved that Matt would be his seat mate, slid over to the wall and rested his left foot on top of the wheel cover. It wasn't particularly comfortable, but it was better than sitting with Pete or Keith or anyone else.

"You know how long the ride is?" Matt asked.

"About two hours," answered Bill.

"Awesome," said Matt. "I'm glad I didn't shower this week." Matt smelled his armpit and smiled.

Bill glared at him and then opened the window. The bus was hot and would soon be cramped and even hotter. He took a deep breath of the crisp air, and it soothed him. Students continued to fill in the remaining seats in the front of the bus. Bill peeked over his seat. A couple rows ahead of him he saw Pete sit down next to Tom. *Poor guy,* he thought. *At least it isn't me.*

After all of the students were checked off and accounted for, Father Stephen announced they were on their way, and the bus rattled forward. Bill stared longingly at the baseball fields full of players as they went by.

Before the bus had even made it to the highway, Bill's foot fell asleep, and his knee ached. It was going to be a long ride. He looked at Matt, eyes closed, head resting back on the seat. Bill envied the legroom in front of him. Matt's eyes opened, and Bill quickly turned his head back to the window.

"I think Rachel might try to come up on Saturday," said Matt.

"Really?" asked Bill out of the corner of his mouth.

"Yeah, maybe." Matt picked at the skin around his fingernail.

Bill squinted at Matt. "Why?"

Matt responded with a shrug. "Why not?"

Bill struggled to understand the point of this possible meeting. "What are you going to do up there?"

Matt shrugged again, this time more slowly, holding his shoulders up for a few seconds before returning them to their normal position. "I don't know. We'll see."

"She's gonna come hang out in your room or...?"

"No. Like maybe we'll go hang out in the woods or something."

"Uh huh." That sounded dumb to Bill. "How will she know where to go?"

"We'll figure it out when we get up there."

"Okay," said Bill, rolling his eyes. He stared out of the window at the passing fast-food restaurants and strip malls. Bill hadn't spent much time with Rachel, and he had no problem with her, but the entire situation just seemed strange to him. Matt couldn't go a few days without seeing her? Maybe he would have understood better if he had a girlfriend.

Matt rolled his head to the left and looked earnestly at Bill. "What?"

Bill shrugged and shook his head. "I don't know. Seems weird and unnecessary."

Matt turned away. "Okay, well, I'm sorry I told you."

"You should be."

"I guess I won't tell you she might bring some friends with her too," said Matt matter-of-factly.

Bill's ears perked up. There was one friend of Rachel's he had met once and instantly fell in love with... Well, he had seen her standing next to Rachel in the crowded bleachers at a football game, in one of the extremely rare occurrences he left his house, and thought she was pretty. He hadn't found the boldness to actually talk to her. "Who?"

Matt stretched and touched the ceiling. "Oh, now you care, huh?"

"Is she bringing Maddie?"

"Maybe."

"Cool," said Bill. He looked out the window and thought, maybe, *just maybe*, he had a chance with her. *Hey, if miracles are going to happen anywhere, it would be on a religious retreat, right?* Bill broke from the daydream with more questions about Matt's plan. "How are you gonna get in touch with her to meet up? They said no phones."

On the paper handout for the retreat, 'no phones' was the only thing in red ink, while all of the other rules, regulations, and suggestions were in black. If found with a phone, you would be basically sentenced to life in detention. This rule was certainly scarier earlier in the school year, but with only a few weeks left, it lost some of its teeth. None of the students were frisked before entering the bus, so it seemed like it would be based on the honor system, and apparently Matt wasn't too worried about breaking it. He took a small flip phone out of his backpack. "With this."

Bill was struggling to comprehend how far this was going. "You bought a burner for the retreat?"

"Gotta do what ya gotta do," said Matt, slipping the phone back into the front pocket of his backpack.

"This is all pretty dumb." Bill turned back to the window.

"You're dumb," Matt said automatically.

The city became a speck in the distance behind them as the bus chugged along the eight-lane highway. Bill stared blankly at the copy of *Jurassic Park* in his lap while Matt dozed on and off next to him. It was one of his favorite movies, so he'd figured he would give the book a shot even though he had always felt that every movie was better than the book—an opinion vehemently opposed by pretty much every other person on the planet. Each time he read the book version, he thought it was too long, had too many inconsequential side plots and characters, and wasn't focused. Movies cut out all of that unimportant fluff and had a narrower emphasis on what actually mattered. So far, *Jurassic Park* was better than most book versions he had read—not quite as good as the movie—but he still couldn't concentrate at all.

Bill thought about how much he did not want to go on this retreat, and he wished that he were anywhere else but on a bus headed there. The regret ate at him, and he longed to go back in time and simply do the one-day retreat. Bill had long thought the idea of religion was rather silly; twelve years of Catholic schooling often had that impact on people. Hardly any of what he'd learned in school made much sense to him. People in earlier times needed to explain the unexplainable: the sun, the moon, stars, storms… everything that science easily explained today. He did appreciate the Romans, Greeks, Vikings, and other polytheistic cultures who came up with gods for everything; that at least seemed a little more fun. Bill felt people got lazy somewhere along the way. It's a lot of work praying and appeasing

33

countless gods; why not just follow one God and only one God? That was much easier. One God to rule over everything and you better behave or else you won't get into never-ending paradise—an easy way to control and manipulate the masses.

He had turned on his religion fairly early on in his life, as it singled him out personally—he was born out of wedlock. It made him a bastard, and if he was born from sin, he must be evil and sinful; at least that's how he felt. He was baptized, so theoretically that would eliminate all of his sins, but it made him feel awful that something he had no control over could cast him in such a negative light. The relationship started off rocky and never improved.

He was one of two students at his Catholic grade school that at no time had served as an altar boy or girl. His classmates would ask him why he didn't do it. The answer was simple: he didn't want to, so he didn't. He never went into much detail. He'd joke he didn't want to get up early or he'd say he was too busy. Even at a young age, he knew better than to say 'I don't believe in God' at a Catholic school, so he played along, aced his studies, mowed down the sacraments, and didn't ruffle any feathers. His mom occasionally sent him to church on Sundays, but she only attended on Christmas. Bill did see some similarities between God and Santa Claus, namely the idea that if you're a good person and generally do good things, you'll be all right. Bill kept those thoughts to himself.

This pattern continued into high school, where pretty much every major religion was represented in the St. Zeno student body. Bill knew the basics about each, but none spoke to him more than any other. They all sounded more or less the same. He wasn't interested in openly bashing anyone's beliefs. If you believed in a higher power and it brought more meaning and fulfillment to your life, then good for you. In that way, he was slightly jealous of those that did believe. It gave people purpose, it seemed to make them happy, and they had a father that loved them. He wanted all of that. And that was what had led him to this retreat.

Maybe, I'll actually learn something about myself, he thought to himself. *Maybe, just maybe, I'll find some sort of answer or purpose or reason to continue… Yeah, right.*

In the very last seat of the bus, Evan and Jerry, St. Zeno's resident stoners and petty drug dealers, had made a crude sign on a piece of ripped-out notebook paper with 'Show me your boobs' written in black marker. Evan was a well-known atheist at the school, and he often argued in class with each theology teacher assigned to him. He referred to the majority of his classmates as 'cannibals,' in reference to Catholics' belief in transformation—the bread becoming the body of Christ and the wine becoming the blood. Each time he was close to getting suspended or even expelled, he would tone it down until the heat was off him. Why would he go on this retreat? "For fun," he said. He couldn't wait to see what type of shenanigans he would see. Why he had been allowed to go on the retreat was a different question, and Bill wasn't sure of the answer. His best guess was the priests still thought they should give Evan the opportunity to change and accept Christ as his savior.

"Oh, here, gimme it!" said Jerry, brushing the jagged, pointy bangs from his eyes.

Jerry took the paper from Evan and held it up to the rear window for two women driving behind the bus. The passenger saw the sign and shook her head no. Other students at the back crowded on top of one another to see, hoping the woman would change her tune. Evan tried egging her on by pulling up his shirt and exposing his pasty thin midsection and pecs. She laughed and began to pull up her shirt to the delight of the students. As the bottom of her black bra began to show, she released her shirt and gave the middle finger with both hands. Jerry stood on the seat, turned around, and pulled down his pants and underwear to his knees, exposing both butt cheeks. He alternated slapping each one as the students cheered him on. The car changed lanes and sped away while Jerry pulled his pants up and received some high-fives from Evan and his classmates.

"Knock it off back there!" screamed Father Stephen from the front of the bus. All of the students scrambled back to their seats and faced forward, trying to contain their laughter.

Two hours into the journey, the bus had long left behind the eight-lane highway and traffic and now drove on a two-lane highway lined with nothing but trees in every direction. The only other car on the road was Father Leo's white sedan trailing the bus. Inside the bus, the long drive had taken its toll on its passengers. Severe discomfort and claustrophobia set in. A handful of students chatted quietly with their seat mates while others read or rested their eyes. A lucky few were able to overcome their surroundings and sleep.

Bill continued to peer out of the window like a zombie at the trees and asphalt whooshing by—back aching, buttocks sore, legs cramped and mind racing. He hoped for a flat tire or to hit a deer—anything to get him out of a few hours or even minutes at the retreat. *Plop*. He felt something hit his head. He combed through his hair and found a wet, crumpled fleck of paper—a spitball.

"Oh, gross," said Bill, prompting Matt to open his eyes. Bill's face contorted in disgust, and he flicked the moist paper to the ground, discharging specks of saliva on the seat back in front of him.

"Spitball?" said Matt.

"Yeah." Bill wiped his fingers on his khakis.

Matt looked over his shoulder to the back of the bus. "Who was it?"

Bill turned to see ole blockhead Keith sitting a few rows behind him, holding a straw.

Keith smiled maliciously at Bill and said, "What's wrong?"

Bill turned all the way around on his seat to face Keith. "Knock it off," he said, in his most intimidating tone.

Keith balled up a piece of paper and put it in his mouth. He placed it into the straw. "Or what?"

The two rows in between Bill and Keith were now fully aware of the situation, hoping to see some action but to avoid a spitball.

Bill lost himself in the moment. "Or I'll kick your ass like I did freshman year in football," he said stone cold.

Matt chuckled, and the only other freshman football player between them smiled, recalling the incident.

The moment flashed in Keith's mind as he held the straw to his lips. He'd been throwing rocks at people's helmets on the sidelines during practice. He hit Bill once, but Bill wasn't sure who had thrown it until he saw Keith launching rocks at other people. The next clank against his helmet, Bill told Keith to knock it off. After Keith responded with "or what" and another rock, Bill walked over, grabbed Keith by the facemask, and pulled him down to the ground headfirst. Keith's helmet thudded against the hard dirt and grass, and Bill jumped on top of him. No damage was inflicted thanks to their protective equipment, and several teammates pulled Bill off Keith before it went any further. Bill had to run a few extra laps after practice, but it was well worth it in his mind. It had been a long time coming. After that, Keith hadn't messed with him until the grandpa incident at the water fountain. And now this.

Even with one of his wrestling goons in the seat beside him, ready to pummel Bill at his call, Keith lowered the straw from his mouth. Bill could see the embarrassment on his face.

"Sit down, Mr. Foster!" called Father Stephen from the front.

Bill did what he was told and turned around and took his seat. Matt offered him a fist bump of congratulations. No more spitballs were sent Bill's way, allowing him to wallow in misery about the retreat in peace.

The last bit of light hung in the red-orange sky. The inside of the bus was dark and completely silent until it slowed, alerting its passengers something was happening. The bus turned onto a dirt path swallowed up by trees marked with a basic green sign with white lettering that read, 'Eternal Springs 2.'

"It's a sequel?" said Matt.

"I think it means two miles," offered Bill.

Matt crossed his arms and sighed. "It's still a lame name."

The bus slowly jostled down the unfinished road, bouncing up and down like a roller coaster—some students cheered and raised their hands in the air, while others felt like they were going to vomit. Bill and Matt gripped the seat in front of them as they constantly banged their shoulders into one another. They couldn't see much more than a few feet of trees in the dark, thick forest.

After a couple of minutes, the bus and Father Leo's car emerged from the forest into a vast clearing. Without the cover of trees, there was just enough light to make out the grounds. The first thing Bill saw was a sign the size of a small car, much more intricate than the street sign at the dirt road entrance. A vivid landscape had been carved into the rectangular wooden sign: jagged grey mountains with streams that zigzagged down to a cobalt lake. The baby-blue sky was filled with puffy white clouds, and doves soared above the treetops. Bill's eyes locked onto a massive cross, encircled by a bright yellow sun, that towered above all and seemingly watched over the land—it made Bill uneasy. The name 'Eternal Springs' was emblazoned in gold metal lettering across the mountains.

Beyond the garish sign, the buses passed a large grass and dirt field and a fenced court for basketball and tennis on the left side. Much to the delight of the students, the courts looked brand new, with perfect hoops and nets. Further down the road a lake, shaded with hints of blue, green and brown, and bordered by a rocky shore, extended into the tree line. Three canoes lay on the grass in front of a short dock. On the right side of the road stood the first of two buildings: a long rectangle made of brick filled with white-bordered windows. A short glass-enclosed walkway linked the brick building to a taller, more impressive square-shaped building made of large colorful stones and concrete. An entirely wooden structure with a pitched roof that ascended to the heavens was attached to the stone building. Dirt walking paths connected the buildings to the courts and wrapped around the lake, trailing off into the woods. Intermittent light posts standing five feet high and glowing yellow lined the paths and made it feel like an old-time main street. The bus slowly rolled to a stop in front of the stone building.

Father Stephen stood up at the front and tried to work out a kink in his back. "All right, we're here. Everyone off."

The students grabbed their luggage and spilled out of the bus, happy to stretch their legs. They formed their usual groups and took in their surroundings.

"Well it ain't the Four Seasons, but it's not so bad," said Matt.

"Yeah," said Scott. "Looks pretty nice."

Butterflies tore through Bill's stomach as he looked around the grounds and tried to convince himself that everything was going to be okay. Down the road a few hundred feet, just at the beginning of the woods, a brand-new blue two-story craftsman style house with white shutters and a half-finished deck sat at the top of small incline. Bill turned back and stood in the shadow of the ominous wooden building that rose in front of him. He was sure it was a church, and it terrified him. Why would they need such a grand church here? He studied the stone structure in front of him— it looked like it had been built decades ago, but the two large windows and the broad, castle-like wooden doors between them appeared to be recent additions.

Father Stephen cupped his mouth and shouted, "Okay, everyone, please move inside. Let's go."

The massive castle doors swung open. Bright light emanated from the void, and two men clad in red shirts and khaki pants appeared. Each held a door as the retreaters passed through, following the light to their hopeful salvation. Bill swallowed hard. The light felt more like a runaway freight train rolling right at him. *Here we go.*

CHAPTER 7:
Eternal Springs

———

THE STUDENTS POURED THROUGH THE DOORS INTO THE ILLUMINATED lobby of the main building—it was large enough to hold all thirty retreaters comfortably. In front of both windows sat a pair of chairs upholstered in green with small circular wooden tables between them. Colossal wooden beams traversed the ceiling, and the stone walls were full of paintings portraying scenes from the Bible. Bill noticed a near-naked Adam and Eve, perfectly covered by well-placed bushes to hide their naughty parts, being tempted by a snake with an apple in the Garden of Eden and a muscle-bound David in tattered clothing standing triumphantly with his slingshot over the body of Goliath. Bill moved further into the lobby and stood next to a small room with floor-to-ceiling windows like a shop at the mall. With the lights off on the inside, Bill couldn't make out exactly what was in there, but he thought he saw several t-shirts and sweatshirts hanging on hooks and countless stacks of books.

"Hello, everyone!" a voice called from the across the room. Bill couldn't see who it came from. A handful of students weakly responded.

Again the voice called out, but this time louder, "I said, *hello, everyone!*"

Bill dipped his head around the person standing in front of him and saw a small man with short, curly red hair and a thin moustache. His large brown glasses made his head look like a peanut. More students feigned excitement.

"That's more like it!" said the man with a smile from ear to ear. "My name is Mr. Jacobs, and I will be your host for the next four days. First things first, we're going to head into the chapel for a short tutorial and meet and greet. So, please, everyone put your things down around the walls of the room to leave a path and head into the church."

"Already with the church?" said Bill, setting his bags on the floor.

"I think you better get used to it," said Matt.

The students made their way into the grandiose church, and Bill felt like he was transported to medieval England. It was an imposing structure, far more elegant and regal than the churches Bill was used to attending. Two columns of pews stretched from the entrance down to the elevated white stone sanctuary which housed the altar—enough seats for ten retreats. Ornate chandeliers hung from the pitched ceiling that rose thirty feet above them. Even the tiles they walked on looked like a piece of art, arranged in a diamond pattern of black and white. The entire building still smelled of fresh-cut wood.

Despite Bill's lack of interest in the faith of the religion, he did have an admiration for the splendor of a church, specifically stained-glass windows. And even with the lack of sunlight, this church's glass didn't disappoint. Three large windows stood behind the altar. The center window, the tallest and widest, rose from the floor to the ceiling ending in a rounded top and depicted a radiant gold sun in a blue sky above a green field. The crucifix that hung behind the altar was perfectly centered in the middle of the sun. The two smaller windows flanking the centerpiece were decorated with a vertical pattern of interlocking blue circles and red diamonds bordered by flowers of pink, purple, yellow and red. The church's west wall, which didn't border on any other buildings, held stained-glass illustrations of the fourteen stations of the cross, starting with Jesus being condemned to death and ending with Jesus being laid in the tomb.

The students filled in the pews, leaving the last twenty or so rows untouched. Bill sat next to Matt and could now get a better look at the small man that ascended the stairs of the sanctuary. Jacobs appeared to be in his late forties and wore very short khaki shorts with knee-high, white socks and brown hiking shoes. His red and purple Hawaiian shirt depicting the Eternal Springs logo was unbuttoned too low, exposing far more of his chest than anyone wanted to see.

A man and woman followed Jacobs and sat in the seats at the edge of the sanctuary. They wore matching red Eternal Springs polos and khaki pants. The man looked to be in his early thirties, with short, parted brown hair and an athletic build. The woman was in her early twenties and caught all of the boys' attention with her wavy dark-brown hair that cascaded to her shoulders like a waterfall.

Pete elbowed Matt in the ribs and stuck his tongue out like a panting dog. "Damn, who is that?"

Jacobs stood at the front of the sanctuary before the altar, clapped his hands, and then rubbed them together. "Okay, everyone settled in?" began Jacobs. "Great! Welcome to the grand opening of Eternal Springs!" Jacobs clapped like the best movie he had ever seen had just rolled the credits. Pete sarcastically clapped along with him, and other students joined in.

Jacobs continued, "I hope you are all very excited, because I certainly am! Just in case you didn't hear before or you already forgot, I am Mr. Jacobs, and I am the owner and operator of Eternal Springs. I bought this facility a little over two years ago, and my dream was to turn it into a place where people could come to be at peace. To take a break. To get away from their normal lives. To learn about themselves. And most importantly, to be with God. And with a little help from the man upstairs," Jacobs pointed up, and Bill's eyes followed, hoping just once to see someone; but alas, he only saw ceiling, "all of my wildest dreams for this place have come to fruition. I really hope you enjoy your time here. It's really going to be… *amazing*. This experience will be quite incredible if you fully give *all of yourself* to the process."

The students fidgeted in their seats—trepidation from Jacobs' speech and aching legs and backs from the long, uncomfortable journey combined to leave them entirely restless.

Jacobs paced along the white stone of the sanctuary. "Now, to go over some of the basics: You will each have your own room. There are bathrooms at the ends of each residential hallway and other bathrooms scattered about the facilities. All meals will be held in the dining room, which you may have seen is located on the other end of the lobby. We have an excellent cook, so you should really, *really*, enjoy the food. We make very healthy dishes, so you get all of the nutrients you need, because at Eternal Springs, we strive to be pure in both mind and body." Jacobs pointed to his head and his small potbelly.

Matt leaned over to Bill. "Must be eat as I say, not as I do."

"During any time that is not spent in prayer and reflection, you are free to roam the grounds. The land around here is quite exquisite, as most of God's creations are. I'm sure you all saw the basketball and tennis courts on your drive in. They are brand new, and I bet that will be a very popular place for you to hang out. We have a small lake with a few canoes that you can paddle around in, or you can take a hike along one of the many paths in the woods. One such path will lead you to Hope Springs, an absolutely gorgeous swath of land that showcases God's incredible majesty. We almost named this retreat center directly after it, but we decided to go with Eternal Springs instead because when you come here, you are preparing yourself to spend *eternity* with God. It's about a ten-minute or so hike from here, and it's a great place to meditate and enjoy nature. Just don't venture too much farther into the woods because they are haunted."

The students stared blankly at Jacobs, who waited with an obnoxious smile on his face for a response but never received one. He carried on, unfazed, "I'm just kidding. They're not haunted. There are, however, deer, snakes, perhaps a coyote... maybe you'll get lucky and see a bear or other wildlife, so please, do be careful. They hardly ever venture into the area around the grounds, but if you take a trail deeper into the woods, you should definitely keep your eyes peeled. If you encounter any wildlife, just back away slowly and leave them be. If you're not very outdoorsy, downstairs beneath the lobby, there is a rec room, filled with table games and board games and all sorts of fun stuff."

Jacobs took a deep breath. "Now for what we don't have and for what you won't need."

The students exchanged quizzical looks.

"We do not have any televisions."

The students muttered amongst themselves.

"We do not have any video games."

The students grumbled louder.

"We do not have any computers."

The students whined.

Jacobs raised his voice to stay above the students, "We do not have any Wi-Fi."

The students booed loudly.

Jacobs gestured with his hands to quiet the crowd. "Although you were told not to bring any phones with you, I'm sure we'll find some over the next few days. There are always a few stinkers in the bunch. You'll survive a couple days without those things, I promise you. It has happened before. The world will still be *there* when you are done *here*."

Jacobs again paced the sanctuary. "Now, one thing you probably won't be used to is that there are no clocks here."

Bill thought about the watch stashed in his backpack as Jacobs continued.

"We don't want you to be rushed or feeling like you are on a schedule. We're simply on God's time. We will make announcements to let everyone know throughout the day what is going on and when. So don't worry, you won't miss a thing. We do start bright and early though, so be sure to get to bed and get your rest.

"Finally, I just ask you to be mindful of your surroundings. This will be your home for the next four days, so, *please*, treat it with the care and respect you would give your actual home. I'm sure you'll all have a wonderful time and if any problems arise, please notify me or anyone else on the staff and we will do absolutely everything we can to help make your stay as close to perfect as possible. Because, of course, the only thing that is perfect is God."

Jacobs presented another terrible smile. The students groaned loudly and shifted in their seats. They'd had enough.

This is worse than I thought, Bill said to himself. He leaned over to Matt and whispered, "I'm gonna go drown myself in the lake." Bill would often make empty and joking threats of killing himself, like anyone else. No one knew there was an unfortunate amount of truth to it.

"Ah, I should probably introduce the rest of the staff," said Jacobs. "This is Delilah."

The beautiful young woman stood with a visibly forced, uncomfortable smile and brushed her hair behind her ear. Her tight polo accentuated every curve. She waved to the students, who each tried their best to keep from drooling. An approving whistle rang out into the air and was followed by several more.

"Now, gentlemen, come on," said Jacobs. "That's no way to treat a lady."

Bill noticed a look of disgust on Delilah's face as she sat down and whispered something to the man next to her. The man only nodded slightly; his face remained stoic and unchanged.

"And this is Mark."

Mark stayed seated and waved with a half smirk. Bill figured Mark's hero must be the David from the painting in the lobby. His polo was at least a size too small, and his arms bulged out of the sleeves.

"I think my little brother wears that same size shirt," Matt cracked out of the corner of his mouth to Bill.

Jacobs' arms pointed to the first pew. "Down here we have Luke."

The tall, slim man swimming in his polo stood and waved. His long, white-blond hair was messily pushed to the sides of his face into his ears.

"And that's Abe."

Abe on the other hand looked as though he had never missed a meal. His polo was painted on, and the students could see every roll. He barely lifted his arm above his waist to wave, perhaps afraid something might rip. His face was covered in a poor attempt at growing a beard—hairless patches lined his cheeks while his neck looked as dense as the forest surrounding the retreat.

"And last and certainly not least, at the back is Ben."

The students turned to see a freckled face smiling at them in the pew behind the last row of students. He tapped his index and middle finger to his forehead and flipped them forward in a sloppy salute.

"We are all dedicated to serving you and making this the experience of a lifetime," said Jacobs. "Okay?"

Jacobs paused, and the students hoped and prayed this would finally end.

"Wonderful. I'm sure you've heard enough out of me. Let's all move into the dining hall for a delicious dinner and then we will get you to your rooms."

Compared to the cathedral-like church, the dining hall was fairly dull and unremarkable. It had been an addition to the building and looked more like the inside of a cabin with its wood floors and three walls of wood beams. The only character was the shared wall made up of the same large colorful stones from the lobby of the building and two long windows that faced the red-brick dormitory. There should have been a view of the woods to the back of the buildings, but the sun had long since set and nothing was visible outside. Long tables with checkered plastic cloths that held eight chairs each stood in perfect rows throughout the room.

Bill sat down at the end of the table with the same group of students with whom he'd waited for the bus. They passed around the family-style platters of roasted chicken, mashed potatoes, and vegetables. It was nothing spectacular, but it hit the spot.

"Aw, man," whined Pete. "There's no more rolls left?"

"Here." Bill tossed his roll the length of the table to Pete. He didn't want the roll to go to Pete per say, but he wasn't going to eat it. "I don't want mine."

"Thanks, Bill," said Pete, catching the roll. "You're the best."

The boys ate their dinner, and the football teammates shared some stories and laughs. Bill, like Tom, added nothing; they just listened, but it at least kept Bill's mind off the daunting task ahead of him. *Four days... Four days of Hell.*

At the end of the meal, the boys broke open their wet naps and scrubbed their fingers clean.

"Yeah, that's when Matt hooked up with Katie Andrews," said Pete.

"I did not," said Matt.

"Yeah, you did," said Pete. "Don't deny it."

"Did you get away unscathed?" asked Scott, mockingly.

"Yeah, I hope you strapped a helmet on." Pete chuckled heartily.

"I didn't need to," said Matt firmly, "because I didn't hook up with her."

"That's not what she was saying," said Pete.

"She just said that 'cause she was trying to get back at her boyfriend for cheating on her," said Matt. "I didn't hook up with her. I swear to God. I have some standards, you barbarians."

"Everybody hooks up with her," said Pete. "It's like a rite of passage. Don't be embarrassed."

"At least you moved on to something better," said Scott.

"Yeah, no doubt there," agreed Pete. "You tell Rachel you boned Katie?"

"Careful guys," said Dee. "The Lord is watching." Dee nodded toward Jacobs as he passed by the table, whistling "Amazing Grace."

CHAPTER 8:
The Many Rooms

DELILAH LED HER GROUP OF RANDOMLY SELECTED STUDENTS DOWN
the second-floor hallway in the dormitory building, giving out room
assignments. Although the building's exterior was made of red brick, the
interior of the dorm was lined with white drywall, broken up with mo-
cha-colored wooden doors on each side of the narrow, dimly lit corridor.
Similarly colored trim bordered the doors and extended the length of the
long hallway along the floor where the wall met the sage carpet.

"Thirty-one. Wilber, Greg."

Greg grabbed his bag and walked into the room.

"Do you know what we're doing tonight?" asked Matt.

"No," answered Bill glumly. He picked at his teeth with his finger, trying to dislodge a piece of chicken. "Just supposed to go back to the lobby
after we get our rooms and put our stuff away." Bill wasn't a fan of all this
secrecy.

"Thirty-two. Fields, Xavier."

Matt figured he already knew what the answer was, but he asked anyway. "Do you want to play cards tonight?"

"Cards?" Bill repeated, shocked. "When?"

"When we get done with everything."

Bill wasn't excited about the idea, but this was supposed to be the start
of the new him. "Who's playing?"

Matt shrugged. "I don't know. I got a couple feelers out there."

Old habits died hard, and Bill instinctively looked for an excuse instead
of an outright refusal. "It's probably gonna be pretty late."

"So what? It'll be fun."

"Thirty-three," called Delilah. "Payton, Keith."

"I'll think about it."

Keith slipped through the other students to get to his room, bumping slightly into Bill, which nudged him into Delilah.

Bill stepped back. "Sorry, I...." The sheepish apology trailed off as he looked into Delilah's gorgeous blue eyes and then down at the ground.

"It's okay," she said sternly. "Keep on an eye out for where you're going." She continued down the hall as Bill paused to let other students go first.

"Nice move," said Matt, elbowing Bill on the arm. He must have missed Keith's push.

"Thirty-four. Bell, Jason."

Pete ambled down the hall, stopped at Keith's doorway for a high-five, and continued to Matt and Bill. "Hey, there you guys are."

"You get your room?" asked Matt.

"Yeah," said Pete. "I'm downstairs. Number twenty-two." He glanced at Delilah. "Oh, of course you guys get her."

"Thirty-five. Simpkiss, Gerald."

"Don't, man," said Matt. He gave Pete a soft thud on the top of the shoulder with his fist, but it was too late; Pete was ready to attack his prey.

"Thirty-six. Foster, William."

Bill shuffled into his room with his massive bag and backpack while Pete leaned against the wall, less than a foot away from Delilah.

"Hi," said Pete.

"Hello," said Delilah, leaning her clipboard against her chest.

"You're Delilah, right?" asked Pete.

"I am," she said. "And you're Pete."

"How did you know that?" asked Pete.

Delilah tapped the nametag on Pete's chest with her pen.

"Oh, right," said Pete. "I keep forgetting about that dumb thing. It's very nice to meet you."

She took a deep breath to calm herself. "It's nice to meet you too."

Subtlety had never been Pete's strong suit, and he just could not stop himself. "You are gorgeous, Delilah. We should hang out sometime."

Her lip curled in disgust. "And why would I want to do that?"

Pete smiled slyly. "We could have some fun together."

"What kind of fun?"

"I think you know." Pete winked at her.

"Like… sex?"

"If you're offering…"

Delilah sneered again and rested both hands on her hips. "Sexual intercourse is for married people and married people alone. Marriage is a sacred bond made before the eyes of God, and sex outside of wedlock is a disgusting sin. You have a lot to learn about your faith."

"Looks like I came to the right place then," said Pete undeterred.

"You certainly did." She turned her back and continued down the hall with the room assignments.

"Okay. Well, if you ever change your mind, I'm in twenty-two," shouted Pete.

"That went well," said Matt, patting Pete on the shoulder as he passed.

"I think it did," replied Pete.

Pete turned to Bill. "She digs me don't you think?"

Bill smiled sarcastically and nodded before slamming the door in Pete's face. Pete jumped back just in the nick of time. He saw Tom come up the stairs at the end of the hall.

"Tommy, my boy!" shouted Pete. "Come here!"

Tom whipped around and jumped down the stairs while Pete chased after him, shouting, "Hey, where ya going?"

Bill took in his new home; he imagined a prison cell would be more comfortable. Directly next to the door was an open closet with a few hangers and two white drawers stacked on top of one another. Bill located what looked like an old intercom speaker above the door. *What the hell is that for?* he wondered.

The rest of the drab room contained a single bed against the wall, and on the opposite side there was a small desk with a lamp and a cheap wooden chair. Bill walked across the room to the square window, covered by a sheer drape, and sighed in disappointment; that wouldn't keep out any light in the morning. He pulled the drape to the side to check out the view. There wasn't much on this side of the building, just darkness and trees. He watched them sway in the light breeze for a moment before checking out the desk. It had a pen, notebook, and Bible resting on the top of it. Bill picked up the Bible and flipped through it.

"Attention, everyone. Attention." Bill's head snapped around to the door at the sound of Jacobs' voice in the room, but Bill was still alone. The speaker did in fact work.

"The gift shop is now open. We'll see you down in the lobby shortly. Thank you and have a blessed day."

"You gotta be kidding me," said Bill aloud to himself. *Thump.* He angrily closed the Bible. He wasn't ready to do any readings, so he opened one of the drawers in the desk, tossed the Bible in, and sealed its fate. Bill retrieved the watch from his backpack. It was almost nine o'clock. He was shocked they were still going to do more tonight. He clamped the brown leather strap around his wrist and ran his finger clockwise around the gold metal rim. He needed to wear it, even for just a few minutes. It immediately made him feel better.

CHAPTER 9:

The Interview

A<small>LL OF THE STUDENTS GATHERED IN THE LOBBY FOR THE FINAL ACTIVITY</small> of the night. None of the retreaters outside of Bill and Matt knew what time it was, but they did know that they were beat and ready for bed. Bill had to leave the comfort of his watch back in his room and again felt alone and terrified. The students listened as their assignments to specific groups and leaders were read off. Bill's hopes of being in the same group with Matt were dashed when Matt ended up in a group with Dee. Bill heard his name called for Mark's group, and much to his chagrin he was placed in a group with Pete, Jerry, and three other students he didn't know very well. Pete walloped him across the back. Bill faked a smile and felt the sting across his skin. He longed to join Matt and Dee's group. *At least I'm not with Keith.* Bill cast a glance toward Keith on the opposite side of the room. He scowled right back at him.

Father Leo, still clad in his casual priest wear of black pants and a long-sleeve black shirt with a white clerical collar, addressed the students from in front of the large wooden doors. "Okay, now that everyone is settled and you've broken up into your groups, we will now conduct the interviews with your counselors. We're going to head upstairs to the main hall. You will each meet one at a time, and this will give your counselor the chance to get to know you a little bit better. He will just ask—"

"Or she," Delilah corrected him from the corner of the room near staircases that led up and down. Her students were by far the most excited to get started.

Father Leo waved to Delilah. "I'm sorry, dear. He, *or she*, will just ask you some basic questions. Be honest. That's the only way you will get something out of this. Feel free to talk about whatever is on your mind. It should only take about five to ten minutes for each student. When everyone is finished, we'll meet in the waiting area upstairs and you will then be dismissed for the night. All right, everyone, follow your counselors."

Bill's leader Mark raised his hand in the air. "Okay, fellas, follow me."

Mark merged into the mass of people going up the stairs, and the six boys followed behind, Bill trailing last. Each step on the wooden stairs echoed through the tight staircase. At the top, they reached a large open space dimly lit by fake flame bulbs. In the center stood a stone fountain surrounded by groups of folding chairs quickly being filled by students. Bill glanced at a few more biblical paintings lining the walls. He didn't notice any repeats from the lobby. Mark led his group to the collection of chairs outside room number five.

"All right," said Mark in not much more than a whisper, befitting the aura of the great hall. "This is us."

The boys sat down in the uncomfortable folding chairs facing the fountain. Bill let out an exasperated sigh when Pete sat down next to him.

Mark checked his clipboard. "Where is... Jerry?"

Jerry raised his hand. "Right here."

"Great," said Mark. "You're up first."

Jerry hopped out of his seat, pulled up his sagging pants, and shook Mark's hand. Mark turned back to the group. "The rest of you just hang out here. Please keep it quiet." Mark opened the door and waved to Jerry with his clipboard. "Come on in."

Bill listened to the splashing water from the fountain and the pacifying instrumental music from the boombox as his eyes wandered around the room. Between the flames, the fountain, and the music, Eternal Springs had really nailed the ambience. But even with all of the tools meant to soothe and relax, Bill felt the nervous energy rising inside him.

"You can't see anything in this place," said Pete in a normal volume. He crossed his arms and slouched down in his chair. "Somebody's going to get hurt."

Father Leo, from somewhere in the dark reaches, popped up behind them. "No talking, please."

Pete promptly sat up in his chair. "Sorry, Father."

Bill tried to calm himself. His hands were soaked with sweat, and his heart raced. He did not want to go into that room. At school, he could avoid talking well enough—don't raise your hand, hide behind other students, don't screw around—but in there, it would just be him. He would have to talk. And even worse, he would have to talk about himself.

Bill locked on to the painting closest to him—an illustration of the great flood. Noah's ark battled the raging waves and rain while people drowned in the water around it. Some found refuge on a rock, but it would not last long. They pleaded and extended their hands towards the ark and to the sky for intervention, but they received none. Bill took in a deep breath and exhaled. *Perfect.* He looked elsewhere at the faces of the students around him. No one else looked as nervous as he felt. He counted the seconds and the minutes until the door finally opened and Jerry and Mark emerged from the room.

Mark eyed his clipboard, and Bill's stomach dropped. "Richie."

Richie, one of St. Zeno's portlier students, went into the room as Jerry took a seat on a folding chair. Bill found a brief moment of peace before he once again realized he would have to go in there at some point. This waiting around and not knowing when was torture. He'd rather just get it over with as quickly as possible. *It could have already been over,* he internally warred with himself.

The time passed, the door opened, and it was Anthony's turn. It didn't take long until Bill went through the agony of waiting and not knowing what was going to happen again. He cracked his knuckles, tapped his foot, and focused on his breathing. Before Bill could really work himself up, Anthony exited the room. *Well, that wasn't too long,* Bill thought to himself, feeling a glimmer of hope.

Mark checked his clipboard. "Peter."

Pete sprang to his feet and entered the room. It was a fifty-fifty chance now. *Let's just do this,* Bill said to himself, trying to rally some nerve. His mind shifted back to the pain in his mouth from the stuck food particle. He once again tried to dislodge the food, but it was packed in too deep. After about five minutes, the door opened, and Pete sauntered out.

"How was it?" asked Bill.

"It started out fine," answered Pete. "But then he started touching me and taking his clothes off."

Pete leaned down and wrapped his arms around Bill. "Hold me."

Bill shoved him away. "Get off me."

Father Leo cleared his throat, getting the attention of the boys. Through the darkness, the boys could barely see his face but could feel his omnipotent presence boring into their souls, and they both returned to behaving themselves. Mark came out and asked for Brandon. Now, Bill knew he was next. The mettle Bill faked dissipated, and the fear returned. His heart felt like it would explode. He couldn't sit still, relentlessly squirming in his chair. Why couldn't he just be normal? Why did every encounter with every person have to scare him so much? He tried to calm down with a few deep breaths. *It's not a big deal,* he kept saying to himself.

Mark and Brandon exited the room. Mark checked his clipboard one last time. "Last but not least, William. Come on in."

Bill's legs wobbled as he got up from his seat and walked to the door. He saw Mark extend his hand, so he quickly wiped the sweat from his palm on his pants and shook it. Mark's grip was too firm, and Bill felt the fingers in his bones compact into one another. *You're strong. We get it.*

Bill entered the cozy, adjunct room filled with the same flickering light bulbs from the meeting hall. Pale moonlight entered through two windows hung with sheer curtains. In front of him two folding chairs faced one another about three feet apart, and next to him three loveseats were positioned in a crescent moon shape. A tissue box sitting on the table in the middle of the couches stoked the flames of Bill's anxiety. *Why would anyone need that?*

"Have a seat, William," said Mark.

"Bill is fine," he said, lowering himself into the chair.

Mark sat in the other chair, which was so close Bill felt like he was right on top of him. He subtly pressed his heels into the floor and slid the chair back a few inches.

Mark crossed his legs and rested his clipboard in his lap. "Okay, Bill it is. My name is Mark. It is a pleasure to meet you."

"Yeah, you too." Bill sat back in the chair, trying to create as much space as possible between him and his group leader. He rested his hands in his lap and interlocked his fingers.

"So, how are you liking it here so far?" asked Mark.

"It's fine," said Bill, with a quick nod, praying the interview would end.

"Just fine?"

Bill exhaled and gave Mark what he thought he wanted to hear. "It's great. I love the… ambience with the lights and the sounds and the pictures."

"Good," said Mark. "We want everyone to be relaxed." He flipped through the sheets of paper on the clipboard.

Bill played with his hands. "Whatcha got there?"

"Oh, nothing," said Mark. "Just your life story."

Bill raised his eyebrows. "It's got all that in there?"

Mark grinned. "Well, of course not everything, but a good amount. Honor Society, ranked sixth in the class, excellent grades, baseball team. Wow! Impressive! You should be very proud."

Bill continued fidgeting with his hands. He became more uncomfortable with every word. "Yeah," said Bill, hoping the praise would end. He never took compliments well.

Mark chuckled. "You don't seem too enthusiastic."

"It's not that big a deal," said Bill.

"Of course, it is," said Mark. "You are on a path to a great future. You are an excellent role model for all of your fellow students."

Bill snorted and laughed. "Okay."

"You may not realize it," continued Mark, "but I'm sure there are a lot of people who look up to you."

"Yeah, sure," said Bill. His face turned bright red. *Good thing it's so dark in here.*

"So, how is everything?" Mark switched crossed legs. "How is life?"

"Excellent." Bill nodded his head. *Lie—punishment: five Hail Marys.*

"Excellent?! Very good! How is your family?"

Bill had trouble meeting Mark's eyes. "Fine. Everything's good." *Lie—punishment: five Our Fathers.*

"Great. That's what we want to hear."

"Yep."

"And school is going well it seems?"

"Well enough."

"Okay. How's baseball?"

"Good."

"Good. What position do you play?"

Bill couldn't tell if Mark was a baseball fan or just making small talk. "Some infield. Some outfield."

"Cool. Do you start?"

"No, I hardly ever play." Bill thought about bringing up the game-winning homer, but he let it pass.

"Oh, well," said Mark brushing a hand through the air, "it's still fun right?"

"Yeah."

"Any girlfriend?"

Bill was taken aback by the lack of relevancy of the question. "Uh, no."

"Oh really? Good looking guy like you…" Mark leaned forward and tapped Bill on the knee. "Why not?"

Because I never leave my house because I hate myself and am terrified of every aspect of life. Bill swallowed hard. "I don't know. Haven't gotten around to it, I guess." The discomfort and awkwardness surged through every fiber of his body, and he accidently blurted out, "Is Delilah single?"

Mark pursed his lips. "I think she's a bit out of your league." Bill furrowed his brow until Mark burst into laughter. "I'm sorry. I'm just having a bit of fun."

Bill took and released a huge breath through his nose. "Well, that makes one of us."

"Ha, you are a pistol, aren't you?"

"I wish I had a pistol."

Mark laughed hysterically and slapped his knee. "You are just too much."

"Thanks." If there were peaks of sarcasm, this was Mt. Everest. Bill just sat and waited for Mark to collect himself.

Mark took a deep breath and sighed contently as he released it. He was at last able to continue. "So, it sounds like life is pretty good."

"Yeah," said Bill after a pause. "It's not bad." Visions of the day Bill quit football overwhelmed him. He felt the warm tears dripping down his face. He heard the splashes of water filling the bathtub. He felt the weight of the sharp paring knife in his hand. Bill reached for his wrist and rubbed where the wound would have been and where the watch should be. He needed it now.

"How about spiritually? How often do you go to church?"

Bill snapped out of it and brought himself back to the present. *And here it comes. Just lie. Just lie and get out of here.* Bill wiggled around in his chair. "Oh, you know, the usual amount." *Lie—punishment: one thousand Our Fathers.*

Mark nodded his head. "And what would 'the usual amount' be?" Mark put air quotes around 'usual amount.'

Bill continued to war with himself as his conscience was tugged back and forth. *Everyone told me to be open and honest. Try it. Maybe it will help you. Something needs to help you. You need to accomplish something here.* "When we go at school, mostly."

"Really? That's it?"

Bill nodded.

"You don't go on your own?"

"Nope." The word barely escaped Bill's mouth.

"Why not?"

Keep going. Bill struggled to swallow. He had no moisture in his mouth, and it felt like his throat was swelling shut. "I'm not really into it. It's just not my thing."

Mark looked completely dumbfounded. His entire body shook with a grunt, and his mouth gaped open. He rested the clipboard on his lap and leaned forward in his chair, closing the gap between him and Bill, which prompted Bill to lean back to try to regain some of his lost space. "Wow! I'm shocked! I did not think this would be the case. Wow! How long has it been like this?"

"I don't know. A while." Bill's heart raced, and he took short, quick breaths.

"You believed at some point though, yes?"

"Yeah. I guess… when I was a kid."

"Well, why not anymore?"

"I guess I've just outgrown it."

"I've hit my thirties—I haven't outgrown it. Your priests have lived longer, and they haven't outgrown it. What makes you think you've outgrown it?"

"I don't know," started Bill. "You get older. You start to see things differently."

"How so?"

Bill thought about it. "Like… do you still believe in Santa Claus or the Tooth Fairy?"

Mark sat back in his chair. "Of course not. No."

"Why?"

"Because they're not real."

"Right," concurred Bill. It was that easy to him. Why didn't Mark see it?

Mark again leaned forward, clipboard dangling between his legs. "I think that's two separate cases."

"Not really. There's no evidence that Santa Claus or the Tooth Fairy exist. They're made up. How is God any different? There's no evidence God exists."

All of the laughter had left Mark. He laid the clipboard on the floor and looked sternly into Bill's eyes. "I think we see evidence of God every-where… every day."

Bill looked down to the floor.

Mark broke his gaze and continued, "There's no concrete evidence that He doesn't exist either, right? You know for certain there is no God?"

Bill lifted his eyes back from the floor. "No, I can't know that for certain."

"Okay. So, you haven't totally given up on the idea?"

Bill thought for a moment, not sure where to go next: let it go and get out of there or press the issue. The voices echoed in his head. *Be honest. It's the only way you'll get anything out of this.* He had a sudden rush of boldness. "I don't know. I just don't understand how God can exist in a place like this. So much death and hate… suffering and destruction… The world's a pretty terrible place. You'd think He'd want to help out or something instead of just letting everything go to hell."

Mark's eyes went wide with surprise. "Wow, that's a lot to unpack there. What do you mean? War? Terrorism?"

Bill couldn't stop. He had never talked like this in his life to anyone, and the words continued to rush from his brain to his mouth. "Yeah," said Bill. "Everything. All you have to do is watch the news for a bit and you get a good idea of what the world is like; terrible things happening constantly. It doesn't make much sense to me if there is an all-powerful, loving God, who seems to have abandoned his children. So, either there is a God, and he's doing a terrible job or there isn't a God… and the world makes a lot more sense."

"It's not a job," responded Mark. "He's not pulling strings like a puppet master. He gives everyone free will. We are free to live our lives the way we want, within the world he has given us."

"But what about God's will? I thought everything that happened was because God willed it. God controls everything. He's all powerful."

"He is. And everything that occurs *is* God's will. But that doesn't mean we're robots predetermined to live our lives like a script. We were given free will, and we have the ability to use it."

Bill snorted. "That's a nice thought and all, but if someone murders me, I didn't really get a say in it, did I? And if God is all-knowing and all-powerful, he certainly saw that murderer coming and could have interceded. I mean, maybe not for me, but for someone better that was going to get killed."

"God doesn't promise us anything in this world. If we follow Him and believe in Him and love Him, we're promised the afterlife with Him."

"I just think this world could be a bit better, that's all. It seems like God has abandoned his children and left them to suffer and die."

"It may seem like that in tough times, but God never abandons us. And if something does happen to you, and you're a true believer, you will spend eternity in heaven with God."

Bill grimaced at the deflection. "Maybe. *If* it exists. It just doesn't make sense to me. Entire cities wiped out by hurricanes and tornadoes and tsunamis? There's no free will there. I guess you could live somewhere else, but it's mostly just bad luck."

Mark paused, contemplating his next words. "Everyone has a different path to walk. No one path is the same. Some have paths that are much harder to walk than others, this is true."

"But why?" Bill quickly retorted. "Some people never even have a chance. Some people were just born to suffer? Do they get a better, more awesome heaven, or do they have to use the same one that a person who lived a normal, happy life gets into?"

Mark focused his eyes directly at Bill. "Life is not a competition to see who can suffer more."

"Are you sure?" What little hope Bill had left to restore his faith was burning in flames. There was nothing left in him but hate and anger and sadness.

Mark sighed. "Well, that's a fairly negative view to take about the world. There's beauty and greatness and compassion everywhere you look. People come together in the worst of times. People help each other. Yes, there are some bad people in the world because, unfortunately, they *choose*, through their own free will, to do bad things. You shouldn't get hung up on those people. You should look more at the positives of the world instead of solely being stuck on the negatives."

Bill shook his head. "I don't think you should ignore all the negatives and just pass them off as some sort of test of resolve. I know people can come together and do great things, but I feel like it would be a lot easier if they never had to."

"So, everything in life should be perfect and everyone should get exactly what they want?"

Bill nodded. "Yeah. Sounds good to me."

"Then why have life at all? Why not just start in heaven?"

Bill pointed to Mark. "Exactly."

"Well, because life is full of incredible possibilities. I have faith that God will bless me and the ones I love and everyone that loves Him, and that He will show them the way."

"I don't believe that." Bill shook his head harder and clenched his jaw. "I can't believe that. My grandpa... he believed. He went to church. He praised the Lord. He was a good person. And what blessing did he get? Het got an incurable disease. He suffered every day and wasted away to nothing and died." Bill choked out the final words as tears welled up in his eyes. "God didn't protect him. God didn't bless him. God didn't give a shit about him."

Bill sniffled and wiped away a tear. He was quickly falling into the quicksand of his emotions, impossible to climb out. And the hate swelled inside him. His throat ached as he tried to hold back the wave of sobs.

"And how about my father? He's the one that was blessed. He abandons me and my mom when I'm a kid, wants nothing to do with me. He's rich and successful now—has his own family. That jerk is the one that gets blessed?"

And there it was—the root of all Bill's issues. He had never said it out loud before. An unloving father discarding an innocent child. The child that grew into a teenager full of anxiety and fear and self-hatred. A teenager that always felt that something was wrong with him, that he was never good enough. A teenager that now looked at himself as worthless and spent most of his time pretending he didn't exist because that's what he really wanted: to no longer exist. He should have never existed in the first place. If his own father didn't love him, why would anyone else? Why would he love himself? Bill could feel the warm stream of tears from each eye.

Bill swallowed hard. Mark left his chair and grabbed a couple tissues from the table. Bill took them from Mark's hand without a word. Mark gave him a moment to collect himself. He knew something had gone off inside of Bill, but he had no idea just how deep down it went.

"I understand your frustration, but God is not trying to punish you personally."

"It feels personal."

"I'm sorry about your grandfather. That's terrible, but God doesn't promise any protection or rewards, if you will, in this life. It's about the afterlife—eternity. It's about receiving salvation through Christ and God.

And you seem to be struggling with the idea of how bad things can happen to good people. Several people in the Bible struggled with the same type of thing. Are you familiar with the story of Job?"

"Yeah." Bill had heard that story plenty of times over the years. "Job is a good guy that loves and follows God and then God lets the devil torment him by killing all of his family members and taking his wealth and he gets sick and other terrible things and God does nothing to stop it. Pretty steep price to pay for being a good, pious follower."

Mark brushed off Bill's interpretation. "You, like Job in the Bible, are mistaken in thinking that there are *good* people. Job thought he was a *good person* and wondered why God would let all of these terrible things happen to him and his family. But no one meets God's standard of good. All fall short of the glory of God."

"Yeah, that's fine. But *no one* can be *good*?"

"No one is worthy of God's standard of good."

"Okay, I understand that God has high standards and that we can't be as good as God... fine. But to not be considered good or worthy at all? That's seems unnecessarily harsh. Why would you want to follow God then, if He says that no one can be good?"

"To redeem ourselves. To overcome our faults and sins and live with God for eternity in heaven. I feel like we're arguing semantics here. We cannot possibly be as good as God, but with God's teachings through Jesus and his help, we can try to be like him. God did not create us just to punish us. He loves us. God is with us. He is on our side."

"Doesn't seem like it. He doesn't have Job's back. He just uses him like a pawn to prove a point to the devil."

"God isn't using Job to prove a point; he's showing Satan that the love of God conquers all. And that even if bad, terrible things happen, we can come to God for peace."

"What peace?" Bill barked back. "God and religion are responsible for the most deaths in the history of the world. I've always wondered about how many wars have been fought and how much blood has been spilled in the name of God... whichever god you happen to follow. Thou shalt not kill, right? Do unto others, as you would have them do unto you, unless of course they are non-believers, in which case, murder them... murder them all, right?"

Mark paused. This fight would not be won tonight. "I'm sorry about your grandfather."

They both sat in silence for a few seconds that felt like hours. How long had Bill been in the room? Bill finally remembered where he was—a retreat with other people. Not some therapist's room where he was by himself. What were the students outside thinking?

Mark finally broke the silence. "So, you have truly lost your faith?"

Bill nodded, staring down to the floor. "Yes."

Mark adjusted his body in his seat. "It seems to me this is the perfect time for you to have this experience. I think you will learn a lot during your time here and maybe even renew your faith."

Bill bit his lip. "I highly doubt that. I'm not promising anything."

"I just ask that you promise to try."

"Okay," responded Bill. *Lie—punishment: eternal damnation in hell.*

Mark rose from his chair, and Bill followed suit. Mark extended his hand out to Bill, and they shook; Mark's grip was much gentler this time around. "Well, it was nice meeting you and getting to know you a bit. If you need anything, let me know. That will be all for now."

"Okay," said Bill. The wave of emotions calmed, and he felt strangely pacified—still embarrassed, but not entirely full of regret. "I hope I didn't freak you out too much. The pope isn't out there waiting to arrest me or something, right?"

Mark laughed. "No, of course not. It is good that you are being honest. It is very important here. It's a crucial first step."

"Okay," said Bill. "Thank you."

"Thank *you*. Have a good night, Bill."

"You too. Bye."

Mark opened the door, and Bill felt an incredible air of relief, like he was floating on a cloud. It came crashing down the moment he stepped into the meeting hall and felt every retreater's eyes lock on him. He must have been the last one. How long had they been waiting for him? He stuffed the tissue into his pocket and took a seat, hoping the darkness covered the redness in his eyes. He slowly lifted his head to see Keith across the fountain nudge the student next to him. Keith raised his two balled hands to his face, put his curled index fingers to his eyes, and turned them back and forth while puffing out his bottom lip to mimic crying. Keith and the student next to him laughed until Father Stephen tapped both of them on the shoulder. Bill clenched his jaw and felt the anger and shame ripple though him.

CHAPTER 10:
The Omen

———

AFTER A FINAL PRAYER, THE STUDENTS WERE TOLD TO RETREAT TO their rooms for the night. Bill joined the mass of people funneling down the stairs, overanalyzing what had what just happened. *I went way too far. Why did I do that? What is wrong with me?* Would his comments go all of the way to Father Leo or Father Stephen? *Maybe Mark will keep it to himself. But what about Keith? He saw me. Why couldn't I just keep my mouth shut like I always do?*

Bill reached the lobby on the main floor and entered the glass breezeway that connected the main building to the dormitory. He caught a glimpse of Matt's head bobbing up and down a few people ahead of him. As Bill picked up his pace and darted between students to catch him, he saw Keith walking shoulder to shoulder with Matt. Whatever they were talking about must have been pretty funny, because Matt threw his head back in laughter. *Please don't be about me.* Bill slowed to a stop at the end of the breezeway and watched the two walk up the stairs together as several other students passed him by. He felt a sharp whack across the back of his shoulders.

"You good?" said Pete without breaking stride.

"Yep," Bill said in little more than a whisper. The last one left in the breezeway, he ascended the stairs shaking his head, literally trying to shake the thoughts from it. *Let it go.* Bill entered his pitch-black room and shut the door. He rested his forehead against the hard wood and whispered to himself, "Three more days."

Bill flipped the light switch on for the ceiling can light and headed for his backpack. He took the watch from the outside pocket and attached it to his left wrist. It slightly calmed his nerves, but he still felt awful physically; he was exhausted and dehydrated—mouth dry as a desert and head pounding. He grabbed the bottle of water from the desk and downed it in a few gulps before he sat down on the bed. His shoulders slumped, and he stared blankly ahead at the white wall, thoughts of the interview creeping back into his mind. *All you had to do was keep your mouth shut.* Out of the corner of his eye he saw the door open and Matt enter.

"Hey." Matt shut the door.

"Hey," Bill said half-heartedly before looking down. He wondered what Keith had told him.

Matt leaned his back against the door. "Sorry... I knocked."

"My bad. I didn't hear you. What's up?" Bill noticed the flip-phone in Matt's hand. "How's your contraband working?"

Matt shrugged. "Service isn't great, but I'm getting texts, so that's good."

Bill nodded, and his entire body rocked back and forth. "Cool."

"Are we still playing cards tonight?"

"I don't know. I'm not really in the mood." It was the same answer Bill had given Matt countless times over the years.

Matt pressed him, determined to get a 'yes.' "Oh, come on. It'll be fun."

Bill thought it over. *Maybe Keith didn't say anything. Maybe Matt's being a good friend.* But then Bill's mind turned negative like it always did. *Or maybe Matt's trying to get me to his room so he and Keith can make fun of me.* "Is anyone else playing?"

"Sounds like it's just Pete," said Matt. "Everyone else is tired." He fought off a yawn.

"So am I," said Bill. He retracted his shoulder blades and leaned into a back stretch. "It's pretty late."

"Yeah, I know. But come on."

Another knock rapped on the door, and Matt quickly slid his phone into his pants pocket.

"Who is it?" called out Bill.

"Father Leo." The voice penetrated the door and rattled the boys' nerves. Bill sprang to his feet. He unhooked the watch from his wrist and shoved it into his pocket while Matt backed a few feet away from the door. They looked at each other anxiously.

"Hello?" the priest called out.

"Oh… you can come in," said Bill.

Matt looked surprised, afraid to be caught in another retreater's room after receiving specific instructions to go back to his own room and go to sleep. Through gritted teeth, he mouthed to Bill, "What?"

Bill shrugged as Father Leo squeezed through the doorway.

"Oh, hello, gentle*men*." Father Leo crossed his arms over his large chest and raised an eyebrow.

They both meekly responded at the same time, "Hello, Father."

"Are we having a little party in here? I thought my instructions were quite clear after the prayer."

"No, Father," said Matt. "I was just on my way out."

"Yes," said Father Leo, matter-of-factly. "You were. Goodnight, Matthew."

"Goodnight, Father." As he exited the room after side-stepping Father Leo, Matt held up a four and a two on his fingers that only Bill was able to see.

Father Leo turned his attention to Bill. "How was your first day?"

Bill's skin started to crawl. *Did Mark tell him?* "Fine, Father," he said, scratching at his cheek.

"Good," said Father Leo with a pleasant smile. "I think this will be a great experience for you."

Bill sighed. "Why am I the only one who doesn't believe that?"

"You just need to be fully open to the experience. You can't shut yourself off or you'll get absolutely nothing out of this."

"Will do, Father." Bill scratched at his shoulder. He was incapable of just being still. "Well, I better get some sleep. Big day tomorrow."

Thankfully the priest took the hint. "It most certainly is. Goodnight, Bill."

"Goodnight, Father."

Bill replaced the watch on his wrist and debated with himself for a few minutes about whether or not to go play poker before cracking the door open and peeking into the dark hallway. It looked clear—no priests, no counselors, no students. Most importantly, no Keith. He tiptoed even on the soft carpet in the hallway, terrified of being caught after curfew. Bill had never been a rule breaker. Then again, he never hung out with people, and he never told the truth about who he really was to anyone, let alone a complete stranger. So, to Bill's own surprise, it seemed he was making an effort to better himself at this retreat. Tonight, he hoped that playing cards would make him feel a little more normal and like one of the guys after his meltdown with Mark.

Bill reached the door with '42' etched on the wall to the side of it. He grasped the doorknob and twisted, causing a slight creak that made himself stop and look back into the darkness of the hallway. Suddenly, the door swung open.

Matt smiled pleasantly while shaking his head in the doorway. "What are you doing?" He waved Bill into the room. "Just come in."

Bill entered the room. It had the exact same layout as the one in which he resided, and he took a seat on the edge of the bed.

Matt rested his backside against the desk and crossed his arms. "So, how'd it go with Father Leo?"

Bill shrugged. "Ah, it was fine. No problems." Even after knowing Matt for twelve years, he was still often uncomfortable around him. Tonight, that lack of comfort was aided by Matt and Keith's earlier conversation in the breezeway. He felt the unease move from his brain to the rest of his body like an advancing army.

"Good. You have to do any penance?"

Bill forced a chuckle. "Not yet." Bill's eyes wandered around the small room. "Where's Pete?" Bill didn't necessarily want him to show up, but cards with two people wouldn't be a whole lot of fun.

"I'm not sure. He probably got lost."

"No kidding." Bill was tempted to ask what Matt and Keith had been talking about on their way back to the rooms, but he didn't want to come on too strong. He settled on a much more benign question. "How'd today go for you?"

"It was fine," Matt said with a shrug. "Whatever. You?"

"Yeah, same. Who's your counselor?" Bill already well knew who Matt's counselor was, since he'd stood idly by and hoped he would be a part of that group.

"Abe. The big dude." Matt opened his arms wide to show Abe's width. "How is he?"

"He was cool." Matt sounded disinterested. "Seems like a nice guy, I guess. I don't know. Who did you have?"

"Mark. Tiny shirt guy." Bill flexed his bicep.

"Right," said Matt with a laugh. "How's he?"

"Fine." Bill studied Matt's face—nothing seemed off; no smirks on the outside, no indication he was secretly laughing on the inside.

Matt grabbed the phone off the desk and flipped it open. "You guys didn't go pump some iron afterward?"

Bill smiled. "Not yet. First thing tomorrow morning. You want to tag along?"

Matt's thumbs frantically sped around the buttons. "Nah, I'll leave you two to your date."

Bill picked at his teeth and let out a groan.

"What's wrong?"

Bill tried to suck out the piece, shredding his tongue across his teeth over and over. "I have a piece of food stuck in my teeth and it will not come out. It's driving me crazy."

"That's a shame," said Matt, focusing solely on the phone.

Bill flicked his head toward Matt. "Rachel?"

"Yeah, sounds like she's definitely coming up on Saturday."

"Awesome."

"I think she's bringing Maddie."

"Sweet." Bill didn't want to get excited. There was still plenty of time for him to chicken out.

"You two met, right?"

Bill tried to downplay the interaction. Earlier he had told a complete stranger personal things that he would never tell anyone, but he couldn't tell his friend that he had a simple crush on a girl. "Yeah, I think so. At a football game. She has blonde hair, right?"

A small smile formed on the left side of Matt's face. "Rachel said you couldn't stop staring at her."

Bill's face twisted with confusion. He probably was staring, but he would never admit it. "What? No, I didn't stare." He ran his hands through his hair as he felt the heat on his face rise.

"It's cool, man. She's smokin' hot."

Bill nodded, staring down at the floor. "Yeah."

"If she comes up here, this is your chance."

Bill flashed a smile. "I'm sure she can find someone better up here."

"Nah, man. You just need some confidence, that's all."

"I probably need a little more than that."

"Look, I'll tell Rachel to put in a good word with her and then it's on. You just gotta seal the deal."

"Sure thing." Bill's gaze shifted down, and he noticed a sheathed knife with a dark green hilt lying on top of Matt's St. Zeno duffel bag—an easy diversion from this conversation. "What's that?"

Matt followed Bill's pointing hand to the bag. "Oh, yeah." He bounced off the desk and retrieved the knife. "My dad just got this for me." He pulled the near foot-long blade from the black sheath. The stainless steel sparkled in the light as Matt turned it over and back. "For our hunting trip next month. Isn't it gnarly?"

Matt handled the knife hilt first to Bill, who reluctantly took it. "Totally." It was lighter than Bill expected, no heavier than his cell phone, and it reminded him of the knife Rambo used in *First Blood*. "Why did you bring it here?"

"Protection," said Matt, slightly insulted at the question. "We're out in the woods. You never know what might happen."

Bill twisted the knife back and forth in his hand, examining the smooth side of the blade and then the serrated side. He imagined what it would take for him to slice it through flesh. He remembered the time when he didn't have whatever 'it' was. "For sure."

Bill handed the knife back blade first to Matt, who wrapped his hand around the serrated side and sheathed it. "You wanna come with on the hunting trip? My dad wouldn't mind. It'll be fun."

Bill, introvert or not, had no interest. "Um, I don't know. I don't think I'd do very well." Bill ate his fair share of meat and knew it was entirely hypocritical, but he didn't understand the fun of hunting, nor was he interested in killing an animal—well anything bigger than a bug. "I don't think I could do it."

Matt raised his voice, tired of hearing the defeatist in Bill. "It's always 'can't do it.' Do stuff!"

Bill's body clenched.

Matt was practically shouting now. "Stop hiding in your house all the time! Go out and do things! It's the same thing with Maddie and hunting. You gotta get some confidence."

Matt had never talked to Bill like this before, and Bill hated where this was going. One potentially life-altering event was enough for one night. He didn't need another emotional meltdown or, even worse, to start crying again.

Matt lowered his voice to a normal volume. "Believe in yourself. Stop with that, 'I can't' crap."

Bill swallowed hard. He couldn't deny that it made him feel better to hear his friend encourage him, even if Bill didn't believe in it at all. "You're sounding like a motivational speaker."

"If that's what it takes."

The door opened, and for a heartbeat the boys thought they were caught for the second time tonight. They both exhaled when Pete entered carrying a wine bottle in his hand and a plastic bag nestled in his arm like a football.

"Hey, it's about time," said Matt. He noticed the bottle of red wine. "What's that? I thought you brought Jack."

Matt slid down the desk so Pete could put the bottle and bag down. "Yeah, sorry, I got caught."

Matt snickered. "What?"

Pete leaned against the desk and his head slightly tilted to his right shoulder like it often would. "Father Stephen found me in the hallway. Took my Jack, gave me a month of jug."

"You serious?" asked Matt with a chuckle.

"Yup," said Pete.

Matt cracked up laughing, while Bill just smiled slightly.

"Yeah, yeah, laugh it up, jerks."

Matt was still grinning ear to ear. "Well, where the hell did you get that?"

Pete wrapped his hand around the bottle of wine and brought to his face to inspect the label. "Found it in a storage room, near the chapel."

Matt's mouth dropped open. "You stole it? You stole sacramental wine on a retreat?"

Pete thought for a second. "Yeah, there were a bunch of bottles. They won't notice."

Matt shook his head. "You're going to hell."

Pete unscrewed the cap on the bottle and took a swig. Bill could tell by the way Pete's lip curled and face scrunched that he didn't like the taste. "I'll make up for it. You want some?" He offered the bottle to Matt. "The blood of Christ."

Matt squinted his eyes at Pete and sighed deeply before taking the bottle. He took a sip and smacked his lips together repeatedly, but his expression didn't change. "Delicious."

Matt held the bottle to Bill on the bed. "Wine?"

Bill never drank—another consequence of never going out. He had tried wine once or twice with his mother's approval. "It's like juice," she'd said. Bill hated it—it was rancid juice. His mother called it an 'acquired taste.'

He took the bottle and weighed the battle between trying to be a normal person with friends and trying to be a good Catholic again. *Jesus is patient... and forgiving—he can wait another day.* He put the bottle to his lips, and the liquid ran past his tongue down his throat. The subtle fruit taste was wiped away by intense burning in his throat and chest. He couldn't stop his lips from puckering, and he winced. Apparently, he still hadn't acquired the taste.

Matt chuckled. "That good, huh?"

Bill forced himself to take another sip before handing the bottle back to Matt.

"I also got these," said Pete, ripping open a bag of communion wafers.

"What the hell are you going to do with those?" asked Matt.

"Eat 'em," said Pete, popping one into his mouth. He underhand tossed the bag to Matt. "Ugh, dry." Pete took the bottle back for a gulp of wine to wash down the cracker and sat on the ground. "Let's play some cards."

Though he'd only taken two sips, Bill began to feel a bit flushed from the wine. He forgot about the interview and joined Pete on the floor. "What are we playing?"

"Hold 'em," said Matt, fishing the pack of cards from his bag.

"What are we gonna use for chips?" asked Bill.

Matt dropped the bag of communion wafers on the floor. "How's that?"

Bill opened the bag and ate one. "Works for me."

Pete took another swig from the wine bottle. "Twenty a game?"

"Sure," said Matt. "You just want to hand your money over now?" Matt completed the three-person circle on the floor.

Matt briskly ran through the rules and determined the correct amount of 'chips' for each player. Bill began to count out the wafers. His hands felt strange as the wine began to hit him, and he couldn't control them exactly how he wanted. He focused extra hard when he raised his watch to his face. 11:47.

Matt dealt out the cards, and they each inspected their hands. Bill came away with a meager four and seven.

"I call," said Pete. He threw his wafers into the pot.

Bill shook his head and slammed his cards down harder than intended. "Fold."

"I'll check," said Matt. He then turned over the flop: three of spades, six of hearts, and a nine of hearts.

Pete thought for a moment. "I check."

Matt nodded in agreement. "Yeah. Check." Matt turned over the two of clubs.

"Check again," said Pete.

"Well, let's at least make it a little interesting," said Matt, throwing in four wafers.

"Big spender." Pete tossed in four of his own. "I'll call that."

Matt turned over the last card: the king of hearts. Pete's face lit up. "What's the max? Ten?"

"That seems like a pretty big tell," said Bill.

"Yep," said Matt.

Bill's hand shook as he raised the bottle of wine to his mouth and sipped.

Pete pushed his wafers into the pot and took the bottle from Bill. "Well, look how much fun you are!" Pete gave Bill a hard shot to his upper arm with his fist.

Bill snorted, refusing to rub the aching muscle while Pete drank.

Matt studied Pete. "Ten, huh? Pick up something good?"

"Don't be scared, homey." Pete's teeth were beginning to turn purple.

Matt took another second to think it over.

"Just play!" interjected Bill. He was growing bored, and his fear of speaking had been flushed down his throat with the wine.

"All right, screw it. I'll call." Matt placed his cards on the floor face up. "Let's see 'em. I got a pair of kings."

Pete joyfully followed. "And on the fifth day God created the flush, and it was good."

Pete started to pull the wafers closer to him until Matt grabbed his hand. "Whoa, wait! You lost!"

Pete shook his head. "No, I won."

Matt rolled his eyes and shook his head. "No. I have a pair of kings and you have... nothing."

Pete pointed at the cards. "I have a flush. It's right there. Are you blind?"

Matt looked closer. "Are *you*? You have four hearts and a diamond. That's not a flush."

"Yes it is!"

"A flush consists of five cards of the same suit, you moron. You have five cards of the same color, which is nothing."

"Yeah," said Bill. "You're a heart short, buddy." Bill gave Pete one of his patented back slaps—it stung his hand more than it did Pete's back.

Pete leaned over to inspect the cards. "Shit!"

Matt grabbed the bottle of wine and set it down next to him. "That's enough for you."

Bill tossed his cards into the pile. "I thought drinking was one of the few things you actually did well." A comment he never would have made sober.

"I'm sorry, okay?" said Pete. "I made a mistake… I don't drink wine. It's shit. It's throwing me off."

Pete grabbed a handful of wafers and chucked them at Matt.

"At least you're not color blind," said Matt.

"Shut up and deal," said Pete.

"Would you like us to go over the rules again?" asked Matt.

"I know the damn rules," said Pete. "Deal the damn cards."

"You sure showed it on that hand," said Bill.

A menacing glance from Pete shut Bill up. "Let's play. I'll have those crackers back in no time."

Bill awkwardly brought his watch to his face. 1:46. The wine bottle had long been empty, but Bill was still feeling the full effects of the alcohol. His body's actions were far more unsure than Matt and Pete's. They made a few cracks about it, but Bill didn't mind all that much because he was actually having some fun. His head pounded, and he needed to sleep though. The only other liquid Bill had had to drink to offset the alcohol was one twelve-ounce water. He was ready for bed. "I hate this game."

Matt dealt the cards to Bill and himself, the former uninterested in looking at his cards.

"Your move," said Matt.

Bill pushed his wafers to the pot. "I'm all in."

"What?" said Pete in complete disbelief. "You didn't even look at your cards."

"I wouldn't recommend it," said Matt, doublechecking his hand.

"I don't care," said Bill, stretching his neck. "I need to sleep. I'm all in."

"Fine," said Matt. "I call. Winner takes all."

"Thank Christ," said Bill.

Matt turned over his cards—a king and a queen.

Bill turned over his cards—a six and a three.

"Yikes," said Matt. "Not looking good." Matt turned over the flop: queen, two, and king. "Two pair for me, kings and queens, baby!"

"Ah, a little foursome… nice," said Pete.

Matt ignored Pete and turned his attention back to Bill. "You got nothing." Matt revealed the next card: a six. "Pair of sixes on the board. I'm still in the lead."

Matt turned over the final card: a six.

Bill threw his hands up into the air. "Yes!" Pete gave him a high-five that stung his hand.

"Ohhhh, that's awesome!"

Matt dejectedly swiped at the cards. "That's ridiculous."

"That's how it's done," said Bill. "It's been fun, gentlemen." Bill grabbed the small pile of cash on the floor and staggered to his feet using the bed as a crutch. The room began to spin as he stood. He focused on steadying himself and jammed the bills into his pocket.

"Three sixes," said Matt. "You better watch out."

"I'm not too worried about it." Bill focused all of his energy on making it to the door. "The Lord shall protect me. I fear no evil. See ya tomorrow." He walked toward the door, stumbling into one of the walls before steadying himself.

"Whoa," exclaimed Matt. "You need an escort?"

Bill put up his hands, and his torso gently rocked back and forth on unstable legs. "Nope, I'm good."

"All right. See ya," said Matt. He smiled as he watched Bill miss the doorknob twice.

Bill quickly glanced into the hall to make sure the coast was clear. He slid his hand along the wall for support and tiptoed down the carpeted hallway, wincing each time the floor creaked, until he made it back to his room. As he opened the door, he heard a thud and a groan echo from down the stairs at the end of the hall. He paused and listened to the faint sounds of two voices, but he couldn't make out the words. Curious, Bill continued to the stairwell and peered over the railing; nothing, but he was able to hear the voices much more clearly.

"Pick him up," rasped one of the voices—Bill still couldn't identify it. "Hurry."

Bill descended the stairs to investigate, gripping the railing hand-over-hand. At the bottom of the staircase, he held the banister for support and saw a figure pushing someone in a wheelchair through the breezeway, with one other person walking alongside them. As they passed a light, Bill recognized the thin, lanky body and flowing blond hair of Luke. He was still wearing his red Eternal Springs polo while he pushed the wheelchair. Bill didn't recognize the young man walking with him—he seemed about the same age as the retreaters, with a huge mop of scruffy dark hair. As he staggered closer, Bill saw Keith's square head tilted to the side, barely rising above the seatback. Three sheets to the wind, Bill could still tell something was off, and even though Keith was Bill's archnemesis, he couldn't just leave him like that.

"Hey!" said Bill. "What are you doing?" He knew he was slightly slurring his words, and he needed to correct it. He wondered if they would notice.

The scruffy-haired person jumped a foot into the air. Luke's head whipped around, and he stopped pushing the wheelchair, which turned slightly, exposing the side of Keith's face.

"What are you doing up?" asked Luke. He let go of the handles on the chair and turned to face Bill.

"I couldn't sleep," said Bill, focusing on every syllable, "and then I heard some noises." Bill stepped further into the breezeway. "What the hell is going on? What are you doing with Keith?"

"Nothing," said Luke in a commanding tone. "He's not feeling well. Please go back to your room."

"No," answered Bill. Liquid courage ran through his veins. "What's wrong with him? You all right, Keith?"

Keith's head bobbed up and down, and his eyelids flittered as he mumbled some incoherent words.

"He's sick," said Luke. "He's been throwing up all night."

"Probably from the food," said Bill. *Or maybe karma,* he thought to himself. Of all the students to get sick, Keith would be Bill's first choice.

Luke scowled at Bill. "He'll be fine. We're taking care of it."

Bill turned his attention to the person helping Luke. "Who are you?"

"Enoch," said the stranger.

"Of course you are," said Bill.

Enoch pushed his glasses from the tip of his nose back toward his eyes. His eyes were too close together and lined up awkwardly with his frames. His dark hair sprung out of his head like a pom-pom.

73

"Please go back to your room," said Luke. "We have this under control."

"Where are you taking him?"

"We have a doctor on staff," said Luke. "He's going to give him something."

"A doctor?" questioned Bill. "Why is there a doctor here?"

"We're an hour away from the nearest hospital," said Luke. "And we have a friend that donates his services when we have people staying here."

"That's nice of him," said Bill. "Why doesn't he just go to Keith's room?"

"My radio isn't working," said Luke. "So, we're just going to bring Keith over there instead of wasting a bunch of time. Like you are. Now, please, go back to your room. You shouldn't be out here. He'll be fine… If you ever let us get him to the doctor."

Bill took one last look at Keith. "Okay. Feel better, Keith," he said half-heartedly.

"Goodnight," said Luke.

Luke pushed Keith through the breezeway toward the main lobby as Bill went back upstairs. He trekked halfway down the dark hall to his room, grabbed his toiletries, and backtracked to the bathroom near the staircase. The effects of the wine had nearly worn off after the shot of adrenaline from his late-night rendezvous. He'd had a decent night, all things considered. The interview had been a train wreck, but at least he'd had fun with Matt, and Keith ended up getting sick, so that was something. Just then, the pain in his gums from the stuck food chunk returned. Was that karma from being happy about Keith's illness or perhaps the work of a higher power? Surely, it was just a coincidence.

He flicked the switch for the lights in the bathroom and set his stuff up at the middle of three sinks. Bill washed his hands and took out his contacts. He removed the floss from his bag, pulled out a good-sized string, jammed it between his teeth, and pulled. A small particle came out. He tried again and finally dislodged the full piece. "Oh, thank God," he cried.

While brushing his teeth, the light above the mirror began to flicker, making him uneasy. *There is just something weird about this place.* He looked around the bathroom with a strange feeling that he wasn't alone. *What is wrong with you?* he thought to himself. *It's just a bad light.* He shook his head and spat into the sink. The spit was half toothpaste and half blood, and it turned the water pale red. *Ew.*

74

Bill rinsed again and spat. "Aw, man," he said to himself aloud. The running water turned deep red and drained. He pulled his bottom lip down and saw the blood oozing out from the gum and pooling in his mouth. Bill rinsed his mouth out a couple more times, each time lessening the amount of blood. He collected his stuff into his bag, mouth aching.

Upon exiting the bathroom, Bill immediately bumped into someone. The dank smell of weed was overwhelming.

"Oh, hey, Bill," said Jerry. He wore sandals, sweatpants, and a hoodie. "What's up?"

"Nothing," said Bill. "What's up with you?"

The two rule breakers walked down the hall, Jerry trailing slightly behind Bill.

"Nothing much," said Jerry casually. "Just getting some extra prayer in."

Jerry sounded completely blazed, like McConaughey in *Dazed and Confused*.

"Cool."

"You?" Jerry brushed the bangs from his eyes.

Bill always wondered what the point of those emo-bangs was if Jerry was constantly brushing them from his face. Not that Bill had any room to judge other people's hair when he was in desperate need of a haircut, but it seemed annoying. "About to do the same."

"Awesome," said Jerry.

They came to Bill's room.

"See ya tomorrow," said Bill, opening his door.

"Yeah, see ya," said Jerry, and he disappeared into the dark hallway, the plume of marijuana wafting with him.

Bill put away his toiletries and took a swig of water from the bottle he had filled in the bathroom. He pushed in the small button on the door-knob which engaged the lock, but it popped back out. He tried again and again, but the lock would not stay in place. A bit of paranoia entered Bill's brain as he remembered Keith being led away in the wheelchair. It was a strange occurrence, but the story made sense, he figured. The more he thought about it the more Bill was sure he didn't want anyone walking in on him during the night or in the morning, so he grabbed the chair from the desk and wedged it under the doorknob. He tried pulling the door open, but just as he planned, it wouldn't budge. *Perfect.* He checked his watch one last time. 2:16.

Bill hopped into bed and tried to get comfortable, but it was a fruitless endeavor; the mattress felt like it was made of concrete. He tossed and turned, but nothing worked. He rolled over once more toward the desk and noticed a small stream of light coming out from the wall across from him. Bill sprang from the bed and discovered the source of the light: a hole the size of a quarter at just about his standing eye-level. He poked his finger through it; nothing, just open space. He lifted up on the tips of his toes and looked through. He saw the wall of what he assumed was the next room maybe three feet away, but he couldn't see the source of the light. Bill backed away and studied the hole, contemplating its possible purpose. *Probably for some wires or something.* He lay back down in bed, continuing to watch the stream of light coming in through the hole until he eventually drifted asleep.

CHAPTER 11:

The First Meeting

"GOOD MORNING, RETREATERS!"** Bill's eyes snapped open at the sound of Jacobs' voice. He quickly sat up and scanned the room as his heart raced—it was empty. He finally realized the voice had come from the speaker above the door. It had tricked him again.

"This is your wake-up call. Time to start this magnificent day. Breakfast will be served shortly, so get dressed and get on down to the dining hall. Thank you and have a blessed day."

Bill sat in bed until his heart returned to a normal rhythm. There was no reason for that type of wake-up call, especially at that volume. His head pounded deep inside his skull, and his parched mouth and throat begged for water. He polished off the last sips from the bottle and looked at the time on his watch—6:18 AM. *I'm so happy I played cards last night.* He hadn't slept well at all; he'd just tossed and turned for most of the night.

Bill rose to look at the hole in the wall—no light was coming through now. He went to the window and pulled the sheer curtain to the side. The sun had yet to rise above the trees, so it was still fairly dark and perfectly calm and peaceful. He suddenly remembered something while he was sleeping—he could have sworn he'd heard someone trying to open the door. The chair was still in place under the doorknob; it must have been a dream. Bill squeezed his eyes shut hard and now felt a mild pain emanating from his forehead. He hoped it was from the dehydration headache, but his fingers felt the true culprit—every high schooler's worst enemy—a pimple. *Great.*

Bill dressed in comfortable clothes—sweatpants and a long-sleeve t-shirt. He tried to conceal the watch beneath his sleeve, but the odds of it slipping out and becoming visible were too great. He took the watch off and put it in the pocket of his sweatpants. The outline of the circular face was blatantly obvious, and he couldn't risk having the watch confiscated. He would have to leave it behind.

Bill heard the chatter of students and the clinking of dishes as he crossed the lobby and entered the dining hall. Bill located his friends but decided to check on Keith first, despite their checkered past. He was certain he was setting himself up for more ridicule and bullying, but he couldn't ignore his conscience. He found Keith at a table with his henchman, Clark, along with Jerry and Evan, whom Bill was surprised to see with Keith. He also found Freddie at the table, a brainy kid that he knew never hung out with Keith. They were all eating from bowls filled with what looked like oatmeal.

"Hey, Keith," said Bill.

Keith lifted his head from his bowl and smiled. "Good morning, Bill," he politely responded.

Bill opened his mouth to continue his conversation but was interrupted by Jerry, no longer smelling of marijuana. "Hello."

"Hey," said Bill.

"Good morning," said Freddie.

"How's it going?" said Bill.

"Wonderfully," said Freddie.

"What do you want?" Clark asked angrily.

Keith patted Clark on the shoulder. "Now, Clark, that's no way to treat a friend."

Bill's mouth hung open. Keith must be trying to mess with him. Bill regretted coming over but finally asked, "How ya feeling?"

Keith swallowed a bite and smiled again. "Very good. Thank you for asking." Keith grabbed a piece of toast and bit into it. The scowl he normally wore whenever Bill was around was replaced with a soft look of happiness, like he was enjoying a fantastic meal at his favorite restaurant.

"You looked pretty crappy last night," said Bill.

"Oh, yes," said Keith. "I was having some stomach trouble, but I am much better today."

Keith took another bite of toast as Bill continued to look him over. "Well, that's good," he finally said.

Keith smiled again at Bill. He had only seen Keith smile this much when he was making fun of somebody. Bill still thought it was a trick.

"Yes, it is. Thank you for checking on me. That is very kind of you." There was no sarcasm or malice in Keith's voice. He tilted his head down and spooned another pile of gray mush into his mouth.

"Yeah, no problem," said Bill.

"Would you like to join us?"

Bill couldn't believe it, and his face crinkled from confusion. "No, that's okay. I'm gonna eat over there."

"Oh, okay. Have a blessed day," said Keith.

What? Why would he say that? He must be messing with me. He examined Keith for a few more seconds, waiting for someone to jump out with a camera and say 'gotcha.' "Are you sure you're okay?"

Keith's face lit up with another smile. "I am better than I have ever been. Truly."

"He said he's fine," scolded Clark.

Bill nodded his head. "Okay, if you say so. See ya."

"Bye," responded Keith.

"Have a blessed day," said Jerry and Freddie in perfect unison.

"You too," said Bill. *They're just mocking Jacobs, that's all.*

"Later, dude," said Evan, his first words of the conversation. He sat next to his pal Jerry, but Jerry seemed entirely disinterested in him, instead giving all of his attention to Keith and Freddie.

Bill sat down at a table with Matt, Pete, Scott, Dee, and Tom.

"What were you doing over there with Keith?" said Matt.

"Uh, Keith was pretty sick last night—stomach issues, I guess. He says he's fine now," said Bill.

"Well, that was sweet of you to check on him."

"The Lord filleth my soul with His goodness."

Scott scooped up a spoonful of pale, chunky mush and let it plop back into the bowl. "I'm sure it's this garbage."

Bill stared in disgust. "That can't be what was intended."

"Anyone else have any stomach issues last night?" asked Dee.

The boys shook their heads no.

Bill looked around and waved to Abe across the room.

"How ya feeling this morning?" Matt said to Bill.

"All right. Head hurts a bit."

"You're not feeling good either?" said Dee, shoving his bowl to the middle of the table.

"It's not the food," said Matt. He grinned. "My boy got a little tipsy last night."

Some small cheers erupted from Pete, Scott, and Dee as Bill's face turned slightly red.

"Atta boy, Bill," said Scott.

"Yeah," said Bill sheepishly. He saw a small look of disappointment on Tom's face. Bill wasn't sure if Tom was disappointed in him for drinking or if perhaps he was sad that he wasn't invited.

Abe waddled his way over to the table. "Yes?"

"Is there anything else on the menu today?" asked Bill.

Abe took a deep breath and sighed. "What's wrong with the oatmeal?"

"I've seen more appetizing things come out of my ass," chided Pete.

"Watch your mouth," said Abe, as the rest of the students snickered. "The cooks work very hard to prepare these meals. It is very healthy and provides you with all of the essential dietary nutrients you need. This is not some fancy, five star—"

Bill held both of his hands in the air. "Okay, I'm sorry I asked. You're right, it's great. Never mind."

"That's better," said Abe, and he left the table.

"No chance that dude got that big eating this crap," said Matt.

Scott dropped his spoon in his bowl. "I have some Cheezits and cookies in my room."

"I'm in," said Matt.

"Yep," said Bill.

They all got up and left the table.

After satisfying their hunger with chips, doughnuts, and cookies, the boys gathered in the chapel for their morning mass led by Father Leo. Radiant sunlight poured through the brilliant stained glass behind the altar, illuminating the sun and colorful flower patterns depicted on the windows. Bill went through the motions: standing, making the sign of the cross, sitting, standing, refraining, sitting, standing, miming singing, sitting, standing, kneeling, refraining, and so on and so forth. He kept an eye on Keith, wondering if he'd keep up his earlier schtick, and he did, standing with perfect posture and singing and refraining loudly. Bill wasn't sure if Keith normally acted like that at church or if this place was already having that great of an impact on him, even before the first real session.

Father Leo, dressed in an Easter-time white cloak with gold trim, went over to the lectern as the students rose from the pews.

"The Lord be with you," said Father Leo, raising his arms.

"And with your spirit," responded the boys, led by Jacobs and Father Stephen. His eyes were sunken, and his face was pale. Bill was sure that Pete's confiscated bottle of Jack Daniels had not lasted the night.

"A reading from the Holy Gospel according to John."

"Glory to you, O Lord," the boys said in unison, with varying degrees of effort on the three crosses to the forehead, lips, and heart.

"Jesus said, 'Do not let your heart be troubled; believe in God, believe also in Me. In my Father's house are many rooms; if *that* were not *so*, I would have told you, because I am going *there* to prepare a place for you. And if I go and prepare a place for you, I am coming again and will take you to Myself, so that where I am, *there* you also will be. And you know the way where I am going.' Thomas said to Him, 'Lord, we do not know where You are going; how do we know the way?' Jesus said to him, 'I am the way, and the truth, and the life; no one comes to the Father, except through Me. If you had known Me, you would have known My Father also; from now on you know Him and have seen Him.'

"Philip said to him, 'Lord, show us the Father, and it is enough for us.' Jesus said to him, 'Have I been with you for so long a time, and *yet* you have not come to know Me, Philip? The one who has seen Me has seen the Father; how *can* you say, 'Show us the Father?' Do you not believe that I am in the Father, and the Father is in Me? The words that I say to you I do not speak on My own, but the Father, as He remains in Me, does His works. Believe Me that I am in the Father and the Father is in Me; otherwise believe because of the works themselves.'

" 'Truly, truly I say to you, the one who believes in Me, the works that I do, he will do also; and greater *works* than these he will do; because I am going to the Father. And whatever you ask in My name, this I will do, so that the Father may be glorified in the Son. If you ask Me anything in My name, I will do it.' "

Father Leo paused. "The Gospel of the Lord."

The room responded, "Praise to you Lord, Jesus Christ." Bill did not even get the last word out of his mouth before he sat back down.

Father Leo walked down the stone stairs of the sanctuary to the tiled floor to address the students. "This is one of my favorite passages from the Bible. Here we have Jesus talking to his disciples at the last supper about faith and trust in both God and himself. Trust is the pillar of our faith in

God. We must trust in God in all times. We must have complete faith in God. In the scripture, Jesus said there are many rooms for the followers of God; all you have to do is follow me. Then Thomas says but we don't know where you're going, so how can we know the way? Thomas thinks he's stranded out in the middle of the woods without his Google Maps app. He can't begin to understand how to find the way. Then Jesus tells him, I am the way. If you know me, you know my Father. We search to find God. We search to find heaven—but there are no GPS coordinates. We can't simply open a map and follow along to an 'X.' Jesus is the map. God sent Jesus to us to redeem us and to show us the way to salvation through Jesus' life and teachings.

"Philip still doubts Jesus. He says to him, 'Lord, show us the Father, and it is enough for us.' He needs proof. Jesus tells him, you've been with me, Philip. You've seen the things I've done. Jesus turned water into wine, healed the sick, brought the dead back to life. He said this is the Father, working through me! 'He who has seen me has seen the father.' Jesus wasn't some sort of X-Man with special powers. He is not a Jedi or wizard or what have you. All of his miracles were the works of God. God showed Jesus his path, and Jesus trusted God and walked that path. Do you think Jesus' path was easy? No way! He was sentenced to death! But he trusted in God and knew it was God's will. He had faith in God and was resurrected and brought back home to heaven.

"I'm reminded of the words from Proverbs: 'Trust in the Lord with all your heart, and do not lean on your own understanding. In all your ways acknowledge Him, and He will make your paths straight.' The setting here at this retreat is a lot like our lives; the paths wind through the woods. We do not know where they go. We do not know what will be at the end. Our lives can go any number of ways. There are so many decisions to be made. So many paths to take. Life is overwhelming. But we trust that God will show us the way and even lighten our burden along the path, for he is always with us.

"Another way we can navigate our lives is with each other. One of the great parts of our faith is our community. Yes, God is always with us, but look around. We are all here for each other: classmates, teammates, friends and family, and our parishes back home. We don't have to do it alone. We need to have faith in one another. We can help each other strengthen our faith in God. We can be there for one another when times are tough. And there will be tough times. God never promised we wouldn't have problems or that we wouldn't be troubled. It's how we handle these troubles that determines our lives. Do we shut ourselves off from God and others? Do we isolate? Or do we open up and trust in one another and trust in Jesus and God to help us?

"Jesus begins this scripture reading by saying don't let your hearts be troubled. Trust in God and trust in Jesus. If we fully trust and believe in God, we have nothing to worry about. Our hearts will be pure and free, and we will find our way to heaven. Our first discussion will be about trust and faith. For this experience to be beneficial to you and for you to grow stronger in your faith, you must have trust in yourself, the people around you, and most importantly, God."

Father Leo walked back up the stairs toward the altar while Bill's stomach turned. It was one thing to open up and share with a single person, but he was terrified of doing it in front of a group of people, especially students who could use any bit of information and turn it against him. No one knew who he really was or how he really felt. If he fully opened up, he felt he would be looked at as a freak and ridiculed ceaselessly.

The mass crept along to Bill's least favorite part—the sign of peace. He was always embarrassed by his warm, sweaty hand and the anxiety leading up to it only made it worse. Every other person's hand was always cool and dry. He could only imagine how grossed out others were when they had to shake his hand. He shook Matt's hand next to him and then shook Scott's hand extended across Matt's body—neither seemed too disgusted by the interaction. Bill was on the aisle, so he figured he was safe from any attacks from that side. But after shaking Dee's hand behind him, Bill turned forward to find Keith standing in the aisle, arm extended.

"Peace be with you, Bill," said Keith.

Bill slowly raised his hand, waiting for Keith to pull it away and childishly swipe his hair and say, 'Gotcha,' but Keith's hand remained, and they shook for far too long as Keith stared directly into Bill's eyes.

"I know I haven't always been the nicest to you. I'm sorry for any hurt I've caused you. I hope we can start fresh here."

"Sure," said Bill. He pulled his hand away. "No problem."

"Great," said Keith. "Just great."

Keith returned to his pew. Matt leaned his head over and whispered to Bill, "You two best friends now?"

"I guess so," said Bill, still unsure of Keith's motives. What could have made Keith that friendly that quickly?

The time came to receive communion, and Bill couldn't help but chuckle at the fact that last night he'd eaten enough communion wafers to last a lifetime, although those weren't blessed, so he didn't get the full effect. He took the wafer from Father Leo and put it in his mouth. He remembered how dry they were and how they were much easier to swallow with a gulp of wine; alas, no wine was offered at the mass. Bill returned to his pew for the conclusion of the mass, and Father Leo dismissed the students to their group discussion rooms.

Bill's apprehension mounted with every stair he scaled. The anxiety and sweats returned as the boys crossed the main meeting hall past the fountain and entered room five.

"Take a seat, boys," said Mark. He sat in a folding chair in front of the semi-circle of loveseats.

Bill sat in the loveseat to Mark's right. Jerry was about to sit down next to Bill until Pete stopped him.

"Do you mind if I sit there? Bill's my buddy."

"Not at all," said Jerry stepping out of the way. "It's all yours."

Pete plopped onto the couch as the other four figured out their spots. Richie had already taken up the entire middle couch by himself, forcing Anthony and Brandon to share the loveseat to Mark's left. Jerry, left without a spot, stood with a hopeful smile in front of Richie. Richie exhaled and slightly leaned his body to the left, and Jerry squeezed his narrow frame into the nook between Richie and the arm rest. He looked awfully uncomfortable with his shoulders smushed inward, and his entire right hip propped up on the arm rest, but he still kept the smile on his face. Richie, tired of touching, slid over a couple inches to the arm rest on his side, allowing both of Jerry's buttocks to hit the cushion.

Just being in this room again gave Bill the creeps. He made eye contact with Mark, who gave him a quick smile, causing Bill to turn away. He flashed back to what happened the previous night. He still couldn't believe all of the things he'd said, and he was terrified Mark would bring up some part of their conversation in front of the group. He would give anything to go back in time and just sit there and say nothing like usual.

Mark began, "Okay, gentlemen, our first topic for discussion, as talked about by Father Leo during the mass, is trust. Trust is obviously a very important aspect of life, faith, and this retreat. Most people have an easy time trusting their families and their friends and people close to them. And you trust God. What we need to do is to be able to trust those we don't know, or at least those we don't know very well, and it starts in this room. We may think we're different. We may come from different backgrounds, neighborhoods, religions, or even varying degrees of spirituality," Mark gave Bill a quick glance, which made him extremely uncomfortable, before he continued, "but we're all in this retreat together. I guarantee you we all have a lot more in common than we think we do. And to have access to one another's thoughts and ideas and experiences is such a blessing. There's so much we can learn from one another. But everyone in this room must be comfortable interacting with each other. That's the only way this will work. That's the only way you will get anything out of this. Everything that is said in here stays in here, okay? Like those Vegas commercials."

"Minus all of the fun," said Pete.

"Not true," said Mark. "By the end of this, I'm sure all of you will have had a ton of fun."

The group sat slouched on the couches with crossed arms, not sure if they could buy it or not.

"I'm having a great time," said Jerry smiling, packed in his nook next to Richie. "This place is wonderful."

"Well, I'm happy to hear that," said Mark.

"Suck up," said Pete under his breath.

"Now, come on," said Mark. "We can't have that. That's not the way to establish trust."

"Sorry," said Pete.

"Now," continued Mark, "everyone should feel comfortable opening up and expressing themselves in this group. We can help each other with our problems, whether they be at home or school, with family or friends or girlfriends. Anything that's troubling our hearts. Whatever it is, we can *help* each other through *trusting* each other. We have to make a promise to one another that we are all here for each other, that we can trust each other, and that we will help one another strengthen our faiths in God and ourselves. Can everyone make that promise?"

Mark popped up from his chair and stuck his hand out towards the students. "I promise." Mark looked at each of the boys square in the eyes.

Jerry sprang to his feet and put his hand on top of Mark's. "I promise."

The other students reluctantly followed suit, each placing his hand on top of the last person's hand and saying the words. Bill could already feel himself reneging on his first promise—to try to renew his faith—as he lied and played along by placing his hand on the top of the pile and repeating the words.

After what felt like an eternity, the session ultimately ended with five out of the six retreaters participating. Bill learned a lot more about each of the other students than he was expecting. Everyone freely entered the discussions, mainly led by Jerry, who had delved into his life story, and described how he had recently strayed from the path of righteousness, virtue, and faith, but had again found the light. The largest breakdowns in trust within the student body seemed to stem from bullying: making fun of others for being different, fat-shaming, being called dumb. Bill heard about the retreaters' good relationships with their parents and siblings and friends, and how they had people who were there for them in their times of need. It only stoked the fires of jealousy within his heart.

Bill wished he could participate. He wished he had the fearlessness to open his mouth and share with them. He wished he could tell them how his father had abandoned him, leaving him without the ability to trust anyone or create close relationships and how he had no faith in himself and felt nothing but shame, worthlessness, and a complete discomfort in his own skin because he never felt good enough. Instead, Bill sat there the entire time with his arms folded and did not say one word. He could not trust these people with the words, 'I hate myself and I want to die.'

CHAPTER 12:
The Path

———

THE STUDENTS FINISHED UP THEIR LUNCH, WHICH CONSISTED OF TUR-
key or ham sandwiches and chips. It was at least edible. Bill, Matt,
Pete, Dee, and Scott walked through the lobby to the main doors, ready to
get some air and toss a football around. A dark green frog speckled with
black spots hopped out from behind a curtain. It paused and squatted on
its long back legs and stared at the boys.

"Aw, look at this guy," said Matt. The frog tried to evade Matt, but he finally caught it and held it in his cupped hands. The rest of the boys circled
around Matt to get a look.

"What's it doing in here?" said Pete.

"I don't know. Should we put it outside?" said Matt, struggling to keep
the unhappy frog in his hands.

"Where at?" said Bill.

"Yeah," said Dee. "You don't know where it lives."

"How about down by the lake?" said Matt. "Don't they like water?"

"Maybe," said Dee. "But what if its home is right around here? It won't
know how to get back."

"I'm sure it can figure it out," said Matt.

"God will show it the path," said Scott. He spun the football on his
index finger.

"What about the distance?" questioned Dee. "It's like… three hundred
yards to the lake. That's like five thousand miles for a human. It will take
forever for it to get back."

"I don't think that math adds up," said Matt.

Dee crossed his arms. "You know what I mean."

"It'll be fine," assured Matt confidently.

"Whatever you say, frog master," said Dee.

Pete opened the door to the outside, and the boys stepped into the glowing sunlight. It was a gorgeous day, continuing the mid-spring streak of excellent weather. The sun was shining, and the basketball and tennis courts were filled with students. The lake took on a beautiful blue color. Two canoes dashed back and forth across the calm water while the third just spun in circles. Up the hill, the retreat leaders were putting the finishing touches on a large deck on the front of the house.

The boys crossed the open field and headed for the lake. They passed a group of students playing hacky sack, one of whom noticed the frog. "What are you doing with that frog?"

"Found it inside," said Matt. "I'm gonna let it go down by the water."

"You wanna give it a kiss and see if you can find yourself a new boyfriend?" said Pete.

"You're such a jagoff, Pete," said the student.

"Don't tell me about what you like to do in your spare time," said Pete over his shoulder.

"That doesn't even make sense," shouted the student.

The boys circled the lake on a dirt path just above the rocky shoreline until they came to a small sandy beach at the edge of the woods. Matt found a three-foot log lying in shallow water next to some waist-high reeds—the perfect new home for the frog. Matt squatted and laid the frog down on the sand.

The frog stood still, its puffy midsection bulging in and out.

"Look," said Dee, pointing to the frog. "It doesn't even know where to go."

"He's fine," said Matt. He gave the frog a light tap, and the frog hopped away. "See?"

Dee shook his head. "You just created a fatherless frog family. I hope you're happy. Those frog-kids have no chance in life."

"The world's a cruel place," said Scott coldly.

Bill was annoyed that such innocuous comments could cut him so deeply.

"Hit me," said Pete. He put his hands up and ran back onto the grass field. Scott hit him with a perfect spiral.

The boys formed into a five-person circle and began throwing the football back and forth. "So, I'm already pretty over this retreat stuff," said Scott, lobbing the ball through the air to Dee.

"For real," said Bill, louder than he wanted.

"It's not that bad," said Pete. He shrugged and tossed the ball to Bill. "Maybe if you actually participated, you might get something out of it."

"Shut up, man," said Bill. He tossed the ball to Matt with much more velocity. Matt could feel the angst in the throw.

"He just sat there and didn't say one word," said Pete with a chuckle.

"Nobody cares," said Bill defensively.

Matt tried to change the subject. "You gettin' anywhere with Delilah?"

"I haven't seen her," said Pete. "She must be avoiding me. She knows she can't resist."

"Obviously," agreed Matt.

That was the last the boys talked about the first session. They tossed the football around for a bit longer before growing bored.

"You guys wanna check out where the trail goes?" said Matt.

"Yeah, sure," said Dee without hesitation.

"All right," said Scott.

"No," said Pete.

"Sure, what the hell," said Bill, solely to spite Pete.

The boys followed the dirt path back along the lake to the beach at the edge of the woods. The trail jogged to the right, deeper into the forest and away from the lake. The trees and leaves were so thick they could barely see the bright blue sky, leaving the trail much darker and cooler than the clearing at the campus. The boys remained mostly quiet. The only sounds in the forest came from the birds singing as they flew from tree to tree and some critters scampering among the bushes.

"Anything poisonous out here?" called Dee.

"I don't think so," said Matt, even though he had no idea.

"I thought poisonous stuff was mostly west," offered Scott. "Or south."

Bill had no idea either. Hopefully they wouldn't find out.

After ten minutes, Pete stopped and whined, "Ugh, how far are we going?"

"Why don't you just go back?" said Matt.

"Well, I mean, what are we doing out here?" asked Pete.

"We're enjoying the great outdoors," said Scott.

Pete dragged his feet along the ground, kicking up clouds of dust. "Well, can't we do that from inside?"

A few minutes later, the path led them to a light gray concrete building about ten feet tall with a single door and no windows. A massive saucer-shaped dish with a long antenna was constructed on the top. The trees around the shed had undoubtedly been cut down, giving the antenna a clear line to the sky. The boys left the cool shade of the forest and walked into the bright warmth of the sun.

"What's this for?" said Dee.

"I don't know," said Matt. "Look at the size of that antenna."

All of the boys craned their necks to look at the large saucer, which dwarfed the building below it, and the four-post antenna that protruded twenty feet from its center.

"They must get every channel on the planet on that thing," said Scott.

"Maybe even other planets," said Matt dryly. "NASA missing any antennas?"

The boys stood in the shadow of the massive structure, wondering what its purpose could be.

"Do you think it's the retreat's or somebody else's?" said Dee.

"It can't be the retreat's," said Matt. "What would they need this for? It's probably some government building."

Dee, Scott, and Matt continued toward the shed as Pete came to a stop on the trail fifteen feet away and kicked his shoe off.

"Where you guys going?" asked Pete.

"Let's see what this is," said Matt.

"It's a shack," said Pete, overturning his shoe; several pebbles fell to the ground. "And a giant antenna."

"Yeah, but what's it for?" said Matt.

Pete slipped his shoe back on. "Who cares?"

"You scared, Pete?" mocked Scott.

Pete rolled his eyes. "I'm not scared. I'm just not interested in trespassing on private property in the middle of the woods. You can get shot out here, ya know?"

"You can get shot back in the city," said Matt.

"I'm gonna have to reluctantly agree with Pete, here," said Bill. "I mean, haven't you guys seen *Deliverance* or any of the *Wrong Turn* movies?"

Matt ignored the warnings and climbed the three concrete steps to the door while Scott and Dee waited idly on the ground. He reached for the doorknob but paused when he heard a rustling in the woods behind the shed. "What's that?"

The sound was coming closer to them. Dee stepped around the building.

"Uh, there's a bear," said Dee, slowly backpedaling.

"What?" said Matt. He jumped off the stairs.

"Yep, small bear. A cub, I think," said Dee still backpedaling. Scott joined him without even seeing the bear.

Matt peeked around the corner of the shed and eyed the small moving bunch of black fur. "Aw. He's so—"

Suddenly, a much larger bear burst through the thicket, and Matt's eyes went wide with fear. He retreated toward the other boys. "Big bear. Much bigger bear. Momma bear."

"Oh, shit," said Scott.

"Just move back slowly," said Matt. "It's just protecting its baby. If we leave it alone, it will leave us alone."

The boys heeded Matt's warning, and each walked backward on the dirt path, trying to make as little noise as possible. The large beast cleared the shed and lumbered toward the boys. Perspiration dripped from their foreheads as each feared their last moments on earth would be as a meal. The bear let out a ferocious growl, showcasing its mouth full of sharp jagged teeth. Pete screamed and immediately turned and sprinted onto the trail and back toward Eternal Springs. The bear lunged forward, and the rest of the boys had no choice but to run as well.

"Pete! You idiot!" screamed Matt.

The bear pursued the five boys down the trail as they ran as fast as they could. Trees whipped by. They jumped over logs and rocks—one wrong move could be the end.

"Get the knife out!" Bill yelled to Matt.

"It's in my room!" Matt yelled back.

"Of course it is!"

Dee, the reigning state champ in the one-hundred-, two-hundred-, and four-hundred-meter sprints, zoomed past Bill and Matt, who exchanged looks of dread. They knew they couldn't keep up. Bill looked over his shoulder and saw Scott had fallen behind, though he still had a sizeable lead on the still charging bear. Dee sprinted past Pete and was the first to escape the woods into the clearing.

"The courts!" said Dee, pointing.

They ran around the lake towards the fenced-in basketball and tennis courts. A group of students near the main building heard the commotion and saw the five boys running from the bear, Scott falling dangerously behind; his lead over the bear was down to ten feet. The students ran into the building for help as Pete, Matt, and Bill followed Dee around the courts to the fence gate and rushed through it, interrupting the basketball game.

"What's wrong?" said Anthony.

Pete pointed to the bear.

"Holy shit!" Fear rapidly gripped Anthony and the other students on the court.

The students watched helplessly as Scott struggled to make the final twenty feet to the court with the bear closing the gap.

"Come on, Scott!" yelled Matt.

Scott huffed and puffed like a bulldog in a marathon and finally made it through the gate and collapsed to the ground. Matt slammed the gate shut and flipped down the lock just before the bear violently crashed into it. The gate bent but held. Another blow like that and the bear would be inside the courts. The students screamed and backed away as the bear stalked around the fenced perimeter, sniffing the air, looking for another entrance to the buffet.

"Now what do we do?" said Matt.

"Hope she doesn't get in," said Bill.

"Thanks for bringing it over here," said Anthony.

The bear nudged at different points along the fence with its head to probe its strength. The bear was losing its patience and growled, frightening everyone stuck inside.

"You always said you wanted a bear as a pet," said Bill.

"I take it back," Matt quickly retorted.

Bang. Bang.

Shots rang out and reverberated across the property. Everyone ducked. A golf cart sped down the hill from the staff house, Ben behind the wheel and Mark hanging off the side with a rifle pointed toward the sky. The bear, startled by the gunshots, turned its head aimlessly trying to locate the source of the loud noise as the golf cart wheeled around the corner of the fence.

Bang.

Mark fired another shot into the sky. The piercing sound vibrated through Bill's entire body. He had never heard a gunshot before in real life. It was much louder than he imagined, and television didn't do it justice. The bear awkwardly stumbled away from the court, alternating between walking and running while the golf cart trailed closely behind. Mark fired one more shot, and the bear vanished into the woods.

"Oh, thank God!" exclaimed Pete as he dropped to the ground.

Bill bent over and rested his hands on his knees to catch his breath, the hum of the gunshots still echoing through his head. He couldn't believe what had just happened.

Matt turned to check on Scott. "You all right?"

Scott was breathing heavily, lying on his back on the concrete. "I don't think so. I might have had a heart attack."

The golf cart cruised back along the fence and stopped at the gate. "Is everyone okay?" asked Mark.

Some responded yes, but most were still too terrified to say anything.

"You know, you're not supposed to run from a bear," said Mark.

Matt glared at Pete. "Oh, really?" he said contemptuously.

"Yeah," said Mark. "They're pretty fast. You're just supposed to hold your ground. And if it attacks, you're supposed to yell and fight back."

"I don't see how just standing around and yelling was going to help," said Pete. "We'd all be dead. Or four of us coulda made it, I guess, while it was eating the other one... Sorry, Scott."

"Shut up," said Matt.

"Thanks for the support," said Scott. He rolled over onto his side and then sat up, clutching his chest over his heart.

Mark stood from the golf cart and walked to the fence. "Well, that's the first time I've seen a bear go after people like that. Usually, you can just scare them off. Did it have cubs?"

"Yeah," said Dee, already back to his normal breathing pattern.

"Well, there you go. It was just protecting its young and being a good mom. A reminder to everyone to keep a look out when you go on the trails. And, hey, now you have a cool bear story you can tell for the rest of your lives."

"Barely," said Matt. He chuckled. "Get it? *Barely*, cuz it's a *bear*."

"Too soon," said Scott.

The boys collected themselves, contemplating their existences after having just looked death square in the eyes.

Pete hopped to his feet. "Well, I'm gonna get a snack." He walked off the court as the others continued to catch their breath.

The students, broken up in their groups, gathered in the large meeting room on the second floor for their evening discussion and sat on the folding chairs facing the trickling fountain while listening to another peaceful instrumental track. After a few minutes of meditation, Jacobs ascended the stairs, prompting Father Leo to stand from his seat.

"Welcome back, gentlemen," said Father Leo. "I hope you enjoyed your free time. It was a beautiful day out there. God has really smiled upon us—some of us more than others from what I hear. It's my understanding there was a bit of a bear encounter this afternoon. Mr. Jacobs…"

Jacobs rubbed his hands together. "Yes, a few students had a small run-in with a black bear protecting its young. No one was hurt, but I just wanted to remind everyone to always be aware of your surroundings. We are in the woods, and there is wildlife, so please keep an eye out. If you encounter a black bear, hold your ground, make yourself as big as possible, and make as much noise as possible. This should scare the bear off. Don't run. Bears don't like sudden movements. They may take that as a sign of aggression."

Matt made eye contact with Pete across the room and raised his eyebrows as if to say 'I told you so.' Pete subtly gave him the finger between his legs.

"Bears are much more afraid of you then you are of them."

I disagree, thought Bill.

Jacobs turned to Father Leo. "I think that about does it. I'll turn it back over to Father Leo. Have a blessed day." With that, he headed down the stairs.

Father Leo stood at the front of the room with a manila folder hanging in his hand at his side. "Thank you, Mr. Jacobs. Now we must get back to work." He raised the folder and opened it. "We will begin with a reading from the first letter of Saint John. 'See how great a love the Father has given us, that we would be called children of God; And *in fact* we are. For this reason the world does not know us: because it did not know Him. Beloved, now we are children of God, and it has not appeared as yet what we will be. We know that when He appears, we will be like Him, because we will see Him just as He is. And everyone who has this hope *set* on Him purifies himself, just as He is pure.' The Word of the Lord."

The students responded, "Thanks be to God."

Father Leo closed the folder. "Who are we? How do we define ourselves as people? Students? Priests? Sons? Brothers? Friends? Athletes? Scholars? There are so many aspects of our lives. What is it that truly defines us? God. We are all children of God. He works in us and through us. We are his humble servants. That should be your main calling. School is important, yes. When you get older, your job will be important. Your family is important. Your friends are important. But the most meaningful part of our existence is being a child of God.

"We learned in Genesis that God made us in his own image—wonderful, incredible beings. We enter God's family through baptism, and we are loved unconditionally by our Almighty Father. God loves us. His love never ends for us. We try and strive each day to be worthy of him, to live as His son Jesus taught us, so that someday, we will be united in heaven. Being a child of God is our most important and rewarding identity. In our discussion, we will talk about how we identify and act as children of God, the many ways we can be distracted from our true calling, and how our faith is what should truly define our lives. Okay, leaders, it's all yours."

The students split into their separate discussion rooms as the word 'father' stuck in Bill's head like it always did. He was incapable of hearing that word and not having a negative reaction to it. It rattled around in his brain, and in his thoughts he dragged it through the mud and spat on it. Bill saw the irony—all of his problems stemmed from the abandonment by his real father, and he was now devasted by the death of his grandfather. And here, another Father, waited with open arms, ready to love and accept him—except he wanted no part of it. Bill fully believed that God had abandoned his children on Earth, and he remembered the talk the previous night, and his past readings, about how no person was good in the eyes of God. Bill laughed to himself—not good enough again for another father.

Bill was the last one into the room, and he took the same spot next to Pete as the earlier session. This time, Richie had left enough room for Jerry to sit on the couch and even have his legs spread a bit. Daylight had come and gone, and the flame bulbs flickered in the room.

Mark took his seat in the folding chair and opened his folder. "Okay, fellas, round two. Tonight, we are talking about identities. How we see ourselves and how the world sees us. Who are we? What is our purpose on this Earth? What are our goals in life? What will we do and how will we do it?

"When we think about identities, there are many things we think about. When we are young, we often think about what we want to be when we grow up. What did you want to be when you were a kid?" Mark pointed to Anthony.

"Uh, an astronaut," said Anthony.

"Great," said Mark. He pointed to Brandon. "And you?"

"Physical therapist."

Mark nodded. "Impressive. Richie?"

Bill didn't like how Mark was going around the room. Earlier you only had to participate if you wanted to. *Now* he was being forced to?

Richie thought for a second with his lips pursed and shrugged. "A firefighter."

Pete looked at the plump boy sitting on the couch and chuckled.

Mark turned to Pete and said, "Quiet," before turning back to Richie. "Very courageous. And you, Jerry?"

"A priest." Jerry interlocked his fingers and rested his hands in his lap. Bill rolled his eyes.

"Oh, wonderful," said Mark "You are on your way. Pete?"

Pete thought about it, and a large smile spread across his face. "Porn star."

"Come on now," said Mark.

"Naw, I'd be great."

Bill was beyond tired of Pete's nonsense and "All-male gangbangs don't sell, man," slipped out.

"You'd buy it." Pete snorted.

"That's enough, gentlemen," said Mark. "Pete? Come on, for real."

"Oh, I don't know. My dad is in construction. That seems pretty cool."

"Wonderful. Bill?"

"Batman," Bill said flatly.

"Bill, can you take this seriously?"

"I am," he said with a shrug. "When I was a kid, I wanted to grow up and be Batman. Fight crime. Cool gadgets. Rich. Mansions and cars. Seems pretty great."

"Fair enough," said Mark. "That does sound great. And you bring up some good points we'll definitely talk about. Each of you had these ideas when you were children. Some of you may still be on your way to achieving these goals. For others, maybe something else interests you now. We often look at our professions as the thing which defines us. If we want to explore and learn about the galaxy and the unknown, we can be an astronaut. If we want to help people, we can be a therapist or a firefighter. If we want to build things, we can be a contractor or architect. If we want to serve others and spread the word of God, we can be a priest. If we want to protect people, we can become... we can join law enforcement.

"A lot of people want to be rock stars and movie stars and athletes because they want that lifestyle. Lots of money, houses, cars, women. People think that those things will bring their lives meaning and will give them happiness. But that's not true. Those things are fickle. Those things are fake. And they can be gone in an instant. What is always there? God's love, as He is always with us. There's a very well-known saying 'money can't buy happiness.' This is absolutely correct. You can have all the money in the world, but if you don't have anyone around you that you love, if you do not have *God's* love, you may act like you are happy, but deep down you're not.

"Rock stars, athletes, firefighters, astronauts—all of these things that sound awesome, but hardly anyone ever says, 'I want to be a child of God when I grow up,' and that's what we should focus on. Our relationship with God, our love for God, should be the most important thing in our lives. We should define ourselves by our faith. We should define ourselves as children of God. That is how we will find true happiness and live forever with Christ."

Bill thought about what it was to be a child—young, naive, flat-out dumb—to believe in fake things, to be scared of authority figures, to struggle with right and wrong and then be punished after doing something wrong. The way he saw it, God was an easy way to keep people in line, to force them to do the right thing. You could break the law and you might not get caught, but God would always know, so you should behave correctly for He is always watching. He thought about earlier humans, before science and knowledge, who tried to understand the world around them and when they couldn't, they attributed things to beings greater than themselves. Humans, when you thought about them, weren't entirely special. They had always tried to create things greater than them: gods, superheroes, characters, artificial intelligence. They wanted to believe in something greater than them because the reality is they were rather quite boring and unimpressive.

Bill came back to the word naive. That was what he wanted. That was what he attributed people's belief in a higher power to—naivete. Couldn't he just believe, without question and accept without hesitation? Couldn't he just be happy as a child of God and enter into the loving embrace of the Almighty Father? Why did he have to think the way that he did? Why did he have to be him? Why did he have to be at all? The negative thoughts defeated him. The hope he'd had for bettering himself slipped through his fingers, and he sat in complete silence for yet another session.

Afterwards, Bill made a stop at the bathroom next to the dining hall to empty his bladder and noticed the sizable red lump growing above his eyebrow in the mirror. *It's gonna be a big one.* Bill entered the dining hall, stomach grumbling, and grabbed a plate from the start of the buffet. He worked his way down the table: burgers, chips, salad. He loaded his burger with all of the fixings and silently sat down at the end of the table with the usual suspects. Bill barely talked during dinner. He was still unable to shake the feelings of sadness and hopelessness. He just faked a few smiles here and there and ate his meal.

Following dinner, the students, free of their religious obligations, had the rest of the night to themselves. Some went back to their rooms for some much-needed sleep, while others hung out at a bonfire by the lake. Matt, Scott, and Pete had had their fill of the great outdoors during that afternoon's bear attack, so they decided to check out the rec room. It took a little convincing from Matt, but Bill agreed to go with, hoping to end the day on a better note.

It was completely quiet as they descended the stairs in the main lobby, Matt in in the lead and Bill trailing last.

"Are you sure it's down here?" asked Scott.

"I think so," said Matt. "Where else could it be?"

The four reached the basement and found the room sparsely populated with students: two were playing ping-pong, two were playing pool, four sat around a table with a Jenga tower, and in the back corner of the room, Jacobs was playing foosball with Father Leo. It wasn't quite as much fun as the kids were hoping.

"It's pandemonium down here," deadpanned Matt.

"Welcome, gentlemen," said Jacobs, focusing all of his attention on controlling the tiny men on the sticks.

Bill and Matt watched the Jenga game while they waited for the ping-pong table to open. The game seemed to have been going for some time, as holes had appeared throughout the tower, and it was leaning slightly. Manny rubbed his ear between his thumb and index finger as he studied the tower. One wrong move would end the game. Manny slowly pulled a piece out, causing the tower to wobble a bit. He held his breath, but it stood.

On the foosball table, Jacobs handed Father Leo a resounding defeat.

"Wow, you're really good at that," conceded Father Leo.

"I've had a lot of practice," said Jacobs, still moving and spinning the sticks full of people.

Bill was less than pleased to see Keith enter the basement, but Keith only said a quick hello before he and his new pal Freddie struck up a conversation with Pete. This led Pete to an incredible opportunity to make some of his money back—neither had any idea how to play cards.

"All right," said Pete. "Let's see what everyone has." The three overturned their cards. Keith showed a pair of tens, and Freddie had three kings. "Wow, that's pretty good, but I have you beat. See, this is a flush." Pete showed off his two spades and three clubs. "It's five cards of the same color. A flush beats a pair and three of a kind, so I win." Pete stuck his hand out for his winnings.

"Oh, wow," said Keith, handing over a dollar. "That's a great hand."

Freddie passed his dollar over. "Yeah, you're really good at this. Do you think we can play again?"

Pete excitedly collected the cards. "We sure can."

Back at the Jenga table, Manny's opponent Colin plotted his next move. "I don't know," he said nervously.

Matt leaned his head over Colin's shoulder and pointed at the tower. "That one there would be good."

Colin pointed to a specific piece. "That one?"

"No, the one right above it," said Matt.

Colin slowly pushed the piece through the tower with his index finger, exposing the block's edge. The tower leaned a bit more, but it stood. He slowly pulled the piece centimeter by centimeter, exposing half of the block before the entire tower crashed to the table.

Colin turned back to Matt. "Good call."

Matt waved his finger toward the pile of pieces. "I didn't mean that one, I meant the one below that one."

Colin shook his head. "I pulled the one out that you told me to. I pointed right at it."

"No, not that one. The one below it would have worked." Matt looked around the room. "Oh look, the ping-pong table's open."

Bill and Matt's ping-pong game went back and forth as more and more students, all complaining of too many mosquito bites, began to file into the rec room. Meanwhile, Scott had challenged Jerry to a game of pool.

Scott sank a ball into the corner pocket.

"That was a really nice shot," said Jerry.

"Thanks," said Scott, repositioning for his next one. He sank another ball.

"Wow, that was great," said Jerry.

"Thanks," said Scott, squinting unsurely at Jerry. He lined up his next shot but failed to sink the red-striped ball when it bounced off the bumper and rolled to a stop.

"Oh, so close," said Jerry, his tone genuinely sympathetic. "I really thought you had that. Do you want to try again?"

"Uh, no," said Scott. "It's your turn."

"I don't mind. You can try again," said Jerry, smiling.

"No, go 'head," said Scott. He took a seat on the bench along the wall beside the table. "It's your turn."

"Fun," said Jerry as he tried to figure out how to use the cue stick correctly. He clutched it awkwardly and clumsily slid it through his fingers

"Nine serving nine," said Matt.

He served the ball over to Bill, who forehanded it back. Matt sent the ball to the corner of the table, making Bill stretch, but he successfully backhanded the ball over the net. Matt easily struck the ball into the opposite uncovered corner, and Bill's next shot struck the net, and came to a rest on his side of the table.

"Yes," said Matt, with a fist pump. "Ten serving nine. Match point."

Bill tossed the ball to Matt, who took a deep breath and then served the ball to Bill. They hit it back and forth several times in a nice and steady rhythm, neither going for a terribly difficult shot. Bill thought he had gained the momentum in the rally and struck the ball hard to the back corner. He thought it was a winner, but Matt lunged and flailed his paddle in his hand at the ball, miraculously making contact. The ball floated just beyond the net to the edge of the table on Bill's side. Bill leaned forward, most of his weight on the table, and swung and missed. The ball fell to the ground.

"That was out," said Bill right away. He picked up the ball.

"Bullshit," said Matt, pointing. "That hit the table."

Bill shook his head "No, it didn't."

"Are you *kidding* me?" said Matt, tapping his chest with his paddle.

"Are *you* kidding *me*?" answered Bill. He mimicked Matt by tapping his chest with his own paddle. "That didn't hit the table."

"Yes, it did. It clearly changed directions."

"No, it didn't," said Bill. "You're full of shit."

"You're full of shit." Matt pointed to a student sitting next to the table. "Didn't it hit the table?"

The student shrugged and shook his head, afraid to be the deciding vote. "I'm not sure."

Matt looked to a different student. "Did it hit the table?"

"I don't know," said the student.

"See," said Bill, "no indisputable evidence that it hit the table."

"There's no evidence it *didn't* hit the table!"

"Ten, ten," said Bill. He tossed the ball to Matt. "Your serve."

"It's not my serve." Matt threw the ball back, and Bill caught it. "It's no one's serve. The game's over."

The situation could have easily been deescalated by any adult, but none were downstairs any longer.

"No, it's ten, ten. And it's your serve." Bill whipped the ball at Matt, who covered his head with his arms and took it in his exposed ribs.

Bill laughed. "It's just a ping-pong ball. Don't be scared."

Matt picked the ball up and whipped it back at Bill. Bill turned at the last moment and ball drilled him between the shoulder blades with a slight sting.

"You're an asshole," said Bill, turning back.

"You're an asshole," said Matt.

"Guys, guys, guys," said Jerry in a calming voice as he walked over to Bill and Matt. "It's just a game. This isn't how friends should treat one another."

"Yeah," said Bill. "You'd think friends wouldn't blatantly lie about balls hitting tables."

"Shut up," said Matt. "You'd think friends wouldn't blatantly lie about balls not hitting tables."

Jerry leaned the pool cue against the ping-pong table and extended one hand toward Bill and one toward Matt. "Why don't you both shake hands and just play the point over?"

Bill and Matt both thought about it, waiting for the other to relent.

"Okay," said Bill.

Matt nodded his head. "Fine."

Bill picked up the ball.

Jerry kept his hands extended to both players. "Now, shake on it first." Jerry beckoned them both toward the middle of the table, where they begrudgingly shook hands. Bill gave the ball to Matt.

"Now that's more like it," said Jerry.

They both went back to their sides and readied their paddles.

"Eleven serving, I mean, ten serving nine," said Matt. "Match point."

Matt tossed the ball into the air and hit his best serve of the match deep into Bill's territory, forcing him to retreat further from the table. Bill's weak return was an easy set-up for Matt to smash the game-winning shot. Matt tossed the paddle onto the table. "Cheater's proof, butthead."

Bill dropped the paddle on the table. "Screw you."

"Guys," said Jerry. "Sportsmanship."

"Shut up, Jerry," said Bill as he passed.

Bill and Matt headed for the stairwell while Jerry went back to the pool table, shaking his head in disappointment.

"Hey, I won," said Scott. He leaned his cue stick against the table.

Jerry looked at the table. Only solid-colored balls remained on the green surface. "Wow. That's amazing!" Jerry leaned his stick next to Scott's and wrapped his arms as far around Scott as he could, gently laying his head against Scott's chest. "Good game!"

Scott stood motionless, arms at his sides, eyes wide in shock. "Thanks," he murmured.

Jerry released him. "Do you want to play again?"

"No thanks," said Scott, backing away. "Someone else can play."

Bill and Matt ascended the stairs into the main lobby.

"What's going on with Jerry, man?" said Matt. "Why was he being such a dork?"

"I don't know," said Bill. "He's getting really into this stuff. He basically led our night session."

"You wanna get a snack?" said Matt. "I'm hungry."

"Sure," said Bill. "Can we? Is the dining room open?"

"I don't know. Let's check it out."

Bill and Matt entered the dark dining hall. The moonlight shining through the two long windows gave them just enough visibility. They went to the kitchen in the back and noticed the pantry door was ajar and a light was on inside. Matt inched the door open with his finger to peek inside, and then pushed it wide open.

Richie and his chubby friend Gus sat on the floor with boxes and bags and food crumbs scattered all around them. White powdered sugar stained Richie's face and Gus was withdrawing his hand out of a Cheetos bag.

"Oh, hey, guys," said Richie, wiping at his mouth with the back of his hand.

"Hey," said Matt. He stepped fully into the pantry, Bill right behind him. "How's it going?"

"Good," said Richie. "Just having a little snack."

"Yeah," said Matt. "We're a little hungry too. What's good?"

Richie licked his fingers. "What are you in the mood for?"

Matt looked to Bill. "Uh, I don't know. Some cookies maybe?"

Bill nodded. "Yeah, maybe some chips."

Gus pointed. "The cookies are on the top shelf there."

Matt looked for a second before finding them. "Ah."

Richie extended the orange bag to Bill. "Cheetos?"

"No thanks," said Bill. He surveyed the rest of the pantry. "Doritos?"

"Yeah," said Matt.

"Regular or Cool Ranch?" asked Gus.

"Cool Ranch," said Bill. He looked over the fruit and took the yellowest banana.

Gus grabbed the blue bag of Doritos and passed it to Bill. As he was grabbing it, Bill noticed the door to the fridge and freezer was open. "Make sure you guys close that door before you leave."

"We will," said Richie. "It's just so hot in here."

"For sure," said Matt. "You guys enjoy the rest of your night. Thanks for the food."

"No problem," said Gus. "Stop by any time."

CHAPTER 13:
The Shed

IT WAS AFTER LIGHTS-OUT. ALMOST EVERY STUDENT WAS ASLEEP IN THEIR beds, but not Bill. He sat in black sweatpants and a navy-blue hoodie at his desk with only the lamp on, writing and waiting. Matt's plan was to go on a scouting mission to find a route and a meeting place for Saturday when the girls arrived. Matt had figured out on his phone that the main road to the highway was just over two miles long—a pretty significant trek by foot. He didn't want to risk the girls driving on the main Eternal Springs road for fear they would be caught, so he figured they could take a shortcut directly through the woods which would lead them to the highway in about half a mile. The plan was set to start at 11:45 PM, and Matt was going to come meet Bill. Bill had been checking his watch almost every minute as the time ticked closer, but it had passed to 11:48.

He had read that writing in a journal could be a cathartic experience—a way to express his feelings and maybe understand them and deal with them. He liked this option much better than the most obvious option, a therapist. Bill hated the idea of seeing a therapist and the stigma that came along with it. Only people with problems saw therapists, and seeing one would confirm that there was something wrong with him. And to see a therapist meant he would have to tell his mom how he felt. He knew his mom loved him and would support him, but he was terrified to tell her the truth. He didn't want to alarm or worry her. She already had enough to deal with.

So, he had decided to try the journal route. He wrote about being over-whelmed and about feeling insecure. He thought about what brought those feelings on. It was always a lack of confidence or an inability to believe in himself just like Matt had said the previous night. He'd come to the retreat with a faint hope that he would have an epiphany and be reborn, that he would have a chance to start over. He was already doubting that anything would happen with him spiritually, but there was maybe some hope he could progress emotionally and socially. He was shocked by how honest he'd been with Mark. He had immediately regretted it, yes, but he still felt somewhat proud that he had done it. Perhaps that proved he could bring himself to see a therapist at some point. He had hung out and played cards and got buzzed on wine, and now he was going to break some rules and socialize some more. There was even the possibility that he would meet a girl in a few days. Bill scribbled away at what it all meant.

Finally, there was a soft knock on his door. He sprang from his seat and exited his room to find Matt, also dressed in dark pants and long sleeves.

"Ready?" asked Matt.

Bill nodded. "You bring the knife?"

Matt tapped his hip. "Yep."

"All right. Let's go."

They walked down the dark hallway and descended the stairs. Everything was perfectly quiet and still in the breezeway into the main lobby and the halls of rooms. Next stop was Pete's room. Bill wasn't thrilled Pete was tagging along. He had already spent enough time with him, and it was only day two. It also meant more competition for Maddie's attention, and he knew Pete would somehow embarrass him.

Matt gently knocked three times on Pete's door, but there was no answer and no light emanating from the crack between the floor and the bottom of the door. Matt checked each side of the hallway and knocked again... Still nothing. Matt let out a sigh and opened the door. It was completely dark, and there was no sign of Pete.

Matt's nostrils flared in anger. He shrugged and shook his head at Bill.

"Maybe he's in the bathroom," whispered Bill.

They moved back toward the breezeway and stopped in the bathroom, but still no Pete.

"Where the hell is he?" said Matt.

"I don't know." Bill wondered where he could be. Did he get caught? Was someone out there waiting for them? "Should we just go?"

"Yeah, I guess so."

Just as Bill swung the bathroom door open, a voice screamed, "Hey!"

Both Bill and Matt jumped a foot into the air. Their hearts raced as Pete heartily laughed. Matt shoved him into the wall.

"You idiot!" said Matt, in a raspy whisper-yell. "Shut the hell up!"

Pete grinned ear to ear.

Bill shook his head. "At a certain point, *we're* the idiots cuz we keep hanging out with him."

"Take it easy," said Pete. "No one heard."

"Why are you even coming with?" asked Bill. "You were terrified this afternoon."

"I wasn't terrified," said Pete as he puffed out his chest. "What else am I supposed to do, sit in my room like some loser?"

"Just shut up, all right?" said Matt. "Come on."

Matt led the two past the emergency exit at the end of the dorm building through the breezeway—there were no signs of people on the grounds through the long windows. They stopped at the main door, and Matt pulled the curtain of the window back and watched. "I don't see anyone out there. But I can't see the house. We'll have to check outside." Matt unlocked the deadbolt on the huge door.

"Wait," said Bill, grabbing Matt by the arm. "What if they lock the door behind us?"

Matt checked the windows. With the screens in place, it would be difficult to remove them and climb through the window. Nonetheless, Matt turned the lock. "We might be sleeping outside."

They exited through one of the massive twin doors and secured it behind them. They each did their best Navy SEAL impression, crouching down, using the stairs as cover, and checking every direction. It was cooler than in the afternoon but still comfortable. The white moon glistened beautifully on the lake and, along with the yellow glow from the light posts, gave a clear view of the empty grounds. The trees swayed in a slight wind, and the sounds of crickets filled the air. Their view of the house, however, was still obscured by trees.

"We'll have to go further down," said Matt. He pointed towards the dorm building.

They hugged the walls of the main building and then followed along the breezeway. Bill's heart raced, and he feared the consequences of getting caught, but he couldn't deny that he was having fun being a bit dangerous. They made one final stop in front of the residence complex as the house at the top of the hill came into view. All of the lights in the house were off.

"Looks clear," said Matt.

"Any bears?" Bill asked wryly.

"Hope not," responded Matt. "I think we want to go just to the left of the courts."

"You think?" questioned Bill. He had hoped Matt planned the route expertly.

Matt pursed his lips and nodded. "Yeah. I'm pretty sure."

The answer didn't instill much confidence in Bill, but the woods weren't that big. How lost could they get?

"Ready?" asked Matt.

The other two nodded, and the three simultaneously dashed through the open field. Bill felt a wonderful rush of adventure and freedom as the cool air ran across his face. They passed the courts, hit the tree line, and hid among the towering trunks. The boys breathed heavily, and the crisp air slightly burned in their lungs. They watched for followers, but the property was clear; no one in sight.

"That wasn't so hard," said Pete between breaths.

Matt pulled his phone from his pocket and brought up a maps app to check the correct direction. "Come on, this way." The other two followed Matt into the forest.

There was no trail to follow, and Matt judged the route the best he could from the tiny map on the screen of his phone. Enough light from the moon filtered through the leaves on the branches to see the ground. It didn't stop them from occasionally tripping over rocks and sticks though.

"Why don't you turn on the flashlight so we can see?" said Pete.

"That would make it a lot easier for someone else to spot us," said Matt.

"Yeah, I guess so," Pete conceded meekly.

"And I don't want to drain the battery. If the phone dies, we're pretty screwed out here."

Bill nodded in approval. They had only been walking for a few minutes, and already Bill wasn't so sure he'd be able to find his way back to the property without the phone. Progress was slow, but they kept moving.

"So, Rachel's for sure coming?" said Pete.

"That's what she says," said Matt.

"And Maddie, right?" asked Bill. A quick vision of the cute girl with green eyes and curly blonde hair flashed in his mind.

"Yeah, I think so," said Matt. "And Sara."

"Mmm, Sara," said Pete.

"Settle down," said Matt. "Aren't you dating Jenn?"

"Yeah... sort of," said Pete unenthusiastically.

They came across a large downed tree, splintered at the base of its trunk. Pete stepped up on the log and jumped to the ground with a grunt. He misjudged the distance in the dark and keeled over.

Matt laughed a few feet ahead of him. "You all right?"

Pete got to his feet and dusted himself off. "All good."

Bill, determined to not make the same mistake as Pete, rested his butt on the trunk and swung his legs over for an easy dismount.

Matt checked the phone—the route still looked correct. "Didn't you guys cheat on each other, like, ten times?" said Matt.

"Yeah, sort of," said Pete.

"I can't believe anyone would be willing to hook up with you," said Matt.

"Yeah, well, your mom did," said Pete.

Matt snorted a small laugh as Bill just shook his head.

"None of you believe in my skills," said Pete.

"That's because they don't exist," said Matt.

"Jesus Christ, there's a ton of mosquitoes," said Bill, swatting at his neck.

"I guarantee you I hook up with Sara," said Pete defiantly.

Matt stopped in his tracks. "I got twenty says you don't."

"You're on!" said Pete. "Twenty bucks!"

Matt and Pete shook hands.

"Whoa, wait," said Bill. "I want some of this action."

"Fine," said Pete. "I'll go twenty with you too. I'll just be raking it in."

Bill and Pete then shook hands.

"Excellent," said Bill.

"Easy money," said Pete. "Ain't even gonna be a bit hard."

"I got a feeling that's what Sara is gonna say to you," said Matt.

Bill chuckled at the back of the single-file line as Pete thought about it in the middle. "Psst, shut up. No way she's turning this big dick down."

"What's the point of having a big dick if you don't know how to use it?" said Matt.

"Oh, I know how to use it," Pete said confidently.

"I'm sure your hand is very impressed," said Matt.

They continued plodding along, swatting mosquitoes, pushing branches, stepping over stumps, making their own path through the darkness.

"So, have you and Rachel... you know," said Pete, pounding his fist into his hand.

"Yes," said Matt at the front of the line.

"Nice. How is it?"

"It's good... It's great. I don't know. I don't really have anyone else to compare to. I mean, I enjoy myself."

Bill was amazed at how forthcoming Matt was.

"Ah, she's your first?" said Pete.

"Yes, Pete," Matt said dully.

"Congrats on finally popping your cherry." Pete stopped, turned around, and tapped Bill on the chest. "Not like us two, right? Regular pussy hounds back here."

Bill felt the rush of heat go to his face as he began to blush. He didn't like where this conversation was going.

"How many have you boned?" said Pete, continuing forward.

"Umm," Bill thought, "ya know, a few." He wondered if Matt heard him—he could end this fabrication instantly.

"Who? Anybody I know?"

Bill said the first name that came to his head. "Cynthia." Cynthia was his elderly neighbor.

Pete winced. "Ooh, old lady name. What's her last name?"

"J-J-... Johnson," mumbled Bill. There was no way Pete was buying this, was he?

Pete ran the name through his brain. "Doesn't sound familiar. Where does she go?"

"Oak Hill. Met her at work."

Matt seemed focused on navigation, and Bill's blatant lies went unchecked.

Pete nodded. "Cool. She hot?"

"Yeah." Bill hastily tried to create this fantasy girl and spouted the first thing that came to mind to get Pete off his back: "Huge tits."

"Nice!" Pete turned around and gave Bill a high-five. Bill hoped that would end the conversation.

Pete picked up his pace to catch up with Matt. "And you got a little thing for Maddie, huh? She is pretty fine."

"Yeah, we'll see what happens." Bill needed to change the subject, so he shouted to Matt, "Hey, are we almost there?"

"I think so," said Matt. "We should be close."

There was still no sign of the highway—just trees as far as they could see. When they stopped, the only sounds were crickets and the lone hoot of an owl in the distance.

Five minutes later, Bill was beginning to worry. They should have found it by now. Every direction looked the same, and he knew Matt must have missed something. "You sure you know where we're going?"

"Yeah," Matt said. His dubious tone made it sound like he was trying to convince himself. "It shouldn't be too much farther. It's just right up here." He pointed forward, but Bill saw only trees.

"We're lost," said Pete.

"We're not lost," said Matt more defiantly. "It's right up here. Trust me."

They trudged through a couple hundred more yards of woods before finally catching sight of a break in the trees.

"I see it!" Matt said.

"Oh, thank you Jesus," said Pete.

Bill, relieved, stepped onto the hard asphalt of the highway. The three stood shoulder to shoulder, watching the completely empty road, lit only by the moon. It extended far to their left, hundreds of yards, but to the right, it curved into the trees after a few hundred feet.

"That wasn't *too* bad," said Matt. "Took about thirty minutes. We *should* shave some time off now that we've seen where to go. Just gotta remember the right way."

Bill checked his watch: 12:27. "Yeah." He looked back into the woods at the maze of tree trunks and branches and vines and darkness and felt nervous about the trek back. "That wasn't difficult at all."

"You got rewetting drops?" said Matt. "My contacts are super dry."

"Yeah." Bill pulled the miniscule bottle from his sweatpants pocket and handed it to Matt.

Matt leaned his head back and squeezed three drops into his eye.

"All right, are we goin' back?" said Pete.

"Yep," Matt said. He pulled the map up on his phone, and they headed back into the woods.

The light from the moon was now blocked by considerable cloud coverage, making it much more difficult to see. The boys felt uneasy as the strengthening winds whistled through the trees. Bill crossed his arms to keep his body heat contained; the temperature seemed to drop by the minute.

"We better hurry." said Matt, "It seems like it's gonna storm."

"Yeah, let's move it," said Pete.

They picked up their pace the best they could. Navigation was much more difficult without the light of the moon. Bill could barely see Pete five feet in front of him. He was concentrating on his feet hitting the ground when he then heard someone stumble and fall.

"You good?" Bill called.

"Yeah," said Matt. He grimaced and rubbed his hands. "Shit, where's the phone?"

"You lost the phone?!" exclaimed Bill.

Pete and Bill surrounded Matt as he stuck his arms out into the grass and leaves, searching for the phone.

"Yeah, I dropped it when I fell. Do you see it?"

"No." Bill dropped to the ground and fumbled around in the leaves. They needed that phone. It was their only hope to get back.

"Got it!" said Matt. He held the glowing phone up triumphantly. Bill and Pete sighed in relief.

The boys continued on. The wind violently howled through the trees, directly into their faces, slowing their progress even more. Bill's ears felt like ice cubes.

"How long since we left the road?" asked Pete.

"About twenty-five minutes," said Matt.

"Shouldn't we be there?" asked Pete, his voice noticeably higher than usual.

"Yeah, we're close," assured Matt.

"We haven't even passed the downed tree yet," Bill said, trying to draw some warmth by rubbing his arms.

"Maybe we passed it and we didn't even know it," said Matt. "We can barely see anything. The map says we're still going in the right direction."

We're close. We have to be, Bill thought to himself. His mind wandered to the possibility that they weren't close, and they didn't know where they were. What if they were lost? Could they die out here? It was cold but was it *that cold*? *No way*, he tried to assure himself.

"I see lights!" Matt yelled from ahead.

"Woo!" Pete howled like a wolf.

Bill lifted his head and saw tiny yellow dots in the distance through the trees, still hundreds of yards away, but they were there, and they could follow them. Bill breathed easier with thoughts of his warm room and bed. Right now, even that hard concrete slab sounded wonderful, if only he could be under the blankets. They navigated their way back to the lake and the grounds, and the two large buildings came fully into view.

"Wait, wait, wait!" said Bill. He grabbed Matt and Pete by the shoulders, pulled them to the ground, and then pointed across the lake. "Look!"

Across the lake, Jacobs led two workers, each pushing people in wheelchairs, along the dirt trail the boys had followed earlier in the day. As they passed the light poles, they were able to get a better look at the faces.

Matt squinted in disbelief. "Is that Tom? And Rob? What the hell are they doing with them?"

"I don't know," said Bill, thinking. "They used wheelchairs last night to move Keith when he was sick. Do you think they're sick or something?"

"I don't know," said Matt. "Maybe."

They watched intently as the figures wrapped around the lake and disappeared into the woods.

"What's going on?" asked Pete.

"I don't know," said Matt. His face was stone cold. "Let's check it out."

Matt rushed out of the woods towards the path.

"Matt!" said Bill, softly yelling. "God damnit!"

Pete watched as Bill scampered after Matt. "Great," he said dejectedly.

He slowly jogged after the other two; he couldn't be the only one who didn't follow, but he could hang back in case they got caught.

They trotted along the path into the woods as the wind continued to howl through the trees. They followed the wheelchair tracks in the dirt, but there was no sign of the wheelchairs or any people before the shed finally came into view. One light above the door illuminated the entrance and steps. Pete caught up to Matt and Bill hiding behind a tree thirty feet from the shed—still no sign of anyone.

"They must have gone inside," said Matt. "Maybe we can get in there."

"Why don't we just call the police?" said Pete. "Where's your phone?"

Matt took the phone out of his pocket and flipped it open to see an exclamation point with a circle around it where the bars showing the strength of connection should have been.

"That's why," said Matt.

"Okay," said Pete, thinking. "Why don't we go back to the dorm and call from there?"

"There's no time for that," said Matt. He combed his hair with his hands as a drop of sweat ran down his forehead.

"What?" said Pete. "There's plenty of time. We don't even know what's going on."

"Well, let's find out." Matt turned to Bill. "You with me?"

"Yeah," said Bill, eyes wide. He had no interest in going into the shed, but his damn conscience wouldn't allow him to leave the students out here under such strange circumstances. "Let's go."

The two walked toward the shed, while Pete looked over his shoulder at the trail back to safety. He didn't like being alone out there. Matt and Bill climbed the stairs and stopped at the door, and Pete scampered to the shed. Matt's hand shook as he slowly reached toward the doorknob. He clutched the cold metal and twisted it back and forth, but it wouldn't budge.

"Shoot!" whined Matt.

"Hey!" a voice called from behind them.

The three boys jumped and turned their heads to see a bright flashlight pointed to the ground just in front of Delilah's petite shadow. She strode toward them and stopped at the bottom of the stairs, shining the flashlight straight into the boys faces. "What are you doing out here?"

They each held their hands in front of their faces to block the bright light.

"Uh, nothing," said Bill.

"I'll handle this," said Pete. He walked directly up to Delilah and stopped less than a foot from her face. "Well, hello. I knew you couldn't resist."

Delilah pointed the flashlight in his eyes at point-blank range, blinding him.

Pete staggered away and blinked repeatedly. "Aw, what did you do that for? I can't see anything." He made a clumsy movement back in Delilah's direction.

She pointed to the other boys. "You better get control of him right now."

Bill and Matt quickly bounded down the stairs and wrapped their arms around the stumbling Pete. "Yeah, yeah," said Matt. "No problem." They pushed him a few feet farther away from Delilah.

"Again, I ask," started Delilah, "*what* are you doing out here?"

"We could ask you the same thing," said Matt. "Why'd they take them in there?" He pointed to the shed.

"*Who* took *whom* in there?" Delilah's mouth hung open after the last word.

"Your friends took our friends in there," said Matt. "They rolled them out here in wheelchairs."

Delilah pointed the light at the shed. "I didn't see anything," she said harshly. "I don't know what you're talking about."

Delilah's assertion didn't convince Matt in the slightest. "Well, you better find out real fast."

The flashlight shone upon Matt's face again, but he refused to look away. He squinted hard and stared straight through it until he got an answer.

Delilah took the walkie-talkie off her belt. "Mr. Jacobs."

The static crackled, and then Jacobs' voice came through. "Yes? What is it?"

Delilah pushed the button. "It's Delilah. I have three students out here by the utility shed and they're very upset about something. They're saying that you took two students in there on wheelchairs."

Silence. Finally, Jacobs answered, "I'll be right there."

"Okay, thanks," said Delilah.

The four waited. The boys were completely uncertain of what to expect. Were they about to end up in wheelchairs too, taken into this mysterious building? Or was it just a strange misunderstanding with a reasonable explanation?

"Be ready," said Matt. He balled his fist.

Bill's face scrunched. "For what?"

The door to the shed opened, and Jacobs emerged from the dark entryway.

"What are you doing with Tom and Rob?" said Matt.

"Yeah," said Bill. "What's goin' on in there, Jacobs?"

Jacobs walked over to the boys and made a gesture toward them with his hands. "Now, everyone just calm down."

"No," said Matt. "You start explaining right now."

"There was an altercation," started Jacobs, "between your classmates. It got pretty rough."

"Bullshit," said Matt.

"Watch your mouth," Jacobs said sternly.

Matt ignored him. "Tom wouldn't get into a fight. And not with Rob."

"Nevertheless, it's true."

The spots in Pete's vision finally faded away and he could see again. "We want to see them."

"Yeah," said Matt.

"Tomorrow," answered Jacobs. "Right now, you should go back—"

Matt shook his head. "*Now.*"

"No," said Jacobs unequivocally. He rested his hands on his hips. "Now, you're going back to your rooms. You have broken *God knows* how many rules. *I* am in charge here, and you will do as I say."

"Okay," said Matt, mimicking Jacobs by putting his hands on his hips. "We'll do what you say. We'll go back to the dorm, and we'll scream, and we'll shout, and we'll raise hell until Father Leo and Father Stephen and everyone else in the building hear us. Then we'll see what's really going on in there."

Bill knew Matt wasn't bluffing, and after Jacobs pondered the situation stoically for a moment, he came to the same conclusion. Jacobs forced a smile. "Okay, follow me."

Jacobs led the boys to the door, removed his keys from his belt, and unlocked it. The boys followed him in with Delilah last. It was dark; there were two recessed ceiling bulbs giving off only enough light to keep the occupants from walking into a wall. A stainless-steel door, entirely too nice and expensive for this unremarkable building, with a numeric keypad lock stood in front of them. Next to it, a few broken-down and dilapidated shelves held various supplies—cans of different bug sprays, towels, brooms, rakes, buckets—all covered in dirt and grime.

Jacobs extended his hand to the red-lit keypad but noticed Matt stretching his neck out to get a better look. Jacobs moved his body to block Matt's view and punched in the numbers. The light on the lock turned green. Directly on the other side of the door was a staircase leading down.

"It was a bomb-shelter," said Jacobs, "built during the Cold War. I bet it came in handy during the Cuban Missile Crisis. I don't know if the missiles could have made it all the way here, but better safe than sorry, I suppose."

The boys grasped the railing and took it slowly down the stairs, barely paying attention to what Jacobs was saying. The boys' nerves were on edge. This building was far stranger than anything they could have imagined. Why would the retreat need this place? Mostly though they just worried about their friends.

"Anyway," Jacobs continued, "we have been remodeling it. We added a small medical facility down here. We're a bit of a ways from a hospital, so we felt it necessary to have one on the grounds. And your friends are taking full advantage of it. One of them had quite a nasty cut on his head."

At the bottom of the staircase was another metal door with another keypad lock. Jacobs covered his hand and punched in the code.

"What's with all of the security?" asked Matt.

"We have some expensive equipment, medical supplies, drugs—can't have anyone breaking in and damaging or stealing anything."

They moved through the doorway into a long concrete corridor that extended fifty or sixty feet. It took their eyes a moment to adjust to the brightness of the overhead panel lights. There were several doors with windows near the top on each side of the corridor, but none of the lights were on inside the rooms, and nothing was visible from the boys' vantage point. The ceiling felt low, only a foot or two above their heads. Bill breathed quickly; a feeling of claustrophobia rushed over him and combined with the adrenaline of the situation. It left him flushed and light-headed—like he might pass out. He paused.

"Are you okay?" said Delilah.

"Yeah." He took some deep breaths and released them. He wiped his brow with his sweatshirt sleeve and the feeling passed. They continued down the corridor.

"How far underground are we?" asked Matt.

"About thirty feet," said Jacobs.

Matt laughed. "This is ridiculous. Why not just build it upstairs?"

"Well, we had this space available," said Jacobs. "We just needed to fix it up a bit. It was a fun project."

"What are all of these other rooms for?" asked Bill, back in control of his body and focused.

"The original owner wanted several areas to serve different purposes— bedroom, bathroom, living room, exercise room—just like a normal house. And he had the means to make it happen."

"And how do you have the means to make this happen?" Matt asked.

"We're very blessed," Jacobs said.

They passed the rooms, hoping to see something cool. None of them had ever been in a bomb shelter before. They each would have pictured a room with a cot or two and shelves stocked with canned goods—nothing anywhere near as expansive or impressive as this. But all of the rooms were pitch-black inside.

"What's in these rooms now?" asked Matt.

"Supplies, mostly," said Jacobs. "And a living quarters for the doctor." Jacobs stopped at the only lit-up room in the former bomb shelter. "Here are your friends."

They entered the room and found Tom sitting on a medical table receiving stitches in his forehead from a middle-aged man in a white lab coat and tan cargo pants. The doctor concentrated on his job without acknowledging the visitors. Rob sat in a chair, holding an ice pack to his jaw, and stared straight at the floor, eyes glazed over.

"You guys all right?" asked Matt.

Rob slowly looked up. "Oh, hey," he grumbled. "Yeah, we're all right. Just got into a little fight, I guess. What are you doing here?"

"We saw them bringing you over here," said Matt. "What happened?"

Rob lowered the ice pack from his face. "I don't remember much. They said I was being a jerk and kept taunting Tom and he finally let me have it."

Pete shook Tom's shoulder. "Atta boy, buddy!"

"Ow!" said Tom. "Stop."

"Can you please *not* do that?" said the doctor in a tone that clearly meant he wasn't fooling around.

"Sorry," said Pete. He put both hands in the air and backed away.

Matt noticed Rob's thousand-mile stare and said, "You sure you're all right?"

"Yeah." He clumsily pawed at his nose. "I feel great."

"I bet you do," said Matt.

"I gave him something for the pain," said the doctor.

"Sweet," said Pete. "Can we get some?"

The doctor lifted his head from his patient to glower at Pete. It was their first good look at him. He had a gaunt face with a dimple in his chin and thinning grey hair combed straight back. His icy stare scared Pete more than the bear did earlier. Pete turned away from the doctor's gaze and he went back to work on Tom.

"Tom?" said Bill. "You okay?" Bill looked over the inch-long cut above Tom's right eyebrow and the dried blood in his blond hair.

"Yeah," said Tom, wincing from the pain of the doctor pinching the gash together, then piercing his skin again with the needle and pulling the thread through the wound. "I'll be fine."

"They'll both be fine," said the doctor in a much less menacing tone than before. "As you can see, Tom here received a pretty nasty gash. He fell down and hit his head on a table. He also has a minor concussion."

Pete tiptoed back to Tom and looked at the gash. "Gnarly." The doctor's glare again scared Pete back a few steps.

"Rob over there," started the doctor, "got slugged in the face a couple of times. His head won't feel great for a bit, and he'll have some bruises, but he'll be fine."

"We contacted their parents," said Jacobs. "They're on their way. We're going to keep them here for now so Doctor Knapp can keep an eye on them and make sure there are no further complications."

"Ugh!" said Pete. "You get to leave? Lucky! Hey, Bill, sock me one. Come on!"

Pete darted from side to side in front of Bill like a boxer, both arms raised to protect his head. He feinted a few left jabs and straight rights.

"Don't tempt me," said Bill.

"What is wrong with you?" asked Delilah, face contorted in disgust. "How many times do you think you were dropped on your head as a baby?"

"Whoa," said Pete, flabbergasted. "That's not very nice."

"Delilah!" roared Jacobs. "Apologize this instant."

"I see why you like this girl," said Matt.

Delilah took a deep breath. "I'm sorry, I shouldn't have said that. It was mean and inappropriate. Will you please forgive me?"

"Of course I will," said Pete. "I can't stay mad at you."

Pete extended his arms to Delilah for a hug. Delilah clenched her jaw and looked to Jacobs, who nodded. She begrudgingly walked to Pete and hugged him. Pete took a deep breath of her hair. He loved the smell. She patted him on the back to signal she was done, and Pete let go.

"How about a quick blessing for your friends here, for a speedy recovery?" said Jacobs. "Come on, let's gather 'round."

Jacobs pulled the boys into a close circle and raised his hands into the air. "Lord, we know there is healing in your touch. We ask that You reach down unto your children, Rob and Tom, and bless them with Your love and strength. You alone have the almighty power to heal. You are our Lord, Savior, Healer, and Friend. We are nothing without You. We trust in You fully and will love You always and forever. Thanks be to God."

The boys backed away.

"Feel better, guys?" said Bill, rolling his eyes.

Jacobs either didn't hear him or ignored him. "Okay, gentlemen, are we about ready to head back to the dorms?"

Bill looked at Matt, who could only shrug.

"Yeah, I guess so," said Matt. "Have fun at home, guys."

"Thanks," said Rob. "See ya."

"Bye, guys," said Tom.

"Have a good night, fellas," said the doctor, locking eyes with Bill.

The hairs on Bill's neck rose. "Goodnight," Bill said softly.

After they exited the medical room, Matt, extremely curious to find out exactly what was in the other rooms, found an opportunity when Jacobs was blocked behind the other two boys in the medical room. He darted across the hall, opened the door, and flipped the light on.

"Excuse me," said Jacobs, pushing past Bill and Pete. "Don't go in there."

The room was filled with large cages made of gray steel wire, lined up next to each other along the walls like a kennel.

"What's this for?" asked Matt.

The boys wandered through the room, inspecting the cages. The front doors were grated and open, but the side panels were covered by pieces of black plastic. Jacobs stopped at the door. "We do some animal rehabilitation: injuries, malnourishment, whatever. We've had some dogs, cats, deer, even a young bear."

Bill wondered if it was the bear that had almost killed them earlier.

"Where are all of the animals now?" asked Matt.

"We released the last one we had this morning," said Jacobs. "A deer. It had been shot. There are a lot of hunters in the area. The shots don't always kill the animals and they get away but are wounded. We can bring them here and try to fix them up."

"Well, that's very nice of you," said Matt. "That doctor in there can treat animals too?"

"Yes," said Jacobs. "Doctor Knapp is very skilled. And our staff helps out too. We are all God's creatures, and we and Doctor Knapp are just doing our part to help out."

"What about the cow we ate for dinner?" said Matt.

"Every being has its place in the world," said Jacobs.

"Yep," said Pete, rubbing his stomach. "And for some, it's in our bellies."

"Let's head back to the dorm, shall we?" said Jacobs.

Jacobs coaxed the boys out of the room, shut the door, and led them down the hall.

"What did you say was in all these other rooms?" asked Matt.

"Like I said earlier, there is a living quarters for the doctor, and the other rooms are mostly storage."

"Well, you didn't mention the petting zoo earlier," said Matt. He walked on his tippy-toes and craned his neck for a better look through the windows on the doors.

Jacobs, Delilah, and the boys made their way up the stairs, out of the shed, and back into the woods. Jacobs stopped. "I would like to apologize. I'm sure when you saw what you saw, you had no idea what was happening and thought the worst. It was probably very scary for you, and I'm sorry for that. I don't blame you for wanting to check on your friends. You're very brave."

The three nodded in agreement.

Jacobs' tone hardened. "However, that doesn't change the fact that you three are out after curfew and are breaking several rules. These rules exist for a reason. You need to show better respect for us and this place. What were you doing out here?"

"We just wanted to get some air," said Matt. "We were tired of being jailed inside."

"This place isn't a jail, and we give you plenty of time throughout the day to go out and get some air and mingle with one another. This time is very important too. You need time to reflect individually. You need time to rest. You need your sleep."

"Yeah," said Matt. "Okay, you're right. Why don't we call it even?"

Jacobs looked at Matt and let out small laugh before guffawing louder. "Okay, we'll call it even." Jacobs reached his hand out, and Matt shook it. As they let go, a bolt of lightning flashed across the sky, followed quickly by a loud clap of thunder that made everyone shudder.

"Holy cow," said Jacobs as it began to pour. "Let's get back to the dorm."

They hurried back along the trail through heavy rain drops. Lightning continued to fill the sky, and thunder rumbled throughout the landscape. They exited the forest into the clearing by the lake, and hail the size of quarters pelted down on them. They covered their heads with their arms, scurried across the muddy field, and took shelter in a nook next to the main entrance. Everyone was soaked to the bone.

"This is quite a storm," said Jacobs. "Sorry, again, about the confusion. I can assure you, your friends will be fine." He unlocked the already unlocked door and swung it open. "I will make an announcement to the students tomorrow about Rob and Tom's whereabouts, and I will keep you posted on any new developments."

"Okay," said Matt. "Thank you."

"You're welcome. And no more running around after curfew. It's dangerous out here," Jacobs said, flailing his arms wildly through the air above his head. The boys looked at him like he was a lunatic.

"Okay," said Matt, completely unamused. He twisted and wrung out the bottom half of his shirt; a small trickle of water fell to the ground.

"Now, go inside and get dry," said Jacobs. "Get some rest. We all have another big day tomorrow. Goodnight, gentlemen. Have a blessed evening!"

They said goodnight, and the boys went into the building. Jacobs locked the door, and he and Delilah scurried back into the storm toward the house on the top of the hill. Bill, Matt, and Pete walked through the breezeway to the dorm building. The warmth inside felt incredible. With each step, water leaked out of the sides of their shoes and left footprints in the carpet.

Pete pulled his drenched shirt away from his torso. "What do you think their deal is? Is she his daughter or niece or are they banging?"

"Maybe it's all of the above," said Bill.

"Is there going to be a normal day at this place?" asked Matt. He wiped drops of water from his brow and watched the sheets of rain pummel the earth through the windows of the breezeway.

"I still can't believe Tom fought Rob," said Bill.

"Yeah, he must be spending too much time with this guy." Matt shoved the back of Pete's shoulder.

"Hey, good for him for sticking up for himself," said Pete. A proud smile spread across his face as if he had anything to do with it.

They came to the stairs in the residence building. Bill and Matt went up and Pete continued down the hall. "Later, dudes."

"See ya," said Matt.

"Later," said Bill.

Bill and Matt struggled up the last few stairs. The entire day crashed down upon them. Their legs burned, and they were completely sapped of all strength and energy.

"Take it easy," said Matt.

"You too," said Bill. "Can't wait to see who almost dies tomorrow."

"No doubt." Matt faded away into the darkness down the hallway, his shoes still squishing with every step.

Droplets of water fell to the floor all around him as Bill entered his room and turned on the main light switch. He kicked off his wet shoes and peeled his socks off one by one, leaving behind a small puddle where he stood. He unclasped the band of the watch and set it down gently on the desk. *What a night*, he thought to himself. *What a day... Two days*, he corrected himself. He had gotten drunk or at least buzzed, almost been eaten by a bear, and been caught out after curfew. Twice he found students incapacitated and being physically manipulated by workers.

Dirty, awful thoughts bombarded his mind before he could stop them. What were they doing with the students?... *This is the Catholic church after all; they don't get the benefit of the doubt anymore. But Tom and Rob seemed normal enough. They weren't struggling or asking for help. And Keith... well, who cares what happened to that jerk.* They could have their way with him for all Bill cared. *No, that's wrong. That's too far.* Bill didn't wish that upon Keith. He was just sick, and Tom and Rob had been in a fight and Bill's mind was running wild with absurd explanations.

Rain pelted down on the window. Bill had never seen rain this heavy last so long— payback for all of the recent perfect weather days. He stripped down naked, body covered in goosebumps; even his undershirt and boxers were completely soaked through. He grabbed a towel from the closet, dried himself off from head to toe, and then wiped up the water on the floor.

After throwing on a dry T-shirt and gym shorts, Bill grabbed his toiletries and made a trip to the bathroom, avoiding the wet footprints on the carpeted hallway like landmines along the way. He flipped on the lights, and again, like last night, the bulbs above the middle sink flickered like a strobe light. He went to the sink on the right which had a properly working light. The red mass on his forehead had almost doubled in size since that morning and was now capped with a pulsating whitehead. Bill's face contorted in disgust. He took out his contact case and large bottle of solution, reminding him that once again Matt had absconded with his eye drops; he lost track of how many bottles Matt had stolen from him in class over the years. He made a mental note to retrieve it tomorrow, spread his right eyelid wide, and pulled out the dry contact.

A huge flash of light shone through the window, and a loud clap of thunder boomed, shaking the room. All of the lights went out—the room was pitch black. Bill tried to quell the fear creeping into his mind. *There's no reason to be scared. It's just a storm. Lights go out all the time in storms. Calm down, you pansy.* He hurriedly finished brushing his teeth and struggled to collect his things, fumbling around in the dark. He timidly took baby-steps toward the door, arm extended. He couldn't see an inch in front of his face as he frantically groped around for the door. Finally, Bill found the handle and escaped the bathroom.

The hallway was no brighter. Bill waited a moment for his eyes to adjust, and slowly the angles of the walls and the shapes of the doors started coming into focus. Bill kept one hand along the wall to guide him. He had only made it a few feet when off in the distance he heard creaks in the floor. Someone was coming toward him. He was able to make out a figure down the hall. *Just a student,* he thought to himself. Bill took another step as the blurry figure came closer. *What about Keith?* The thought stopped Bill dead in his tracks. *What about Tom and Rob?* Two nights in a row, students had been detained and taken away. The stories concocted by the Eternal Springs workers suddenly seemed too farfetched to Bill, and fear overtook him. They must be hiding something. Was he next?

Bill suddenly found himself backtracking to the bathroom. He hid in one of the stalls as a person entered the bathroom. Bill quietly dropped the lid on the toilet and stood on top of it, clutching his toiletries to his chest. Whoever it was flipped the light switch back and forth several times to no avail. The person gave up and stumbled to the urinal. Frequent flashes of lightning lit the bathroom. As Bill raised his head above the stall to see if he could identify the person, the power suddenly came back on, and the bathroom filled with light. Bill quickly ducked his head.

"What the hell?" said the person. "Who's in there?"

Bill didn't know what to do. He heard the urinal flush, and he turned the lock on the stall door.

"Hey, who's in there?" The person knocked on the door. "Hello?" The person pulled the door hard, shaking the entire stall and then began pounding with his fist. "That ain't cool, bro. You can't be spying on people in the bathroom."

"I wasn't spying," said Bill. "I'm sorry." He wasn't sure who it was. He thought Carter maybe, but he wasn't positive. All he had seen was a flash of dark skin through the crease between the stall door and wall.

"Well, what the hell are you doing in there?"

His voice was strained with anger. Bill was sure whoever was on the other side of the door wanted to smash him into oblivion.

"Just using the toilet."

"Who is that? Foster?"

"Uh, hi."

"What were you doing peeking your head over?"

"I wasn't. I was worried about the lights."

"That's some weird shit, man. You're into that, that's cool. I'm not though."

"I didn't mean anything, I'm sorry," Bill pleaded.

"Yeah, you better be sorry. Hiding in bathrooms, getting off watching people piss."

"That's not what was going on."

"You're lucky we're at this retreat. Normally, I'd kick your ass. But with God watching and all, and the spirit of the place, I'm gonna let you off with a warning."

"Okay. Thank you. I'm sorry."

"You can't be doing this shit again."

"I won't."

"You better not. Damn pervert. Hiding in bathrooms, looking at dicks."

Bill heard the door close, and he stepped down from the toilet. *I can't believe that just happened. I'm screwed.*

Bill returned to his room and dropped his stuff on the desk. He sat on the bed, and his mind ran wild. This embarrassment would never end. *Will he tell anyone? Of course he will. Everyone will know, and then I'll be known as the guy that spies on people while they pee. I can just explain that the lights went out and I thought someone was trying to get me, so I hid in the toilet. Yeah, that's much better than spying on people peeing. I'm not a sexual deviant, I'm just a pussy, exactly like Keith said.* No one would believe him anyway; they'd all believe the student who found him in the stall. He dropped his head into his hands as his entire life flashed before his eyes. *When this gets out, there's no coming back from it.* He just wanted to be normal, to hang out and make friends, and then this had to happen. If he had just stayed in his room by himself like usual, this wouldn't have happened. *This is why you don't try to get better. This is why you should just end it.* The feelings of shame and hatred overwhelmed him, and the tears ran down his cheeks, like the rain on the window, and the line repeated over and over in his head: *I hate myself.*

After a little while, the rush of feelings dissipated, and Bill started to calm down. He convinced himself the best he could that it was not a big deal—just enough to try to sleep. If he could have stayed awake and continue to beat himself up about the bathroom incident, he would have, but he was beyond tired. His body ached, his head pounded, and he was chilled to the bone. Bill had forgotten to inform anyone about the broken lock, so he secured his makeshift doorstopper underneath the doorknob. He flicked the light off and lay down in bed to the sound of light rain pattering against the window. He pulled the covers over him and was reminded of just how uncomfortable the bed was. Bill lay motionless on his back and stared at the ceiling. *Not gonna work.*

As Bill rolled over, he saw the whites of an eyeball staring at him from across the room in the darkness. Bill froze, his mouth hung open. "What the…" The eyeball blinked, and Bill let out a terrified grunt.

Bang, bang, bang! Bill looked to the door and then back to the hole in the wall, but the eye was gone—now just a stream of light shone through. There was another knock on the door, snapping him out of his daze. Bill slowly got up, completely focused on the hole.

"Who… who's there?" called Bill. His entire body was clenched tight.

"It's Matt."

Bill removed the chair and opened the door. Matt extended the small bottle of eyedrops towards him.

"Sorry, I stole this." said Matt. "Wasn't sure if you'd need it or not."

Bill didn't take the bottle. His entire focus was on the hole and the eye. *Was that real? There's no way that was real. It had to be my imagination.*

Matt waved the bottle. "Hello, Bill?"

Bill turned to Matt and snatched the bottle before returning his focus to the wall. Should he tell Matt? No, he would never believe him.

"Thanks," said Bill, staring at the hole.

Matt leaned against the doorframe. "You all right?"

Bill could hear the concern in Matt's voice. "Yeah… Just tired." He paused and gently massaged his eyeballs with his palms before looking back at Matt. "Going a bit crazy here."

"I hear ya," said Matt. "Hang in there. Just a couple more days."

Bill took a deep breath and exhaled. "Yeah."

Matt patted Bill on the shoulder. "Get some sleep, man. See you tomorrow."

"See ya," said Bill.

Bill closed the door and went over to examine the hole. *It couldn't have been real,* he thought to himself over and over. He needed to convince himself of that. He raised his hand to the wall and hesitated, fearful of what could be inside. He slowly pushed his finger in down to the knuckle on his hand. He pulled it out and knocked on the wall—sounded hollow. Bill grabbed a pen from the desk and slid it through the hole. He heard it hit the ground after a second, landing on the same level on which he was standing.

"What the hell is going on with me?" Bill whispered to himself, unable to remove the vision of the eyeball from his mind. He stood there and stared at the hole for a few more minutes before turning off the light and sitting on the bed. The stream of light continued to shine through the hole while Bill watched wide-eyed. *Was it real? Where did it go? Who was it? I must have imagined it. No one could fit in there, could they? Could they? Why would they be in there? What the hell is going on?*

Bill did not sleep for the rest of the night.

CHAPTER 14:

Slipping Away

EVEN THOUGH BILL WAS AWAKE, THE SOUND OF JACOBS' VOICE STARtled him. It emanated from the speaker box above him like God's voice from heaven. "Good morning, retreaters. It is time to start this magnificent day. Last night's storm has given way to a glorious morning. Breakfast will be served shortly. Have a blessed day."

Bill sat on his bed in a sleepless void, head and back resting against the wall. He clutched his watch in his hands and stared at the hole in the wall across the room. He had not slept the entire night—he couldn't after what he had seen. He was too terrified. The light had gone off a little after 3:00 according to his watch. Was it Jacobs watching him last night? The omniscient ever-present God, constantly watching his subjects and talking to them from above? *Why would he watch people? Why me? Was he some sort of pervert? Like I am, watching people in the bathroom.*

Bill shook his head. He couldn't handle the negative thoughts. *The eye had to be fake. It had to be my imagination. I was just tired and freaked out and I imagined it.* Bill was always terrified of people's attention. He couldn't handle the eyes watching him in the batter's box. He couldn't handle the eyes of people looking at him in school or at this retreat. And now he was seeing eyes watching him from behind walls. It had to be imaginary. It was just his psyche messing with him like always. Even if it were real, who would believe him?

Bill thought about going to the bathroom, and his mind gave up on agonizing over the eye for a moment to become transfixed on the other incident from last night. Would he be able to get to Carter before he told anyone and apologize and explain what really happened? He wasn't even positive it was Carter. And if he was too late, how many people would know by now that he liked to hang out in bathrooms and watch people urinate, hoping to catch a glimpse of…? Bill closed his eyes and took a deep breath. He could easily see how this story played out, and he had no interest in living it. *I don't need to pee that bad… I don't need to shower… I got a shower in the storm last night.* He put on a pair of jeans and switched out his T-shirt for a fresh one. He thought about getting some food. *I'm not that hungry. I'll just have some water.* All of the justifications made enough sense for him to stay put in his room.

Bill paced back and forth in his room for a few minutes, ultimately summoning the courage to go to breakfast, aided by his excessive hunger. The hallway, staircase, and breezeway were empty. So far, so good. The closer Bill got to the dining hall, the more he thought it was a bad idea. He envisioned the scene: he walked in, and everyone dropped their silverware to point and laugh together at him, the peeping Tom, the freak, the guy that liked to hide out in bathrooms and watch you hold your junk. Bill tried to calm himself as he arrived at the dining hall doors and heard the loud chatter of the students.

Never mind. Bill did a one-eighty and hurried back to his room to wait for the next announcement from Jacobs.

Bill hurried down the main aisle of the chapel and rushed to the open spot next to Matt in the pew. Bill sat down in a huff and began rubbing his hands together while he scanned the students in front of him.

"Hey, man," said Matt.

"Hey," responded Bill. His leg bounced up and down with enough force that everyone in the pew could feel it.

"Where were you for breakfast?"

"I wasn't hungry." Bill quickly glanced over his shoulder.

"Well, you missed it," said Matt, smiling.

At once, Bill halted all body movements. "Missed what?" he said, terrified.

"They were giving out muffins and doughnuts for breakfast," said Matt. "Everyone wanted more; turns out those two dumbasses left the fridge open last night. The motor overheated or something and the fridge and freezer broke. All of the food—the meat, eggs, milk—spoiled."

"Really?" said Bill, relieved; it wasn't about him.

"Yeah," said Matt. "Jacobs was pissed. Kept asking if anybody knew anything."

"Richie or Gus confess?"

"Hell no," said Matt with a chuckle.

"And no one said anything?"

"Nope."

"So, now we're out of food?"

"Jacobs said they would have to go get some stuff later. He's not angry, just really disappointed and blah, blah, blah. You know the spiel parents do."

"Right. So, nothing else?" Bill sounded too overeager. His leg erupted back into spastic bouncing movements.

Matt looked quizzically to Bill. "What do you mean? What else would there be?"

"No other news?" Bill's eyes shifted throughout the church, looking for anyone who might be looking at him and laughing.

"You mean the Tom and Rob thing?" Matt shook his head. "No, Jacobs hasn't said anything yet. I think most students know by now, though. It was going around at breakfast."

The words poured out of Bill's at mouth one hundred miles per hour. "Father Leo or Father Stephen say anything to you about getting caught after curfew?"

"Nope. Nothing yet. Maybe Jacobs didn't tell them."

"Yeah. Did you talk to Carter at all this morning?"

"Carter?" Matt threw his head back aggressively in confusion. "No. Why?"

"No reason," said Bill.

Matt watched Bill blink incessantly as he scanned the church, his eyes darting all over the place. He looked like a junkie needing a fix. "You all right?"

"Yeah," said Bill quickly. "Why?"

"You look terrible," said Matt, eyeing Bill over.

Bill tried to calm down. He gave up on his search. It didn't sound like the news had spread, and no one was hinting that they knew anything. "I feel terrible." He rubbed his eyes. "I didn't sleep much. I don't think I slept at all."

"That's no good," said Matt.

"Nope," said Bill.

"Well, I'm having the worst acne outbreak of my life," said Matt, pointing to his face. His chin and jawline were riddled with tiny red and white spots.

Bill pointed to his forehead at the massive red blob with the white bubble in the center. "I take it you've seen the second head I'm growing? It's not like you can miss it."

Pete sat down in the pew directly behind Bill and Matt.

"Hey, Pete," said Matt with a quick glance over his shoulder. "What's going on?"

"Not much," said Pete. "Just walking the path. My eyes have really been opened."

Matt chuckled. "Yeah, right."

"This place truly is magnificent," said Pete. "I've learned a lot about myself. I love it here."

"All right, man, you can knock it off," said Matt.

"And to share this amazing experience with you guys… it truly is a gift," said Pete. "I'm so grateful."

Matt, completely bewildered, looked to Bill and then turned back to Pete. Matt had never seen Pete's hair perfectly combed before. It was always a mess. "Are you being serious, man? What the hell are you talking about?"

Pete's face lit up with a smile. "We've been going about this all wrong. You especially, Bill."

Bill's head jerked to the side at the sound of his name. Pete leaned forward and rested his hand on Bill's shoulder.

"You need to believe in what Mr. Jacobs is doing here. You need to give yourself to God."

"I do, huh?" said Bill.

"Yes," said Pete, removing his hand. "That is the only way to salvation."

"You feelin' okay?" asked Matt. "You're starting to freak me out a bit."

"I honestly have never been better," said Pete. "I love you guys."

Pete leaned forward and wrapped his arms around Bill and Matt. Matt patted him on the head. "Love you too, buddy."

Pete sat back in the pew with a smile on his face. Bill raised his eyebrows at Matt, hoping for an explanation. Matt was dumbfounded and could only put his palms up and shrug.

Jacobs stood at the front of the church, today sporting a white polo and tan khakis. "Excuse me, everyone. Excuse me! If I could have your attention for a moment, please. Quiet down."

The students obliged and sat quietly.

"Thank you. Thank you. Hello again, everyone. First, I just wanted to say that I still have not heard anything regarding the food in the pantry and fridge. We've already learned here that some of the most important pillars of our faith are honesty and trust. I'm deeply disappointed that no one has come forward yet. I'm sure whoever did it didn't mean to leave the door open. It was an accident. Please, *please*, come see me in private if you know what happened. No one will be punished, I promise.

"Now on to our second bit of news. I wanted to make an announcement about something that happened last night. Two of your fellow retreaters were involved in an altercation. Thomas and Robert got into a fight with each other last night and were sent home this morning."

Most of the students had heard the news by the end of breakfast. Tom and Rob were missing, and Matt knew why—he was there. He told Scott and Dee, who told one or two others, and it spread like wildfire. The remaining students who were hearing the news for the first time conversed with those who had heard earlier and exchanged their comments and looks of disbelief. It was a shock to those that heard at breakfast, and it was a shock to those hearing now.

Jacobs gestured to the students to settle down. "Gentlemen! Gentlemen, please quiet down! Quiet down, please!"

Jacobs regained control of the room. "Thank you. They are both fine now. They were sent home this morning with their parents to rest and recuperate. We just wanted to let everyone know so you weren't wondering what happened to them. They are fine. Okay? Wonderful! Well, we shouldn't waste any more time. We have so much to do today! I'll turn it over to Father Stephen. Have a blessed day!"

The students were still buzzing from the news as the first notes of the entrance hymn began for mass. Bill jumped from the pew and cut Jacobs off in the aisle.

"Hey, Jacobs."

Jacobs winced and held a finger up to Bill. "I think Mr. Jacobs is more appropriate."

"Sure," said Bill. "Sorry."

Jacobs put his smile back on. "It's all right. What can I do for you?"

"There are a couple things wrong with my room. They were already messed up before I got there, so don't blame me. First, the lock's broken on the door. It's a bit of a security risk. Can someone fix that?"

"Sure can," Jacobs said pleasantly. "And what else?"

"There's a hole in the wall in my room. There's a light coming out and it is very distracting and I'm having a hard time sleeping. You of all people know how important rest is for this experience. Can someone please fix it?"

"Absolutely," said Jacobs. "What room number is it?"

"Thirty-six."

Jacobs took out a pen and pad and wrote it down. "Thirty-six. I'll have someone come by and take a look at it."

"Great," said Bill. "Thanks."

"You're welcome," said Jacobs. "Have a blessed day!"

"And you too, *Mr.* Jacobs," said Bill.

Matt turned to Bill as he sat down. "You have a hole in your wall?"

"Yep."

"So what's the big deal about a hole in the wall?"

Bill sighed. "Nothing. It's just distracting. Don't worry about it."

Matt shrugged and turned back to the front of the church as Father Stephen knelt before the altar. The mass passed Bill by, as he was still too focused on his humiliation from last night. He subtly looked around the room to see if anyone was staring at him, keeping his head pointed forward while his eyes danced from person to person. No one gave him any looks back. Bill's stomach let out a growl loud enough for the people around him to hear. Now, everyone looked at him. Bill played it off like it wasn't him—turning from side to side to find the culprit—while his face turned red.

Father Stephen walked over to the lectern, and the students rose.

"The Lord be with you."

"And with your spirit," the students responded.

"A reading from the Holy Gospel according to Matthew."

The church responded in unison, "Glory to you, O Lord."

Bill didn't bother with the words or the crosses.

"Then Jesus was led up by the Spirit into the wilderness to be tempted by the devil. And after He had fasted for forty days and forty nights, He then became hungry. And the tempter came and said to Him, 'If You are the Son of God, command that these stones become bread.' But He answered and said, 'It is written: Man shall not live on bread alone, but on every word that comes out of the mouth of God.'

"Then the devil took Him along into the holy city and had Him stand on the pinnacle of the temple, and he said to Him, 'If You are the Son of God, throw Yourself down; for it is written: He will give His angels orders concerning You; and on *their* hands they will lift You up, so that You do not strike Your foot against a stone.' Jesus said to him, 'On the other hand, it is written: You shall not put the Lord your God to the test.'

"Again, the devil took Him along to a very high mountain and showed Him all the kingdoms of the world and their glory; and he said to Him, 'All these things I will give You, if You fall down and worship me.' Then Jesus said to him, 'Go away, Satan! For it is written: You shall worship the Lord your God, and serve Him only.' Then the devil left Him; and behold, angels came and *began* to serve Him. The Gospel of the Lord."

"Praise to you Lord, Jesus Christ."

Father Stephen descended the stairs to address the boys. "Temptation. We've all faced it. Jesus faced it. Jesus went into the desert for forty days and nights to pray and fast... tough enough alone."

Bill's stomach reminded him it was empty. *I feel ya, Jesus.*

"Now, the devil comes 'round to tempt Jesus. He wants Jesus to turn against God, to take the easy way out, to give in to cravings of flesh and pride and materialism. Jesus rebukes the devil, that repugnant creature, each time and stays strong in his faith of God. Are we tempted by Satan? Of course we are. We are tempted by Satan every day. Gluttony, greed, sloth, lust, pride, envy, wrath. Do we eat and drink ourselves to excess?"

You do, thought Bill.

"Do we want as much as we can have? Do we waste away and not give our lives to God? Do we have cravings of the flesh? Do we think better of ourselves than others? Do we want what others have, forsaking what we do have? Do we let it anger us so that we then hate one another?

"We are tempted every day. We sin every day. It's easier to give in to sin than it is to fight it, and we've become apathetic to it. We allow it. We need to start fighting back. We need God and God alone to fight back. God will give us the strength to avoid these temptations if we believe in Him. We speak it every time in the Lord's prayer: 'lead us not into temptation.' If we have strong faith in God, like Jesus did in the desert, he will help us. We do not need to possess riches or kingdoms or power or tons of women. We don't need the cravings and indulgences of this world because if we love God and stay true to Him, we will be welcomed into His kingdom with everlasting life. If we truly trust in God, He will give us the strength to beat temptation and overcome sin."

The boys returned to their group discussion rooms after mass concluded. Bill took his usual seat and waited for Pete to sit next to him. He was shocked to see Pete hug Jerry, and then he watched the two boys sit down next to each other on the same couch. They both sat with perfect posture, shoulders back and hands folded in their laps, smiles from ear to ear as they eagerly awaited the discussion to begin. Richie stood in front of Bill.

"Can I sit there?"

"Yep," said Bill. He slid over to the arm and felt the mass of flesh squeeze him into the couch.

"Thanks," said Richie.

Mark welcomed everyone back. "Yesterday, we talked about living our lives through God. How we should see ourselves and represent ourselves to the world. How we must have ultimate trust and faith in God. This afternoon, we will discuss some of the things that can lead us astray in our lives: the things that can tempt us, the things that can make us forget our commitment to God. And even though God gives us the strength to overcome these temptations, sometimes we are still unable to.

"In the Gospel story, Jesus was tempted by the devil. Jesus fully believed in God and God gave him the strength to beat those temptations. Now, it's one thing for the Son of God to overcome temptation, but what about the rest of us? Can anyone think of any stories in the Bible in which someone fell prey to temptation?"

Jerry swiftly responded, "Adam and Eve."

"Absolutely," said Mark. "Probably the most famous story of temptation. Adam and Eve are given paradise and need only follow the rules but can't because of temptation and end up banished. Good choice, Jerry. Any others?"

"How about Judas?" said Pete.

Bill was shocked Pete had answered something correctly.

"That's another good one," said Mark. "Judas was tempted by money and power. He did not truly believe in God or that Jesus was the Son of God. He took the silver and betrayed Jesus. Good job, Pete."

Pete nodded delightedly, and Jerry gave him a high-five.

After a tedious and uninspiring lecture about how you should want nothing, have nothing, and be no one, Bill entered the cafeteria. He had still not heard anything about the bathroom incident from the previous night, so he felt it was safe enough to grab a bite to eat. His stomach desperately needed it. Bill sat down with Matt and Scott.

"Hey, guys," said Bill.

Matt and Scott replied with a "hey."

Bill bit into his peanut butter and jelly sandwich. "This menu really took a hit."

"Yeah," said Matt. "How was Pete in your group session? Still acting like the pope?"

"Yep," said Bill. "He was super into it."

Matt nodded over his shoulder. "Now he's sitting over there with Jerry and Keith and Freddie and them. He never hangs with them."

Bill looked over to the table of ten seemingly random students sitting together, all of whom had become much more pious over the course of the last two days. "What's going on?"

"I don't know," said Matt. He looked at the spots previously held by Pete and Tom. "Our table is dropping like flies."

Bill, Matt, Scott, and Dee played two-on-two basketball at the courts. Bill had been considering heading back to his room to hide and rest, but Matt once again talked him into hanging out—they absolutely needed a fourth with Pete AWOL, and Bill could always rest later.

It was another beautiful day—baby-blue sky, white puffy clouds, and bright sunshine. The grass areas and dirt paths were still flooded from the heavy rains the previous night, however.

Pete and his new fellowship comprised of Jerry, Keith and Freddie, walked along the outside of the fence, all of them barefoot and splashing in the mud and water.

"What are you guys up to?" said Pete as he stopped at the fence.

"Jerking each other off," said Matt. His shot clanked off the side of the rim. "What does it look like?"

"That's inappropriate, Matt," said Pete. "You're better than that."

Matt's eyebrows quickly shot up. "Okay."

Pete rested both hands on the links of the fence and peered through with a subtle smile. "Do you guys want to go for a walk? We're going to the springs to meditate."

"No," said Scott. "I've had enough walking."

"Yeah," said Matt. "Don't you remember what happened yesterday?"

"Oh, that was nothing," said Pete, swiping the air.

"Nothing?" said Scott. "I almost died."

"No," said Pete. "We weren't in any danger. It was just one of God's creatures. It meant us no harm."

Pete's usual harsh tone and vulgar language had been replaced by much more eloquent speech. Matt hadn't heard Pete swear all day. "It's kind of hard to make that argument after being chased by it," he said. "But, hey, you have fun out there!"

"All right," said Pete.

"Bill, would you like to come along?" said Keith.

Keith had not said one bad thing or done anything mean to him since that first night. Perhaps Keith had legitimately turned a corner and wanted to be friends with him. Bill was glad he no longer had to consider him an enemy, but he still had no intention of being friends.

"No thanks, dude," said Bill. "I'm just gonna hang out here."

"Fair enough," said Keith. "Whatever makes you happy."

"Have a blessed day," said Pete.

The four playing basketball froze and watched Pete lead the students on the muddy path into the woods.

"What the hell was that about?" said Matt.

"I have no idea," said Bill. He grabbed the ball and swished a long three-pointer.

"Nice shot, potty peeper!"

Bill turned his head behind him and saw a group of five students walking from the dock to the main building. Among them was Carter... He must have told. Some of the group waved to Bill.

"Woooo, potty peeper!"

Bill turned away, trying to keep a straight face, playing it off like he didn't know what they were talking about, and readied for his next shot.

"What was that about?" said Matt, squinting at the group and trying to comprehend what they had said.

"No clue," said Bill. He airballed the next shot.

After playing basketball, Bill expertly snuck in and out of the bathroom to shower, then took a mac-and-cheese dinner back to his room to enjoy alone. Now that he was the 'potty peeper' he had to avoid everyone at all costs—an impossible task at a retreat. He thought about faking an illness or just flat out refusing to do anything else and forcing his way home, but he was afraid of drawing even more attention. He thought about hanging himself in the shower—that would make Carter and the others feel bad they had made fun of him—but spite wasn't a strong enough conviction to make him go through with it, and he figured he was just being overdramatic anyway. In a few months he'd be out of here, and he would never have to see any of these people again.

Bill now found himself slowly mounting the stairs to the main meeting space, nerves once again rising. He kept his head down, avoiding all eye contact, and plopped down in a chair within his group. No one talked; the only sound in the room was the fountain splashing. Something had to be up. Usually dinner came after the night session, but today, the night session followed dinner. And none of the group leaders were present. What could it be?

Father Leo received word that all the students had arrived and went to the center next to the fountain with his scripture book. A bald priest the students did not recognize stood with him.

Father Leo read the story of the prodigal son and then gave his homily on forgiveness. Bill was completely checked out. None of the words registered until he heard Father Leo say, "Reconciliation." Bill's ears perked up and he listened with the rest of the students.

"Father Stephen and I, along with Father John, will be open for business. First, we are going to give you about fifteen minutes or so to reflect and think about what you would like to confess. When you are ready, please come into one of the rooms we are in. You do not need to line up, just keep an eye on when one of us is available and come in. Please, do not be afraid to discuss anything, no matter how big or small. We are all God's children, and we all sin. Okay? All right. Let's turn on some music, and you guys can meditate peacefully and think about what you would like to say."

The soft, somber music began to play, which reminded Bill of a funeral—his grandfather's. He thought about how much he missed him. He thought about how his grandpa went to church every Sunday. Could his grandpa see him now? Would his grandpa be ashamed of him for his behavior and his lack of faith? The thought devasted Bill. He turned his mind to his possible confession. He hadn't confessed in two years. Since then, when the school held confession every couple of months, he just sat in the pews until everyone was done. Did he want to take one last chance at resurrecting his faith here? He could confess everything and start completely anew. Maybe there was a light at the end of the tunnel, and he could be happy.

The fifteen minutes passed, and Father Leo emerged from a room. "If anyone is ready, we can begin." He went back into his room and shut the door.

Two students rose from their seats, and one went in with Father Stephen and one with the ringer Father John. Jerry and Pete both stood up at the same time and took a step toward Father Leo's room.

"Were you going in?" said Jerry.

Pete laughed. "Yes, I was, but you can go."

"No, please, you go first," said Jerry.

"I would feel bad. Please, you do the honors," said Pete.

"No," said Jerry. "You were up first. By all means, go ahead."

Anthony, sitting between them, had had enough. "Jerry, you're closer, why don't you just go first?"

Jerry agreed and shook Pete's hand. Bill secretly thanked Anthony for ending the conversation.

Bill watched students exit and enter the rooms. Some took a couple minutes, while others seemed to be confessing their entire life stories. Bill waited it out. No spiritual feeling came over him. No epiphany that he needed to confess sang through him. He was fine with his sins. The retreat leaders weren't present, and the priests had no way of knowing who did or didn't confess. Instead, Bill rubbed the festering pimple on his forehead. The lump had grown considerably, and he couldn't stop touching it. He could feel every heartbeat pulse through it.

Father Leo emerged from the room. "If anyone else still needs to go, we will give it another five minutes or so."

Father Leo returned to his room, and a student got up and entered. After that, students entered the other two priests' rooms as well.

A few minutes later, Father Stephen opened his door. "It looks like a couple of people are still finishing up, so we'll give it a few more minutes. This is the last, last call."

Nope, nobody left, thought Bill. *Shut it down.*

The students waited for the last two to finish, and Father Leo was ready to call it a night.

Free and clear. Bill exhaled in relief.

Pete stood up. "Bill didn't go."

Bill's eyes stabbed a thousand daggers into Pete. *Are you kidding me?*

"Bill? Do you need to confess?" asked Father Leo.

Bill looked at Father Stephen and then Father John. Both stared back at him blankly. He knew they wouldn't lie for him.

"Yeah," said Bill. "Yeah."

Bill rose from the chair and walked toward Father Leo's room. He dipped his shoulder and bumped Pete as he passed by. He heard someone in the darkness cough and whisper, "Potty peeper." Everyone giggled. Bill clenched his teeth. If he had known who said it, he might have attacked them right there. Maybe he would just attack the entire room.

Father Leo led Bill into the room. "Take a seat, Bill."

Bill entered the room and saw the black screen divider between two folding chairs for anonymity. *What does it matter at this point?* Bill sat down in the chair directly across from Father Leo, face to face. The only light in the room came from a lamp off to the side, leaving half of Father Leo's round face covered in darkness.

Father Leo began making the sign of the cross around Bill's body. "In the name of the Father, and the—"

Bill put up both of his hands to stop Father Leo—he had made his decision. "You don't need to do that. I don't want to confess. I don't want to do any of this stuff anymore. I'm through with it."

"What do you mean?" Father Leo folded his hands in his lap.

Bill shook his head and looked around the room. "I'm done with this stuff. I shouldn't have come here. I should have just done the one-day retreat and kept my mouth shut."

"What stuff?"

"Religion. God. *You*. All of it."

Father Leo's lips curled in disappointment. "Why do you feel this way?"

Bill's voice rose in volume and intensity. "I don't want to talk about it anymore. It doesn't matter."

"Of course it matters. I'm worried about you. I want to help you." Father Leo rested his hand on Bill's knee.

Bill quickly moved his leg to the side, and the priest's hand slipped off. "Well, you can't. You can't help everyone. You can't save everyone."

Father Leo sighed. "Is this about your grandfather?"

Bill ran both hands through his hair and thought about telling Father Leo about the bathroom incident and being made fun of. It would be even worse if he tattled on the students and got them in trouble. The ridicule would never end. "Yes… No… I don't know. I just want to go home. That's all."

"Well, we can't let you go home yet. Maybe there's still time for you turn things around."

"No, there isn't. It's not working. I tried."

"That's not what I heard from your group leader. He said you were having some issues with your faith and maybe you weren't taking this as seriously as you should."

Bill's blood boiled. "No, I did."

"Are you sure?"

Bill turned defensive. "Yeah, I'm not sure why he'd say that."

"He says you don't say much. And when you do, it's mostly in a dismissive tone."

"I don't think that's true. And now he's ratting me out to you?"

"No, he was just concerned."

Bill crossed his arms. "Oh, okay, sure. That's fine then. Where's the trust? I thought that was important here."

"You don't need to get upset about it," Father Leo said calmly.

"I'm not upset. I'm sorry. I'm just tired." Bill wiped at his eye and breathed heavily.

"All right. There's nothing else you would like to discuss?"

"Nope," Bill said stubbornly. "That about does it."

"Very well, Bill. You can go."

"Thanks." Bill bolted from the chair to the door. He walked back to his seat, ready to tear Pete apart, but Pete paid no attention to him. He sat with his eyes closed, meditating.

"All right," said Father Leo. "We are finished for the evening, please think about what you confessed tonight. We will pick up in the morning. Goodnight, gentlemen."

Bill walked down the stairs into the main lobby, where he found Matt waiting for him.

"Wanna play some ping pong?" said Matt.

"Eh," said Bill, thinking it over. "Nah, I think I'm just gonna go back to my room."

"Come on," said Matt. "Just a couple games. I'm bored."

"I'm really not in the mood. I'd rather not be around people anymore."

"Please," pleaded Matt.

"Play with somebody else."

"I don't want to play with somebody else. I want to kick your ass."

"I don't care," Bill snapped. He watched Pete and Jerry descend the stairs from the upstairs meeting hall and continue down to the basement.

Matt grabbed Bill by the shoulder. "Just for a little bit."

"Fine," said Bill, filled with hate.

The rec room was sparsely filled. Four students were playing pool and two more occupied the foosball table. Pete, Jerry, and Freddie sat with Mark and Father Leo at a table, talking about scripture. The ping-pong table was open, and Bill and Matt began their game.

Halfway through the game, another group of students came down the stairs.

"Oh, no," said Carter. "Bill's down here. Watch your junk, cuz he is."

The others laughed.

Bill let Matt's shot bounce by him. He stepped in front of Carter, and said, "It was a misunderstanding. I wasn't watching you. What happened—"

"Get away from me, you scumbag. I saw you watching me. You're disgusting."

Carter bumped Bill with his shoulder as he passed him.

"What happened in the bathroom?" said Matt. "I heard someone talking about it."

Oh great, him too, thought Bill. He felt the burn in his eyes as the tears welled. "Nothing, I swear. It was a weird misunderstanding and now it's…" Bill swallowed hard. I'm just gonna go back to my room."

"No," said Matt. "I believe you. Just finish the game."

Bill waited. Father Leo had left, and now Pete and Jerry had begun a chess match while Mark played a board game with two other students— still a chance to confront Pete.

"Fine," said Bill.

Matt easily finished the match against an indifferent Bill.

"You truly are the best," said Bill.

"I know," said Matt. "I think I might try going pro."

Keith patted Bill on the shoulder. "Good game. You tried your best. God is proud of you."

"Spare me," said Bill. Everywhere he turned, people were constantly in his face. He was ready to explode.

Mark had left. There was no authority figure in the basement, so Bill went to Pete and Jerry's table.

"What's going on, fellas?" said Bill.

"Hey, Bill," said Pete.

"Hello, Bill," said Jerry. "How are you?"

"I'm great… Feeling extra holy after confessing, ya know?"

Pete studied the chessboard, seemingly unaware of Bill's foul mood, for which he was responsible.

Jerry nodded his head. "I always feel better after confessing. It feels like the weight of the world has been lifted off my back and I am free again."

"Mmm, yeah, for sure. Now tell me though, if you rat someone out, do you have to confess that?"

Pete looked up to Bill. "I didn't rat you out. I wanted to help you." Pete reached out for Bill's arm, but he pulled it away.

"Help yourself, Judas. Don't worry about me," Bill growled.

"You won't get anything out of this experience if you don't participate."

Bill's shoulders hunched up. "So what! I don't care! I don't give a shit about any of this!"

Now, everyone in the basement was watching Bill's meltdown.

Pete remained perfectly calm and spoke gracefully. "That's a really poor attitude. I've learned so much about myself here. I've grown so much. It's really disheartening to hear you say that."

A vein bulged in Bill's forehead and his entire body shook with every word. "Oh, cut the bullshit! Is this some sort of joke?" Bill raised his palms in the air before pointing one hand to his chest. "Are you just messing with me?"

"Faith is never a joke. I am committed to this process. I want to be one with God."

Bill knocked over one of Pete's chess pieces with a quick backhand. "Give me a break, dude. I'm not buying it. You're full of shit."

"I was once like you, but now I have seen the light. I now know what it takes to be truly happy in this world. It is through God—"

"Oh, shut the fuck up!" Bill flipped the table over, and the chess pieces flew across the room. Bill pointed his finger directly in Pete's face. "You're full of shit."

The students heard footsteps rushing down the stairs, and Mark peeked his head through the doorway.

Matt grabbed Bill and pulled him back. "Settle down, man."

Bill pointed his finger around the room. "You're all full of shit. I'm tired of this nonsense." All of the students stared at him in shocked silence.

"What's wrong?" asked Mark.

"Stay away from me." Bill barged past Mark and stormed out of the rec room, knocking a bag of Doritos out of Richie's hand along the way. "Can you stop eating for like five minutes?" he called over his shoulder.

As Bill walked through the doorway to the stairs, someone shouted, "Potty peeper!"

Another shouted, "Pizza-faced potty peeper!"

Bill heard all of the laughs as he went up the stairs.

Mark caught up to Bill in the breezeway. "What's going on, Bill?"

Bill hurried his pace. "Nothing."

Mark tried to keep up. "Something is clearly wrong. I think we should talk about it."

"I don't want to talk." Bill leapt up the steps, two at a time, but Mark kept following him.

"I don't want you to feel this way."

Bill hustled down the hallway. "You don't know how I feel."

"Then explain it to me."

Bill made it to his door and turned to face Mark "No." Bill put up one hand to stop Mark from advancing any further. "Please, just leave me alone. Please."

Mark stopped. "Okay. Okay. If you need anything let me know."

"Sure, I will."

Mark noticed Bill's forehead. "You're bleeding."

"What?" Bill touched his fingers to his forehead and felt the blood and pus leaking down his face from the broken pimple.

"Do you want me to get you—"

"No," said Bill. He entered his room and slammed the door behind him.

The room was dark, except for the light streaming in from the hole in the wall. "God damnit," he whispered to himself.

Bill grabbed the towel hanging on the inside of the closet, held it to his head, and sat down on the bed. He removed the towel to see a red stain the size of his thumb. As he put the towel back to his head, he fully felt the shame and embarrassment of his actions. It hurt deep. He felt his throat harden, and he swallowed. *I hate myself.* He repeated it over and over again in his head.

Eventually, the blood stopped spurting from his head and the pimple flattened, but the wound still ached and pounded. He checked the hall to make sure it was empty and ran quickly back and forth to the bathroom to brush his teeth and use the toilet. Luckily, it was empty. Upon returning to his room, it came as no shock to him that the lock on the handle wasn't fixed either. He tightened the watch around his wrist, flipped the light off and lay in bed. He closed his eyes and tried to relax, but the moment when he flipped the chessboard flashed repeatedly in his mind—all of the students watching in amazement and then laughing at him, shouting out insults.

Bill didn't know why, but he felt a sudden rush of fear, like he wasn't alone. He sat up and he looked to the wall across from him.

Terror gripped him—the eye was back! Bill shot up from his bed and leapt toward the hole, but the eye vanished and now it was only light. The eye had never been there; his mind was playing tricks on him, and his sanity hung by a thread. There was no way he would be able to sleep tonight. Bill flicked on the light and looked at the watch. 11:17. Seven hours to kill... and then another twenty-four. How would he do it?

Bill paced between the door and the window for a bit before doing some pushups, sit-ups, chair dips, squats, and lunges. After his shirt began to fill with sweat, he decided he had had enough. 12:02.

Bill took out a notebook and a pen, thought for a second, and wrote 'Super Bowl Winners' at the top. He started listing the winners working backward but, apparently, Bill didn't remember many Super Bowl winners. He ripped the paper out, crumbled it up, and threw it into the trash can. He started a new list: 'Best Picture Winners.' He again worked backward, this time making much more progress. Bill got all the way back to 1970 but was stumped again. *Whatever, there weren't any good movies before 1975 anyway.* He checked the watch—12:46. Bill let out a long sigh. *What to do?* He got up and looked out the window at the dark woods and cloudy sky.

Bill went back to pacing. He could faintly make out the stream of light coming from the wall with the ceiling light on. He flicked the light switch off and looked at the stream of light. He flicked the light switch back on. And then off. And then on. And then off. And then on. Faster and faster until finally leaving it on. He rubbed his face and eyes, completely exhausted. 1:28.

Bill lay down in the bed. *I need to sleep. I have to.* It was coming up on forty-eight hours since he had last slept. The harder he tried, the worse it was. He tossed and turned while the thoughts of embarrassment and shame and humiliation continued to enter his head. *Nope.* He hopped out of bed and went back to pacing. 1:53.

Bill's stomach grumbled. *I could eat.* He opened the door and peeked into the dark and perfectly still hallway. A chill ran up his neck, causing him to close the door and sit down at his desk. He tapped his forehead over and over as he tried to come up with something to do. He played tic-tac-toe against himself; each game ended in a draw. He flipped his hat into the air and tried to land it on his head. He went through each professional sports league and set up a tournament to see which real life mascot would win in a fight… Bears, of course. *Maybe I'm a bit biased.* 2:55.

Bill tried drawing even though he'd never been good at it. He drew the woods and lake and the buildings. *That sucks. A blind person could do better.* He tore out the sheet of paper, crumbled it up, and threw it in the trash can. 3:13.

Bill nailed every U.S. state and capital. *Damn, I'm good.* He worked his way through the other continents. He was pretty happy with his progress until Africa. *Who the hell can keep up with all those? They change every five minutes.* 4:19.

Bill leaned back in his chair and rubbed his eyes. He thought about his future. Was there hope for him? This retreat obviously hadn't turned out the way he wanted, but he could start again at college. He could be an entirely different person. This didn't have to mean the end of the world. He stared straight ahead at the wall and actually dozed off here and there. Each time his head fell, it woke him. And then his head drifted to the left, and he noticed the light in the hole was gone. He jumped from his chair to take a look. *How the hell did I miss that? Unbelievable.* He inspected the hole for a minute, but nothing was different—it was just an empty, dark hole. Bill took in and let out a deep breath and went to the window. The black sky began to brighten to a dark grey. *Almost there.* 5:37.

Bill moved the chair in front of the window and watched the sun slowly rise and the sky turn from gray to purple to dark blue. He checked his watch every five minutes as more and more bird chirps filled the air. He was happy to not be alone. 6:10. 6:11. 6:12. 6:13. 6:14. 6:15. "Finally."

Bill pointed at the speaker box as Jacobs' voiced cracked over it. "Good morning, retreaters. Time to wake up! It is our final day! Hasn't it just flown by? Everyone up and at 'em! Breakfast will be served shortly. Have a blessed day!"

CHAPTER 15:

Hold It Together for a Few More Hours

BILL AGAIN WEIGHED HIS HUNGER AGAINST HIS DESIRE TO AVOID PEO-ple. He could hear the students passing by in the hallway, while he remained safe from their quips and snickers inside his room. His stomach grumbled as he thought back to the night before, screaming at Pete and flipping the chessboard. He thought about being the 'potty peeper.' Once again, Bill went hungry.

Bill lay on his bed for a bit, eyelids heavy, until Jacobs's disembodied voice came in over the speaker. "Attention, retreaters. Mass will begin in ten minutes. Please do not be late. Thank you and have a blessed day."

Bill sat up and looked at the hole. He was now completely convinced that the eye was a figment of his imagination, a figment of his fear of people looking at him, a figment of his fear of this place, and a figment of his fear of an all-knowing, all-seeing God. He rose from the bed. *Here we go. Last day.*

There was a knock on the door, and Bill opened it to see Father Leo with a big smile on his face. "Good morning, Bill."

"Good morning, Father." Bill's eyes fell to the floor. He didn't want to deal with this right now.

"We missed you at breakfast this morning. Are you feeling all right?"

"Yeah, I'm okay. Just getting a little extra rest." Bill tapped his fingers on the doorknob.

"Ah, okay. These have been some long days," said Father Leo, nodding.

"They sure have been."

Father Leo leaned his head down to make eye contact with Bill. "But you're sure everything is okay?"

Bill looked into the priest's eyes and said, "Yep." He quickly looked away.

Father Leo's large stomach heaved out with a deep breath and retracted in a sigh. "I heard that you had a bit of a dust-up with Pete and Jerry last night."

"Um, yeah. Sorry about that. I just got a little..." Bill paused and swallowed, replaying the scene in his head, "...heated and carried away."

"You don't say?"

"Yeah. Pete cheated during the game. I don't take cheating lightly."

Father Leo raised his eyebrows. "I bet."

"It's a, uh, game of honor."

"It sure is," said Father Leo, nodding.

Finally, Bill gave the priest what he wanted. "I'll apologize to them."

"Yes, you will."

"Thanks, Father. I should probably get ready." Bill turned to close the door, but Father Leo blocked it with his hand.

"Bill, I know you're going through a really tough time right now, and it's very understandable. But you can't take that out on others. We're all here for you, and we all want you to feel welcomed and loved. Is there anything I can do for you right now?"

Bill's entire world felt like it was crumbling around him, and he was desperate for help. If it had been offered by anyone other than a priest, he may have accepted it. "No, I'm okay." Bill looked to the priest and nodded. "I'm okay. I'm sorry for the thing with Pete and Jerry, and I'm sorry for what happened during confession. I'll talk to Jerry and Pete at my group."

"Okay. If you want to talk about anything, please don't be afraid to come to me." Father Leo crossed his hands over his heart.

"Okay. Thanks, Father."

"Okay. Have a good day, Bill."

"Thanks, you too."

Bill was the last person into the church, and he took a seat in the back by himself, three rows away from any students. It didn't seem like anyone noticed him back there. He saw Pete and Jerry seated ten or so rows ahead of him and thought about apologizing. His heart pounded rapidly through his chest. *After mass.*

The mass plodded along with Bill's head constantly bobbing up and down as he tried to focus and stay awake. The awe and admiration of the magnificent church had worn off. He tired of listening to the words and trying to find an important meaning. He had to stand as Father Leo went to the lectern to read the Gospel. Bill heard some words and phrases here and there—'love your enemies' and 'turn the other cheek.' He had heard it a thousand times. It was just white noise at this point. He finally got to sit down while Father Leo gave his homily about the 'Golden Rule' and 'love.' The priest spoke about loving others. Bill hoped the people at this retreat would take it to heart and stop being so mean and just leave him alone. The priest spoke about loving God. Whatever feelings inspired so many of Bill's classmates to embrace this retreat were lost on him. Bill knew God was another father he would never love. And the priest spoke about loving yourself. Bill couldn't. It was just impossible.

The boys sat down for their group session. Today, like yesterday, Pete sat with Jerry, but now Richie eagerly took a spot with an approving Anthony, leaving Bill with Brandon.

"Welcome back, gentlemen," said Mark. "Before we get too far into our topic today, there is something I would like to discuss first. And as it turns out, it is quite topical."

Bill's stomach dropped, and he watched Mark out of the corner of his eye.

Mark continued, "There was a small altercation amongst some of our group members, and I think it would be good to discuss what happened. Bill, do you have anything you would like to say?"

Bill glanced up and nodded. He cleared his throat and said, "I would like to apologize to Pete and Jerry for my actions yesterday." His head cocked to the side as he bashfully looked at both Pete and Jerry. Bill was embarrassed by his actions, and he felt they were completely out of line, but he still wasn't entirely sorry for what he did. A large portion of him still felt that Pete deserved it. At least it would get some people off his back if he apologized. "Um, guys, I'm sorry. I got a little heated yesterday and, um, caught up in the moment, and I acted like an idiot. It was totally unaccept-able and I'm sorry."

"Wonderful," said Mark.

"It's okay," said Jerry. "I forgive you."

"Me too," said Pete. "It happens. You're a great person."

"It is very impressive of you to take accountability and apologize," said Mark. "This is exactly the stuff we've been talking about. Sometimes we lose our tempers. Sometimes we disagree. Sometimes we fight. But we must always find in our hearts the ability to forgive and the ability to love. Often the hardest part is admitting *we* were wrong. It's always easy to point the finger at someone and say, 'They wronged us.' It takes courage to ask for forgiveness. So, thank you, Bill, for being a man of honor. And Pete and Jerry, thank *you* for showing the forgiveness and love that God teaches us—for putting into action exactly what we have been learning here. Well done, gentlemen."

Mark started to clap, and Pete, Jerry, Richie, and Anthony joined in while Bill and Brandon remained still on their couch, arms folded across their chests.

"Maybe we should share an embrace," said Mark. He stood and extended his arms. "Just to bury the hatchet."

"That's a great idea," said Pete as he popped up from the sofa.

"Absolutely," said Jerry, joining him.

Every fiber of Bill's being said no, but he sheepishly stood. "Okay." The combination of the sleep deprivation and the lack of food and water had caught up with him. His knees went weak, and he felt light-headed and disoriented.

The three wrapped their arms around Bill, who didn't move. The room spun around him, and then darkness closed in on him.

"I would like to get in on this too," said Richie.

"Me, six," said Anthony.

"Sure, fellas," said Mark. "Hop on."

They joined the six-way hug with Bill crammed in the center. There was nowhere to escape. All around him, bodies held him tightly and smothered him. He closed his eyes and tried to fight off the feeling of claustrophobia as a piercing pain shot through his head.

"Brandon?" said Mark. "Would you like to join us?"

"Nope," said Brandon. He stayed on the couch and turned his head away.

The hug continued, and Bill felt like he would be suffocated. He began to struggle and called out for them to get off, but his muffled cries went unheard.

"Oh, just a couple more seconds," said Mark.

"Stop!" Bill pushed his way out of the group hug and staggered back.

"What is it?" asked Mark.

The entire room pitched back and forth. He extended his arms out for balance while he tried to catch his breath. "I don't feel good."

"Oh my." Mark moved closer and grabbed Bill's arm. "Take a seat here."

Mark helped guide Bill back to the couch as Brandon jumped out of the way. Bill sat, and the room keeled from side to side like he was on a boat in rough waters. He closed his eyes and felt the pain in his head intensify the harder he closed them.

Mark rested his hand on Bill's shoulder, while the others looked on in concern at his pale, ghostly face. "Are you all right?"

Bill swallowed hard to keep what little food he had in his stomach down. Everything kept spinning. "Yeah, just give me a second. Give me some space."

Mark backed away as Bill took several deep breaths.

"I'll get some water," said Pete before he darted out of the room.

Bill started to settle down, and everything came back into focus.

"How are you feeling?" asked Mark.

"Better," said Bill. The color had returned to his face. "Just felt a little light-headed."

"No problem. Take your time."

Bill looked around the room at the concerned faces. "I'm okay. It's all right." Bill waved his hands to convince them.

Pete returned with a glass of water. "Here."

Bill took the glass from Pete. "Thanks."

"You're welcome." Pete stood at Bill's side and watched him down the entire glass of water in a few gulps.

The cool water instantly made Bill feel better. "Much better." Bill nodded and feigned a smile to the rest of the room. "I'm okay."

"Okay," said Mark with a sigh of relief. "That was scary."

The students returned to their spots and sat down while Mark grabbed a folding chair for Brandon. "You sure you're good to go?"

"Yeah, I'm okay." More embarrassment flooded Bill and all he could do was meekly say, "I'm sorry."

"Nothing to be sorry for," said Mark. "Could have happened to any one of us. We just want you to be okay."

Bill swallowed. "I am. Thanks."

"All right, guys," said Mark. "That was exciting, huh? Good work with the water, Pete."

Pete nodded to Mark and received a pat on the back from Jerry.

"Now, let's get back to it."

The morning group session ended, and Bill bolted out of the room after assuring Mark he felt fine. He could barely walk straight or keep his eyes open, and he went promptly back to his room. He needed sleep much more than food or company. Bill dropped his notebook on the table, kicked his shoes off, and collapsed face first onto the bed. He didn't think about God or faith or shame or embarrassment. He didn't think about the hole or the eye. He didn't think about anything. He closed his eyes and immediately fell asleep.

Bill was awakened from a deep sleep by someone patting him repeatedly on his back. He removed the pillow from over his head and squinted in the sunlight coming through the window to see Matt.

"Hey," said Matt. He sat down on the bed at Bill's feet.

"Hey," said Bill. He pulled his legs toward himself and sat up against the wall.

"What's going on? I've been looking for you."

"Nothing. Just taking a little nap."

Matt took a closer look at Bill. "You look terrible."

"I haven't been sleeping well," said Bill, trying to hold back a yawn.

Matt furrowed his brow. "The hole in the wall?"

Bill thought about how much he should say to Matt and decided not to tell him about the eye. After all, Bill was convinced the eye wasn't real, so there was no reason to bring it up. "That's part of it." He also didn't want to bring up anything even remotely related to peeping.

"Where?" said Matt as he stood up.

"There." Bill pointed to the wall across from the bed. "Do you have one in your room?"

Matt inspected the hole, putting his face right up against the wall. "Not that I've noticed. Weren't they supposed to fix this?" He backed away.

"Yep." Bill's eyes were sunken, and his head still pounded.

Matt bit his lower lip. "Yeah, that's weird."

"Yep." Bill shrugged and tried to come up with an explanation that didn't involve someone spying on him. "Maybe they used to run cables or something through there."

"Yeah," said Matt. He sat in the chair at the desk. "Or maybe it's the world's smallest glory hole."

"You wish," said Bill.

"*You* wish," said Matt. "You all right, man?"

"Yeah… Yeah," said Bill, rubbing his eyes. He dropped his hands into his lap. Here Matt was, Bill's best friend. If there was anyone on the planet he could confide in, it would be him. "You know, I came here to try to save myself, but I feel like I'm slipping further away."

"Save yourself? That seems a bit melodramatic. You're just tired."

"Yeah," said Bill. He turned and looked out the window and quickly spaced out. If only Matt had any idea what Bill was actually thinking about. But Bill dared not mention it.

Matt rose from the chair. "Just one more day," said Matt. He tapped Bill on the shoulder, snapping him out of his stupor.

"Yeah." *One more day*, Bill thought.

"Pete still acting like an idiot?"

"Yep. I had to apologize during group. Then we hugged."

Matt snorted loudly. "Sounds awesome."

"Yeah. A lot of people are acting weird. Like almost everyone in my group is fully buying into this stuff way more than before. Richie and Anthony now too. Brandon still seems like himself, though.

"The others don't? How are they acting?"

"I don't know," said Bill shaking his head. "They're all… nicer and getting along with each other. It's strange."

A quick frown showed on Matt's face. "Isn't that a good thing? First step towards world peace." Matt pumped his fist.

"Yeah, I guess so, huh? Is that what's happening in your group?"

Matt thought it over. "Well, today Evan said he wanted to be baptized."

"Really?"

"Yeah, so they're gonna baptize him at the lake this afternoon."

"Seriously?" Bill's mouth hung open.

"Yeah…" Matt held Bill's gaze. "…What?"

"You don't think that's a bit strange?"

Matt shook his head. "Not really. If that's what he wants to do, why not?"

"He always talks about how dumb religion is and how dumb everyone is that follows it. He hates it."

Matt pondered it. "Maybe he had a change of heart. It happens."

Bill angrily shook his head. This place couldn't have had a positive effect on Evan. There was no way. "What about the rest of your group?"

Matt shrugged. "Everybody's participating. I don't think anyone is acting strangely though. You know… there are some people who believe in this stuff more than you do."

The realization saddened Bill. "Yeah." Maybe that was all it was—people doing what they wanted to do, people of faith following what they believed. Bill did go to a Catholic school after all.

Matt headed to the door. He could see the disappointment on Bill's face. "I'm sure it's just this place. It may take a day or two, but once we get the hell outta here, everybody will be back to their normal, miserable, debauched selves."

"I hope so. I liked them better that way."

"Me too. And, hey, maybe tonight you have some fun with Maddie, huh? Get your mind off this religious stuff." Matt jabbed at Bill's midsection. "I mean, if that's what you're into."

Bill turtled and protected his ribs with his arms. "What do you mean?"

Matt let up. "I just heard some things, that's all. And if you're not into girls, it's no big deal. You can still come and hang out."

"What are you talking about?"

"Nothing." Matt could tell he'd hit a nerve.

"What did you hear?" said Bill forcefully.

"I heard you were in the bathroom spying on Carter… trying to look at his…"

"I was not," pleaded Bill. His heart sank. "It was a mistake. I wasn't looking at him."

Matt put his hands up to calm Bill down. "Okay! Okay, I didn't mean anything. That's just what I heard. *I* believe you." He could see the tears welling in Bill's eyes, so he tried to change the subject. "I'm starving. All they had for lunch was rice and veggies. You got any food?"

"No," Bill said angrily.

"All right." Matt wished he hadn't said anything. "I'm gonna check Pete's room. He's gotta have something. You wanna come with?"

"No."

"Okay, I'm sorry. I didn't mean anything."

"It's fine," said Bill, staring at the floor. "I'll see you later."

Matt exited the room, and Bill lay back down on the bed. He tossed and turned—thoughts of failing at the retreat raced through his mind. This experience had worked out for so many people here. So many of his class-mates had bettered themselves and strengthened their relationships with God and each other and themselves, while Bill had done nothing but em-barrass himself and find new reasons to hate himself even more. He had no interest in going back to his normal life and pretending everything was all right—to continue to live as the same terrified awkward loser that he had built up in his mind. He was completely exhausted of dealing with it. As he realized that there was no hope left in him that he would ever change, a moment of clarity and peace came to him followed by one thought—it had to end now.

CHAPTER 16:
Sacrifice

B ILL THREW ON A PAIR OF JEANS AND A DARK HOODIE AND SLIPPED INTO his shoes. He reached for the doorknob with his left hand and saw his grandfather's watch on his wrist. He couldn't take it with him. He didn't want any part of his grandfather there when he did it. Bill unclasped the watch and laid it down on the desk.

The hallway was empty. A feeling of complete numbness overcame Bill, and he felt weightless walking to Matt's room, almost like he was floating. He knocked on Matt's door and waited, watching each end of the hallway. He knocked again and entered the cluttered room. Matt was gone, and Bill found clothes strewn about the desk and floor and bed. Bill didn't even think to look if there was a hole in the wall; he was too focused on his objective. He located Matt's backpack in the corner of the room and rifled through the various pockets.

"Good afternoon, retreaters!"

Bill flinched. No matter how many times he heard the voice through the speaker, he never got used to it. Bill stared at the box above the door, as if it were Jacobs himself standing there, and said under his breath, "I hate you."

"In just a few moments, we will be having a baptism ceremony for your classmate Evan down at the beach by the lake. It would be so wonderful if everyone could show their support and attend. So come on, retreaters! Head outside and witness the glorious sacrament of baptism and officially welcome Evan into our family as he begins his new life with Christ. Thanks, and have a blessed day!"

"Pass," Bill said to himself as he held Matt's knife in his hand, then secured it in his waistband by his back. He left Matt's room, speed-walked down the hallway, and hopped down the stairs before ducking into a corner of the stairwell by the breezeway. He waited, calmer than expected. He was finally ready to do it. He watched and listened; there was no sign of anyone, so he traversed the sunlit walkway. Just as he entered the main lobby, Bill ran into Nick and Jake, former football teammates, coming up from the rec room.

"Holy shit," said Jake. "It's the potty peeper. Haven't seen you around in a while. I figured you offed yourself."

"Not yet," said Bill. His face was empty of emotion.

"Good for you," said Jake.

"I missed last night's meltdown," said Nick. "Do you have any scheduled for today?"

Bill's face remained completely blank. "I'm working on it. The day is young."

"Yeah," said Nick. "I'm sure you'll find some way to embarrass yourself."

"Most certainly," said Bill. He moved toward the main door.

"Hey, where's this pimple everybody's talking about?" Jake leaned toward Bill's face and saw the flat red spot on his forehead with a hole in the middle, lightly leaking clear pus. "That's it? I heard it was like you had a second head."

"It used to be bigger."

"Yeah, I bet." Jake's face snarled. "Now it's just a disgusting open wound."

"Great talk, fellas," said Bill and he brushed past them.

"Later, potty peeper," said Nick.

Bill exited the large door and felt the warm sunshine on his face. Another bright blue sky soared overhead with sporadic puffy white clouds. He could see a large crowd gathered at the beach by the edge of the woods, leaving him a free path to the woods on the other side of the lake. He followed the path that would take him into the woods and then to the spring. He kept an eye over his shoulder to make sure no one was following him, until he hit the tree line and took cover behind a thick trunk. Across the lake, he saw Evan standing barefoot on the wet beach in a white gown next to Father Leo and Father Stephen, each wearing white cloaks of their own. The two priests dwarfed the diminutive Evan. He resembled nothing more

156

than a small child from far away. Jacobs and his workers stood above them on the grass with what looked like most of the student retreaters.

Bill watched as Father Leo and Father Stephen led Evan into the dark green water, their cloaks floating behind them on the surface. They stopped in waist-high water and positioned themselves on both sides of Evan. Bill couldn't hear the words, but the next thing he knew, Evan disappeared backwards into the water with a small splash and then came up again, soaked. A big smile shone across his face, and the audience erupted in applause. Evan would now begin his new life, while Bill turned his back and walked into the forest to end his.

Bill kept a good pace along the path. He could feel the hilt of the knife digging into his lower back. He still felt calm and at peace with his decision; he was ready, and he didn't want to start having second thoughts. He needed to get there and get it over with.

Bill made it to the spring, no larger than a backyard pool, pulled the knife from his waistband, and sat down against a tree. He closed his eyes, holding the knife in both hands between his legs, and took in a deep breath, which he slowly let it out before opening his eyes and taking in the scene. The view was like something out of a painting. The light blue spring was bordered by trees all around, all perfectly reflected in the calm water like a mirror.

His thoughts drifted to his family, his grandfather and mother. He knew his grandpa would be ashamed of him, giving up like this, but there were no tears. He thought about how devasted his mother would be upon hearing the news and the pain she would feel caused solely by his actions, but there were no tears. He had reached the end. He was the one who had carried the burden and pain for so long. He could no longer endure it. He had tried to change. He had tried to fix himself, and it only ended in disaster. He wanted to finally be at peace.

Bill grasped the dark green hilt and pulled the knife from the sheath, watching the sunlight reflect off the blade. He wrapped his hand around the wide blade, his fingers barely reaching his thumb, and squeezed. It left an indent in his palm but didn't break the skin. Was it even sharp? He ran the blade along the tip of his index finger, opening a small cut, and winced. He watched crimson red blood leak down his finger to his palm.

Bill wiped the small spot of his blood off the tip of the knife—Matt's knife. The one he had brought here for protection, and now his best friend was going to use it to kill himself. Would Matt be able to handle it? Would he blame himself for what happened to Bill? How many others would blame themselves and say they should have known, and they should have done more? These were the thoughts that had stopped Bill in the past, but it wasn't about anyone else anymore; it was only about him.

Bill needed to act before the guilt overcame him. He pulled the sleeves of his hoodie toward his elbows and held the blade perpendicularly to his forearm, imagining it slicing the vein open and blood pouring out everywhere. He took a deep breath and readied to cut but chickened out at the last moment, only making a quick, halfhearted slash. He missed the vein and opened a small nick a few centimeters long. Even with such a small cut, a steady stream of blood trickled down his forearm to his elbow. This would be a huge mess. Bill felt bad for whoever would find him.

The time had come, and fear and uncertainty crept into his mind while tears filled his eyes. He again held the blade to his bloody arm and looked to the heavens, hoping for a signal for him to stop. "Show me You're real. Show me I shouldn't do this. Give me one sign that my life is worth anything."

Bill waited, breathing heavily, with the steel touching his skin. "Nothing?" He waited another moment. Who was he to demand God to show Himself? He gripped the hilt tight and started to cut across his flesh. Bill had only made it half an inch when he stopped at the sound of rustling leaves in the distance. Someone was out there. He quickly sheathed the knife and hid it behind his back. The cut wasn't deep and only a half an inch long, but it bled, and he smeared it all over his arm. He heard the rustling again—this time with a faint whimper—and stood to check the trail and surrounding trees. "Hello?" he called out but there was no answer.

Bill now pinpointed that the rustling and whimpering were coming from deeper in the woods. He took the knife out and trudged through the forest toward the noise. There, in a thicket of bushes and trees, he found a stag lying on the ground in a pool of blood. Bill moved slowly toward the great beast, knife held out in front of him for protection. The startled stag cried out and tried to stand, but collapsed and let out another meek whimper. Bill noticed several wounds on the animal's midsection leaking blood. Bill looked away from the gruesome sight. The stag lay defeated, weakly moaning.

Bill walked closer to the stag, struggling to look and listen to the animal. "I'm sorry," he said to it. He sheathed the knife and stuck it in his waistband.

Should I get help? he thought to himself. *Jacobs said they can treat animals. Maybe they can fix it.* Bill examined the stag. *They can't fix that. You have to do something. You can't let it suffer like this.*

Bill watched the stag, hoping it would just pass, but it continued to writhe and cry. It made him feel awful to watch the animal suffer. How could it be a coincidence that he came across this animal at this exact time? Was this the sign from God that he asked for? Was this a sacrifice prepared by God, and all Bill had to do was offer it?

Bill reached for the knife in his waistband and took it out from the sheath. "I'm sorry, but this is all I can do." Bill walked behind the immobile stag and positioned himself by its throat. Whether this was a sacrifice or a mercy killing, Bill was not sure, but there was only one thing to be done.

You're helping him. He's suffering. He put the knife to the stag's throat, tears welling up in his eyes. *You have to.* Bill grabbed the stag's head and pulled it back. The knife cut into the stag's flesh, and blood spewed out everywhere. The stag gargled and made horrible, disgusting sounds. Bill continued to cut deeper until the stag went limp.

There were no more sounds. Bill wiped the tears from his face on his shoulders and looked at his hands and the knife covered in blood. "I'm sorry," he said again to the lifeless stag.

It had to mean something.

He stood at looked at the horrible mess he'd made of the elegant creature. *This could have been* me. *Someone would have found* me *like this.* Bill sobbed. He backed away from the spreading puddle of blood and fell to the ground.

By the time Bill had finally calmed down, the sun was quickly setting below the trees. Bill was exhausted. He couldn't believe what he'd almost done, and he promised himself that he would never do it again.

Bill covered the stag with as many leaves as he could push and kick over the body. He went back to the spring to wash himself off. His hands and arms were covered in blood, but miraculously his clothes looked untouched. He scrubbed his hands hard to rid the blood from the creases in his skin. The self-inflicted wounds on his forearm had stopped bleeding and didn't look like they would require stitches. He dipped the knife in the water and carefully cleaned it, scraping the dried bits with his fingernails until the blade looked immaculate.

The woods were dark by the time he'd started off on the trail back to the campus. He didn't have much daylight left, but the dirt path was easy to follow regardless. He was late though. The final session had to be starting any minute. He wondered if people would be worried about him. He didn't have to wait long to find out.

"Bill," a voice called out.

Bill jumped and saw a gangly figure further down the path. The red Eternal Springs polo and long blond hair came into view.

"What are you still doing out here?" said Luke. "Everyone is waiting for you."

"I'm sorry," said Bill. "I lost track of time. I dozed off."

"Hey, I got him. I'm bringing him back," Luke said into his radio.

"Roger that."

"Let's go," Luke said to Bill.

Bill followed Luke back to the main building where Father Leo, Jacobs, and Mark were waiting outside. Bill knew he was going to hear it, and he knew that if he told them why he'd been out there, everyone would feel sorry for him, and he wouldn't get into trouble. But he wasn't ready to admit it quite yet and decided to keep his mouth shut.

"Where have you been?" said Father Leo. Tension filled his voice.

"I'm sorry, Father. I went for a little walk, and I lost track of time. I'm really, really sorry. I didn't mean to."

"No one knew where you were. We were scared sick."

"I'm really sorry, Father. I—"

"I thought we talked about this," said Jacobs. "We were supposed to be on our best behavior."

Bill could accept taking a scolding from the principal, but he wasn't too interested in hearing it from Jacobs. "Look, I'm sorry, okay? I don't know how many times I can say it."

Father Leo pointed his index finger at Bill's chest. "The last thing I want from you right now is attitude. 'Sorry' seems to be your word of choice at this retreat. I don't know what's gotten into you here, but I am very surprised. Enough is enough. Go into the dining hall and eat something... *Quickly.*"

"Yes, Father," said Bill.

Bill sat in the church with his group, the hunting knife slowly falling further down his waistband into his jeans, poking him in the lower back and buttocks. It was a constant reminder of what had just happened. He had come so close, closer than he ever had before. Bill had thought he finally had it in him, and perhaps he had... until the deer. How could that possibly be a coincidence? What were the odds? Had he actually received a sign from above? Bill didn't believe it, but he didn't completely dismiss the idea either.

Bill's eyes scanned the church as Father Leo gave a talk, and finally the thought occurred to Bill that he had to get the knife back to Matt's room. Would he be able to do it? There was no time. Maybe he could sneak it back in there when Matt went into the woods to meet Rachel. But Matt would probably want the knife when he went out there and he'd find that it was missing. Bill could just give Matt the knife; it didn't need to be a secret. Bill could just tell him he took the knife for protection when he went on his hike. There was no reason for Matt to believe that was a lie.

The last session involved all of the group leaders giving speeches on what it meant to be a leader and how everyone in the room could be one moving forward. They talked about how this experience was just the beginning and now they had to take what they had learned about themselves, God, and others and put it into use in their lives. Bill drifted in and out of the speeches—sure he was no better a leader than when he arrived—with visions of the mutilated deer running through his head and thoughts of how, if the deer weren't there, it would have been his lifeless body lying in the woods. He couldn't believe what he'd done, and he couldn't believe what he had almost done. He would carry that shame for the rest of his life. Now, all he could do was move on the best he could. Maybe he would finally seek the help he needed. First, he just wanted to get home. This retreat had gone so wrong for him when it had gone so well for so many other people. Bill was bitter and jealous, but he was glad he was still alive.

Bill entered his room, barely able to stand, and turned on the light to see a large collection of gnats flying around by the desk. He pulled the knife from his waist and laid it on the desk next to his watch. He couldn't bring himself to put it on. He was too ashamed. On the floor behind the desk, Bill found the banana he'd taken from the dining hall the first night—black, decayed, and covered in even more bugs. "Ugh." He crushed some gnats out of the air with his hands, picked up the banana, and tossed it out in the bathroom garbage can.

"Hey," Matt called out to Bill in the hallway.

"Hey," said Bill. He paused and let Matt catch up to him.

"It's all set for tonight," said Matt as he wrapped an arm around Bill's shoulder. "10:30."

"I don't think I'm going," Bill said somberly. Trying to impress a girl was already so foreign to him, and in his current state of mind it seemed absolutely impossible. It would only lead to rejection and humiliation.

"Oh, come on," pleaded Matt. "It'll be fun. This is your chance with Maddie. I'm sorry about what I said before. I believe you. Carter was just being a dick… I mean a jerk. Come on, man!"

They stopped at Bill's door.

"I'm *so* tired. I just want to sleep," Bill groaned.

Matt looked at his phone. "It's 9:15. They're getting here around 10:30. Take a little nap and you'll feel better."

Bill sighed. "I don't think so."

"Why not?"

"I said, I'm tired."

"So what?"

"Anybody else going?" Bill hoped someone could take his place.

Matt shrugged. "Just Dee. Pete and Scott don't want to."

"Well, you don't need me."

"I always need you," Matt grabbed Bill for a hug, and despite his determination not to, Bill couldn't help but smile.

Bill pushed Matt away.

Matt made a sad face and said, "Please."

Bill knew he would fall back into his usual vicious cycle: try to make progress, fail repeatedly, and completely break down. Could this be the time he finally got it right? He doubted it after the day he'd had, but he went against his better judgment and finally relented. "Just stop by when you're leaving."

"Yes!" Matt loudly clapped his hands together. "Atta boy." He gave Bill a tap on the shoulder. "You're gonna have a blast."

"I doubt it." Bill opened his door. "See ya in a bit."

"Later." Matt continued to his room.

Bill closed the door and saw Matt's knife lying on the desk. He thought about running it down to Matt but figured he could just give it to him later when Matt picked him up. Besides, a quick nap sounded like a great idea. He secured the chair under the doorknob so there wouldn't be any disruptions 'and killed a few more gnats. He went to the desk and held the watch in his hands. He whispered, "I'm sorry. Please forgive me," and clasped the watch around his wrist. He was fairly sure his grandfather couldn't hear him, but it made him feel a little bit better about himself. If his grandfather did hear him, Bill knew he would forgive him. He turned off the ceiling light and dropped into bed. He kept the desk light on, though it made him feel like a child needing a nightlight. The room was warm—too warm to sleep—so he opened the window to the overwhelming sound of crickets chirping. He debated which was worse: the heat or the noise. He tried the noise for a bit and lay back down. It was 9:21—he could get a good hour of sleep, and maybe his fortunes would change.

CHAPTER 17:
Lost

———

*W*HERE AM *I?*
Bill found himself in the middle of the dark woods. He had no idea of how he got there; he'd never left his room. The frigid air reminded him that he was only wearing his pajamas—shorts and a T-shirt. He didn't even have shoes or socks on. *What the hell is going on?* Bill rubbed his arms and shivered. He was freezing. It was far colder than any of the other nights when he'd gone outside and far colder than he had expected tonight to be. He looked around—darkness and trees surrounded him in every direction. He had no recollection of leaving the building with Matt or meeting anyone else outside and now no one was around. He was completely alone in the middle of the forest. He cautiously called into the darkness, "Hello? Is anyone there?"

No one responded. The only things Bill heard were the wind coursing through the trees and the leaves rustling on the ground beneath him as he took short shuffling steps. He checked his shorts pockets but had nothing else on him. Even his watch was missing. Bill's heart pounded in his chest as his terror grew. He saw nothing he recognized in the woods—the lake, the spring, the downed tree, the shed—nothing from his previous excursions, nothing to give him a clue of where to go. He called louder, "Hello? Is anyone out here?"

I need to get back to my room. I'll be okay in my room. Bill tried to formulate a plan, but he didn't know which direction to go, and he spun around and around, which only disoriented him further. *Why is this happening?*

Bill stood still and rubbed his arms. The trees seemed to grow taller

164

and close in all around him. He couldn't waste any more time—he had to pick a direction. He chose a gap in the woods that looked slightly brighter and began maneuvering his way through the forest, stubbing his toes on logs and stepping on sharp sticks. After a few minutes of finding nothing but more trees, he gave up on that route and turned to the left. He tripped and fell face first to the cold ground, breaking his fall with his hands. He picked himself up, dusted off his skinned knees and palms, and continued. In the distance, Bill heard the faint hooting of an owl. *At least I won't be alone.* He followed the sound.

The hooting grew louder as Bill staggered through the woods, cold and broken, but he was at least going in the right direction, which gave him a bit of hope. He searched the trees for his new friend—his only friend. "Where are you?" he shouted into the forest. Bill finally saw the yellow, glowing eyes and white feathers of the owl sitting on a low branch. "Hey, buddy. How's it going?" Bill looked at the majestic bird who seemed to watch over the forest. "You wouldn't happen to know which way the dorm is, would you?" He walked closer and the leaves crunched under his feet. The owl suddenly leapt from its perch and flew into the black abyss of the night.

Bill meekly whimpered as his last hope abandoned him. He was frozen to his core. He checked his aching bare feet, which were cut and bleeding. The blood looked black in the pale light of the moon. He leaned against a tree and kept rubbing his arms, desperately trying to create some warmth. *What do I do? I'm gonna die out here.*

Bill rallied the little strength he had left to scream, "Hello! Is there anyone there?" He gathered his breath to shout again. "Please! Please, someone help me!" He fell to the ground on his knees and palms, crying. "Please," he whispered. "Please, someone help me. I don't want to die."

Bill lifted his head and opened his eyes, his vision blurred from the tears. Far out in the distance, he saw something move. At first, he thought it was a branch swaying in the wind, but he wiped the tears from his eyes and realized the shape resembled the figure of a person. Bill struggled to his feet and squinted into the black forest. "Hello?" he called and immediately regretted it. The figure moved suddenly toward Bill, gaining ground quickly—no person could move that fast. Bill gasped. His heart lodged in his throat. What was it? He spun around and limped as fast as his shredded feet would carry him in the opposite direction. He looked over his shoulder and saw the dark figure in a black flowing cloak rapidly catching up.

Was it a priest? Why wasn't he responding? Bill didn't know what to do. He just kept moving, grabbing the tree trunk in front of him and pulling himself forward.

The figure was within twenty feet, and Bill knew he could not get away. He put his back against a tree trunk and watched the cloaked figure gracefully move through the forest. It didn't trip or stagger or break stride. It just floated above the ground toward him. It was inhuman.

Bill closed his eyes and whispered, "You're not real. You're not real. You're not real." He opened his eyes, and the figure was fifteen feet away. Bill closed his eyes and repeated more loudly, "You're not real. You're not real. You're not real." The figure glided to him, only ten feet away. Fear coursed through Bill's veins, and he closed his eyes and said even louder, "You're not real. You're not real. You're not real." When Bill opened his eyes, the figure was right on him. He saw nothing in the cloak but blackness. He closed his eyes and screamed, "You're not real!"

Bill opened his eyes, and the figure was gone. He scanned the woods… Nothing. *Where is it? What happened?* Bill tried to calm his breathing with still no sign of the figure. He turned and the black cloak engulfed him, swallowing his scream.

CHAPTER 18:
The Proverbial Shit Hits the Proverbial Fan

———

BILL SCREAMED AND AWOKE. HE SAT UP AND SAW THE DESK AND CHAIR and realized he was perfectly safe in his room at Eternal Springs. He breathed deeply to settle himself as his heart raced. *It was just a dream.* He rested his face in his hands and rubbed his eyes. The deafening chorus of crickets overwhelmed him. His watch read 12:53. Where was Matt? Had he not come by? Had he slept through it?

Bill rose from his bed to close the window, but then heard a faint scream, from the hallway perhaps. His mind was playing tricks on him again, he thought. First the eye in the wall, then the dream, and now he was hearing voices. This place was really doing a number on his sanity. He heard another faint scream and shook his head. "It's not real," he whispered to himself. He shut the window and heard another scream, but louder and closer. They were real—outside his door.

"Help me! Help me!"

Bill went to his door and suddenly a loud thump and bang sent him jumping back as someone slammed into the door on the other side. The handle turned back and forth, and the door wedged on the chair. The person pounded on the door.

"Help me! Bill! Open the door! Bill!"

It was Matt! Bill removed the chair, and Matt hurried inside. Bill peeked his head into the empty hallway and was aggressively pulled back into the room.

"What's going on?" said Bill.

167

Matt pressed the lock on the doorknob, but it popped back out. He then pressed his head against the door to listen. Bill could see the perspiration on Matt's forehead. Matt tried the lock again. "What's wrong with this thing?"

"It's broken. They still haven't fixed it. What's wrong?"

Matt went to the desk and began pushing it across the floor.

"Matt, what the hell are you doing?" Bill couldn't understand what had Matt so spooked.

The desk thumped against the door, and Matt backed away.

Bill put both hands on Matt's shoulders. "Matt. What is going on?"

Matt pushed himself from Bill's grasp and paced through the room. "They tried to kidnap me."

"What?" said Bill. "Who?"

"I don't know," said Matt, desperately trying to catch his breath as he finally stopped pacing. "I was waiting for Rachel. She said she was gonna be late because of a flat tire, and I fell asleep. The next thing I remember, I woke up in a wheelchair outside. They were pushing me through the field."

"Who was?"

"The staff. It was the staff. Mark, Abe, Luke. I didn't know what was happening and they tried to restrain me but I fought loose and I ran back to the building and they chased after me. I don't know what happened to them. I don't know where they…"

Matt trailed off, his mouth left wide open. A look of sheer terror overtook him. Bill's head snapped to the wall as he followed Matt's gaze.

The eye was back. It *was* real! Matt could see and it was staring right at them! There was no denying it anymore: something awful was happening at this retreat. Bill grabbed the knife from the desk and moved to the wall as Matt stood frozen, staring at the eye. It blinked, and Matt finally snapped out of his daze with a guttural grunt. Bill panicked from the overwhelming fear. He tightened his grip around the hilt of the knife and plunged the tip of the blade into the hole and into the eye. A horrific, ear-piercing shriek erupted from the wall, and blood spurted out and sprayed across the room and onto Bill's arm. Bill backed away from the wall, the knife still stuck in the hole as blood dripped down the white drywall. The screeching finally stopped.

"What the hell was that?!" Matt was hysterical now, hyperventilating, and pulling at his hair. "What did you do? What did you do?!"

Bill was in shock, completely unable to process what just happened. "I don't know… I don't know… Holy shit." Bill looked at the blood on his arm and hand. His mind flashed back to his arms and hands covered in the stag's blood.

Both boys' heads slowly turned to the door as they heard the knob turn. The door banged against the desk, but it remained closed. A loud thud on the door made them both jump. And then another. And then another. Someone was trying to break down the door. The desk wouldn't protect them for long.

"Here," said Bill, moving to the bed.

More and more bangs and thumps hit the door, which started to crack in multiple places. The boys pulled the mattress from the frame and dropped it on top of the desk. Bill added his large bag of clothes to the barricade. Then the pounding on the door stopped and a voice called to them from the hallway in a calm, encouraging tone.

"Fellas? Guys, it's Mark. Are you all right in there?" Bill looked to Matt, unsure of whether to reply. "Hey, guys, I'm really sorry about this. It's all just a misunderstanding." Matt, untrusting, shook his head no at Bill. "Can you please come out so we can talk about it?"

"Go away!" shouted Bill.

"I'm afraid we can't," said Mark, in a pacifying voice. "We need to talk about this. Just open the door."

"What do we do?" whispered Matt.

Bill searched the room. The only ways out of the room were the door or the window, which opened onto a fifteen-foot drop to the ground.

"Boys?" called Mark. There was a hint of anger in his voice, as if his patience was beginning to wear thin.

The boys stood still, hoping they would be left alone and that this nightmare would end.

Mark's deep voice now sent a chill down their spines. "Boys?"

Silence… and then violent blows rained down upon the door, smashing and cracking the wood. Through the broken remains of the door, Bill could see several faces of fellow classmates—Scott, Richie, Keith, all perfectly calm and stoic as they destroyed the barricade in front of them. *Oh my god, what was happening?* He grabbed the knife from the wall.

Matt tried opening the window, but it would only go up about a foot— not enough space to fit through. The desk skidded across the floor; it wouldn't be long before they fully breached the door.

Bill grabbed the lamp from the floor and ripped out the cord from the outlet, sending the room into total darkness. "Watch out." He threw the lamp though the windowpane, and the glass shattered.

Matt cleaned out the remaining shards of glass with a T-shirt and looked down below to the ground. Several bodies now climbed over each other and the desk and mattress to get into the room. Their only choice was to jump.

"Go!" shouted Bill,

Matt climbed through the opening and dropped from the ledge. Bill saw him land awkwardly and tumble to the ground. He clutched the knife in his right hand and worked his way through the window. As he held onto the ledge, hanging out of the window and looking back into the room, Bill saw multiple figures lunging at him in the darkness. One grabbed a hold of his left wrist and the watch. He quickly brought the knife over and sliced the hand on top of his, not stopping to think about which classmate's hand he was slashing. The intruder cried out and released his grip. Bill fell backwards from the window.

The fall felt like an eternity, and Bill waited for his body to painfully meet the earth. His fall was broken by Matt trying to catch him, and they fell hard to the ground. Bill looked up to the window—the silhouette of a person looked down at them from the broken window and then disappeared back into the room. They both staggered to their feet in pain. But their bodies still functioned properly.

"What the hell is going on?" said Bill.

"I don't know," said Matt. "I..." Matt paused. "Oh, shit," said Matt. He pointed down to the other end of the building. In the moonlight, Bill could see a group of ten to fifteen people walking toward them.

"Come on!" yelled Matt as he grabbed and pulled Bill. They ran along the dorm building toward the main building and the large group sprinted after them. Matt stopped to check the door attached to the dining hall, but it was locked. They ran past the three huge stained-glass windows of the church and turned the corner. They now raced along the length of the church, looking for anywhere to hide, but there were no doors, just more stained-glass windows. They cleared the church and paused. The Eternal Springs house stood ominously above the hill to the right. They couldn't go that way. They ran to the front of the main building.

"Let's go to the woods!" said Bill.

"No, we won't make it!" said Matt. He could see more people running to them from the dorm. He went to the main door, but it was locked. He pulled and pulled as hard as he could. "No!"

The horde from the back of the buildings turned the corner of the church and zeroed in on the boys. They were coming at them from both sides. There was no escape.

"The window!" Bill said. It was their last hope.

"Give me a boost," said Matt.

Bill secured the knife in his waistband and cupped Matt's foot in his hands to help propel him up to the window. Matt ripped the screen off and lifted the window—which was fortunately still unlocked—and pulled himself through. Bill jumped up, and Matt caught his arms. Bill scaled the stone wall with his feet as Matt pulled him up. Bill climbed through and fell to the floor of the lobby. Matt slammed the window shut and flicked the lock home.

They looked around the dim lobby. There was no sign of anyone inside and no sounds of anyone outside.

"Where'd they go?" Matt crept to the window and pulled back the curtain.

The crowd smashed into the door on the outside, and Matt jumped back. They backed slowly away from the door toward the breezeway.

"Now what?" said Bill.

There were plenty of options: the church, the dining hall, the rec room. But which was the best one? They didn't have time to decide as the door began to come off of its hinges.

"This way!" Matt pulled Bill into the breezeway, and they both suddenly stopped. All along the outside of the glass hallway, students stood and watched them. They didn't make any movements or say anything, and their faces looked pleasant and content. They remained completely still and just stared at them, like perfectly trained watchdogs waiting for their master's call to strike.

"Holy shit!" said Matt. "That's Pete! And Jake! And Tom! It's everyone!"

Bill looked on in disbelief at the faces staring back at him. He waved to them, and Pete waved back. It sent a chill down Bill's spine. That wasn't Pete.

The breezeway ended, and they found themselves by the staircases at the start of the dorm building as the bangs from the front door echoed to them.

"What do we do?" said Bill. "Should we try to get out the other side of the building and run to the woods?"

"I don't know." Matt was too scared to think.

"Do you have your phone?"

"No. It's in my room."

Bill looked up the stairs toward the dorm hall from which they had just fled. It didn't sound like anyone was up there, but he couldn't be sure. Did they dare venture back there and risk getting caught for the phone?

Then a single figure came running toward them through the breezeway.

"Someone's coming!" Matt clenched his fists in front of him and Bill stood next to him.

The person came to a sudden halt at the end of the breezeway at the sight of the boys.

"Oh thank God!" said Matt. "Father Stephen!"

"Stay back!" he shouted. The priest extended both arms in front of him. "Stay away from me!"

"We need your help," said Bill. "Something's happened! Please!"

"Stay back!" Father Stephen sidestepped the boys. "You've all gone nuts. Don't come any closer to me."

"No, we're normal!" shouted Matt. "You have to help us! You're the only one left!"

"I'm not helping you. I can't trust you. You're all crazy. Leave me be." Father Stephen eyed the emergency exit. He didn't see anyone through the glass. "I have to get out of here!" He lunged for the door.

"No!" yelled Bill and Matt in unison.

Father Stephen pushed the door open, and the alarm blared. The boys covered their ears to block out the piercing sound and watched. Father Stephen didn't make it ten feet from the door before he was tackled and swarmed by students.

"Can't go that way," said Bill. He pulled the emergency door closed and backpedaled to the stairwell.

Matt followed. "Now what?!"

Bill saw a pack of students enter the lobby. "Down!" he screamed.

They hopped down the stairs to another long corridor. Dorm rooms lined the left side every few feet, while only a few sporadic doors were on the right. The alarm reverberated throughout the hallway; it made it difficult to concentrate on anything else. Bill, still clutching Matt's knife, tried the first one, but it was locked. They saw a shadow coming down the stairs and scurried to the next door, but it was locked. They dashed to the end of the hall, hoping to find an exit to the outside, but there was none. The figure reached the bottom of the stairs at the end of the hallway. Bill turned the knob on the door in front of him, and it thankfully opened. They flipped the lights on—it was a cluttered storage room filled with tables and chairs and stacks of boxes. They navigated through the maze of crap and found a door at the back of the room that led to an outside staircase. Bill stood on top of a chair and peered through one of the small windows at the top of the wall just above ground level and saw several students standing, motionless, along the field, facing the building; too many to escape. "God damnit! They're everywhere!"

"What are they doing?" asked Matt. He cupped his hands over his ears.

Bill continued to watch them. "Nothing, really. They're just standing there. They're not moving."

The alarm finally went silent, but the sound continued to ring in their ears. All of a sudden, the door to the storage room swung open wildly and hit the boxes behind it. Bill jumped down from the chair and joined Matt hiding behind a stack of clear storage crates as the person entered the room.

"Who is it?" Bill whispered to Matt.

Matt tilted his head around their cover, then his chin dropped to his chest. "Scott," he said, defeatedly.

"Great," said Bill.

The behemoth walked through the maze of boxes and supplies, hunting his friends. It felt like the earth shook with each of his steps. Bill and Matt crouched low and shuffled around, trying to stay below Scott's eyeline.

"Guys?" Scott called. "You wanna play some pool or something?"

Bill and Matt ignored the invitation. They thought they could make it to the door to the hallway, but another stack of chairs blocked their path. Scott was right on them now, just on the other side of a tower of boxes. He paused, and the boys held their breath. He continued around the corner, and the boys crawled into the center of the room.

Scott suddenly lashed out and knocked over a stack of boxes. He violently threw tables and chairs out of his way, sending the boys scurrying back toward the door they'd entered through and the last stack of boxes to hide behind. They crouched down and searched the room. Bill clenched the knife in his hand. He didn't want to use it, but he would if he had to. They could no longer hear or see their huge friend. Matt peeked out around the boxes. He mouthed, "I don't see him."

Bill cautiously rose from behind the box, only for Scott to grab him and hurl him across the room. Bill slammed into a mess of tables and chairs that collapsed around him and he lost his grip on the knife. He searched for the knife in the clutter before he felt two huge hands grab him from behind and throw him backward through a stack of boxes to the ground.

Matt leapt from a table onto Scott's back and yelled at him, "Scott! It's Matt and Bill! We're your friends! What are you doing?"

Scott didn't respond. He instead began to thrash around furiously. Matt's legs whipped into the wall and knocked over more boxes. Scott reached behind his back, trying to grab a hold of his attacker. Matt slipped his arm under Scott's chin and around his neck and squeezed. Scott grunted, and his face began to turn purple. He desperately grasped behind him and finally secured a hold of Matt's shirt. Scott ferociously flung him over his shoulder like a stuffed animal to the cluttered ground.

Matt could no longer defend himself. His back and hip radiated pain. Scott grabbed him by the throat, lifted him up, and held him against the wall a foot off the ground. Bill worked his way back to his feet, blood dripping from his nose, as Matt fervently tried to break Scott's grip. Bill saw a brand-new baseball, glowing white, touching his bare foot.

"Scott! Stop!" Matt barely choked out the words out with Scott's meaty paws tightening around his neck. In a last-ditch effort, Matt kicked Scott in the groin, causing him to release his grip. Matt fell to his knees and grabbed his throat. He gasped for air. Scott clutched his crotch, and just as he turned around, Bill whipped the baseball directly at Scott's forehead. The ball thudded against his skull, sending Scott stumbling around the room like a drunk, crashing into boxes and tables and chairs while the boys stayed an arm's length away. Finally, Scott collapsed face first through a table. The entire room shook, and an avalanche of boxes fell on top of him.

Bill checked on Matt, who seemed to be okay apart from the massive red handprints on his neck. "You okay?"

"Yeah," said Matt, gently rubbing his throat. "You?"

"Yeah," said Bill. "Sorry, Scott."

The boys looked at Scott's unconscious body lying under the pile of debris.

"Now what?" said Bill.

Matt went back to the wall and stepped onto a chair to peer through the window at the top. All of the students had left the area. "I think they're gone."

They opened the door and ascended a few concrete stairs to the ground level. The campus was completely empty.

"There's no one here," said Bill, unbelieving. "Where'd they all go?"

"I don't know," said Matt. He checked vigilantly in every direction. "But if we're gonna run for it, now seems like a good time."

Bill nodded. "Let's do it."

"Okay, on three," said Matt, readying himself. "One... two... three!"

They ran as fast as they could, sprinting the entire way, never looking back. The ground was wet and slick beneath Bill's bare feet. He expected to get tackled at any moment, but they made it unmolested to the tree line and hid behind two trunks. They looked back at the serene grounds. There was no sign of the havoc they had just escaped.

"Where are they?" asked Matt. "They couldn't have all just disappeared."

"I don't know," said Bill. "As long as they're not coming after us, I don't care."

"Yeah," agreed Matt.

"Shit!" exclaimed Bill, frantically patting his body and hoping for a miracle.

"What?"

The truth sank in. "I lost the knife."

"It's fine. We'll make it to the highway. Maybe Rachel's out there waiting for us."

"Okay," said Bill. "I'm sorry." He'd let both Matt and himself down.

"Don't worry about it," Matt assured him. "I'll get a new one. It's all right."

They paused to catch their breaths.

"What is going on here?" said Bill. He tried to work it out in his head while he kept his eyes fixed on the clearing. The students had become so nice and docile... so friendly. But now they were acting like maniacs, hell-bent on capturing them and even hurting them.

"I don't have a damn clue," said Matt, the realization sinking in that he had lost friends to... what? He had no idea.

Bill thought aloud. "Was it something they ate or drank? Maybe they're hypnotized somehow. They were all acting very strange, even before today."

"Hypnotized?" Matt couldn't believe that—it was impossible.

Bill ran with his theory. "Yeah, the staff changed them somehow. Maybe we can change them back."

Matt quickly dismissed the idea. "We aren't saving anyone with just us two, and we have no idea what's happening. We find Rachel and then we call for help. That's our only choice."

Bill didn't like the idea of leaving anyone behind, but Matt what right; what help could they be right now?

Bill wiped the dried flecks of blood from his arm. "Who do you think I stabbed?"

Matt replayed the scene in his head and closed his eyes—he didn't want to think about it—the blood, the scream. "Hopefully Jacobs. He has to be responsible for all of this."

They each took a few deep breaths to gather themselves as they watched the still-empty campus before they would enter the woods. The adrenaline finally started to subside, and they thought they might just make it out of Eternal Springs.

"Ready?" asked Matt

"Yeah," said Bill. "Wait... look."

Bill pointed to the clearing at one person running from the dorm building across the open field to the woods, directly to where Bill and Matt were. Fear returned to both of them.

"*God*, who is *that*?" whimpered Matt.

"I can't tell." The person wore shorts and a T-shirt. Bill was sure it was a student. He crept deeper into the woods, and Matt followed, watching the dark-skinned person pass the trail lanterns and then disappear into the darkness of the open field. They each took cover behind a trunk as the student made it to the woods.

"Bill? Matt?" the person whispered. "Where are you guys?"

Bill and Matt looked to each other, unsure of what to do. It could be a trick.

The person continued to search. "Bill? Matt? Where are you?"

He was right on them, so Bill jumped out, both fists clenched in front of him. "Who's there?"

"Oh, thank god," said Dee. He stumbled toward them, but Bill and Matt were still ready for a fight.

"Wait!" said Bill, extending his arm. "Stay Back! How do we know you're you?"

Dee stopped in his tracks when he saw their fists clenched. "Well... I'm not attacking you."

Bill's eyes rolled to the top of his head as he thought about it. "Good point." He slowly lowered his hands and then quickly raised them again. "But it could be a trick. You could be stalling until more people show up."

Dee inched closer to them. "Shut up, idiot. It's me. The real me. I have no interest in talking religion with you."

Matt began to relax. He wanted so badly for someone else to be on their side. "Seems legit, I guess. How did you get out?"

Out of the corner of Bill's eye, he saw a group of people return to the front of the buildings. "Get down!" he said and pulled them both to the ground.

They hid low behind the trees and watched as Mark came forward from the handful of students and searched the horizon with a pair of binoculars. There was no way he could see them in the darkness, could he? They each lay flat on the ground while their heavy, worried breaths puffed dirt into their faces. With one eye, through the clutter of leaves in front of him, Bill saw Mark lower the binoculars and scan the area with just his eyes. Mark paused when he looked in the boys' direction, and Bill felt like his eyes were fixed directly on him. Mark then barked out a few inaudible orders, and two students from the group followed Mark into the residence building while four others remained outside.

"Is it safe?" whispered Matt.

"Mark went back into the building, but there's still a couple people out there," responded Bill. "I don't think they saw us. I think we're okay."

They slowly rose to kneeling positions and glanced at the four sentries posted in front of the dormitory.

"What's going on?" asked Dee.

"We don't know," said Bill. "They're doing *something* to us. So far, we have ingestion of a substance or hypnosis. We're certainly open to other suggestions."

"Hell, if I know," said Dee. "I thought people were just getting into the setting and the retreat, but now they're all psychos."

Matt, still unsure of Dee, said, "How did you get out?"

"I went to the bathroom, and when I came back Abe was at my doorway with a few students. He wanted me to come with them, but then I heard a bunch of screaming and banging and a window break. They came at me, and I ran away and hid in the dining room. Then I saw you two running out here and I thought it was my only hope. I waited till it was clear and here I am."

Dee sounded normal—and he certainly wasn't spewing uber-religiosity like the others had been—but maybe this was just another version of the retreat's plan, designed to capture them. Matt still didn't fully buy it and repeated, "*How* did you lose them?"

Dee's tone rose in panic. He needed them to believe him, to trust him. "I told you, I outran them and hid in the dining room."

Bill and Matt exchanged an unconvinced glance. That was it? There had to be more.

"I won state, man," said Dee. "One hundred, two hundred, and four hundred meters. Give me some credit."

"Right," said Matt, nodding. "He seems all right."

Bill agreed.

"Yeah, no shit, guys, I'm fine," said Dee. "Thanks for asking. How'd your slow asses get away?"

"Violence, mostly," said Bill. He rubbed his eyes. Exhaustion was creeping over him again. "And some luck, I guess."

They checked back on the four guardians, who were still watching over the grounds.

Bill continued, "Why aren't they doing anything? They aren't even moving. It's like they can't think for themselves."

"It's so weird," agreed Dee.

"Did you see anyone else?" said Matt.

"No, just you," said Dee. "What are we gonna do?"

"We gotta get to the highway," said Matt. "Hope we can find Rachel and get some help."

"She's still coming?" Dee asked. "I figured it was off. You never came to get me."

"Sorry, I fell asleep then all hell broke loose. But she's here... somewhere."

"Where?" asked Dee.

"That's the problem." Matt paused and gulped. "We were supposed to meet her at a spot on the highway, through the woods." Matt pointed to the foreboding forest.

"Hell yeah!" Dee jumped to his feet. "What are we waiting for?"

Matt's head drooped. "But I don't have my phone with the GPS. It's in my room, so I don't know how to get there."

"So?" said Dee, with a shrug. "We'll figure it out."

"It was difficult even with a map," argued Bill. "It will be almost impossible without one. And none of us are wearing shoes."

"Who cares?" exclaimed Dee, louder than he should have, prompting Bill to shush him. Dee then whispered, "It's better than being here."

The three thought it over—and Bill remembered the dream of the black cloak devouring him in the forest—before Matt broke the silence. "Our plan before was to get to the highway. One more person shouldn't change that. We can't stop whatever's happening here with three people. We need more help."

Bill and Dee nodded in agreement and the decision was made.

Matt took one last look at the grounds and saw something he couldn't believe he had missed. He'd been so focused on watching for bodies he never even realized it was there. He squinted hard and knew for certain that the car parked next to the retreat workers' house was Rachel's.

CHAPTER 19:
Well, That Didn't Work

"THAT'S RACHEL'S CAR," SAID MATT. "SHE'S HERE."

Bill turned and saw the back of the white car he had once taken a ride in parked next to the house. "Are you sure?"

"Yeah," said Matt between quick breaths. "I have to get her." He lunged forward but was stopped by both Bill and Dee. They struggled to restrain him.

Matt tried desperately to break free. "I have to go. They have her!"

"You can't go," said Bill, arms wrapped around Matt's torso.

"I need to! It's Rachel!"

Bill and Dee each secured an arm, but Matt continued to try to shake them off violently.

"I know you need to get her," said Bill. "And we will. But you can't just go running in there. You'll get yourself caught and you'll be no help to her. We need a plan."

The words started to register in Matt's head—Bill was right.

"Calm down, Matt." Bill let go of his arm and put a hand on his chest. "Calm down."

Matt relented but breathed hard. He was ready to tear someone's head off. "Let's figure out a plan. Quick."

They crouched down and watched the grounds—the same four people stood guard and that was it.

"I don't like it," said Dee. "Where is everyone else?"

"They must be in the buildings looking for us," said Matt.

"Maybe that's what they want you to think," said Bill. He'd rather they all be out there. At least he'd know where they were. They were about to reenter hell, and at any moment those devils would descend upon them.

"How do we get to the house?" said Dee.

"Quickest route is straight through that field." Matt pointed to the route they'd taken to the woods, directly towards the students standing guard.

"Right," said Bill. "But we need to avoid people."

"I don't care," said Matt. There was no fear in his voice. "I'll go right through them."

"We need to be smart," said Bill. "We can go around the lake the other way. That will give us better cover with the trees and darkness, and then we'll be right at the house."

"Okay, let's go." Matt didn't care what the plan was as long as it started immediately. Matt charged into the forest and took huge steps, the other two trailing behind him.

The boys stayed well inside the tree line, always keeping an eye on the lake, their guide. It was a rushed walk through the trees and foliage. The sweat on their skin chilled in the cool air and wind, and their feet ached from cuts and scratches, but they marched on until the house's lights came into view. The lights were on inside on the main floor, but no one was out front. They circled around the side of the house through the trees to do some quick reconnaissance.

Bill's legs burned and cramped; he wasn't sure how much longer he could go on. He wished he had stuck with football instead of baseball. Matt showed no signs of fatigue. All of the weightlifting and conditioning kept him strong, and he was about to start the fourth quarter. His eyes were wide, focused solely on the goal of recovering his girlfriend, and he was ready to fight every single person there to get her back.

"I see two people inside," said Matt.

"Me too," said Dee "What's the plan?"

"We're going in that house," said Matt, still planning to rely more on brawn over brains. He felt that time was his greatest enemy.

Bill wanted to be a bit more tactical. "Let's check the car first. Maybe there's something we can use."

"All right," agreed Matt.

The three crawled toward the car in a single-file line led by Matt, followed by Bill and then Dee. They reached the small white sedan; all four of its windows were rolled down. Matt opened the driver's door and slid into the seat. He tried to keep his head below the dashboard while Dee watched at the trunk of the car for anyone that might come from the main buildings, and Bill watched at the hood for anyone that might sneak up behind them from the house or woods. There was no sign of the keys and no purses or phones. There was nothing inside the car that would be useful as a weapon. Matt gently pulled the latch by his feet, and the trunk popped opened.

Matt met Dee at the trunk, and they looked inside as Bill watched the two figures in the house; it was Abe and Luke. The juxtaposition of their body types—four Lukes could fit inside one Abe—made Bill quickly smile, but then he again realized where he was and what he was about to do. The contents of the trunk were slightly more helpful. There were at least a couple of objects they could hit people with: a tire iron and an ice-scraper. Not ideal weaponry, but better than nothing. Then there were paper towels, jumper cables, and some small orange cones. Matt grasped the tire iron and gave the ice-scraper to Dee. Bill met the two at the trunk, and Matt handed him the jumper cables.

"What the hell am I supposed to do with these?" whispered Bill, as he tried to corral the cables sliding through his arms.

"I don't know," said Matt. "Pinch them." He closed the trunk with a soft thump, then nodded to the other two.

They slowly crept toward the house, climbed the stairs, and crouched next to a window. Matt saw Abe and Luke inside, standing at a table, rummaging through the contents of a green purse. He whispered, "Bill, go tap on the window over there and get their attention."

Bill didn't like being the bait, but he supposed it was better than actually breaching the house, so he nodded and crawled along the deck on all fours under the windows to the corner of the house. He gave a thumbs up to Matt, who returned the gesture. Dee kept his eyes on the empty trail leading to the house; his view of the buildings was blocked by trees. Bill's heart raced as he raised his hand to the glass and knocked three times.

Inside the house, the tapping on the window attracted Abe and Luke's attention, but they remained at the table. Matt looked to Bill and motioned for him to hit the window again. Bill took a deep breath and knocked three more times. This time, both Abe and Luke moved towards the window. Matt waved his hand for Bill to join them, and Bill gladly scurried back to meet his friends. Matt whispered to Dee, "Take Luke; I'll take Abe." Dee nodded, and Matt opened the door. They entered the house into the large living room.

It was bedlam as soon as Matt made the first move, lunging at Abe with the tire iron. There was no time for Abe to react, and the solid metal clanked against his head, sending him to the ground. Luke made a quick dash towards the walkie-talkie on the table, but Dee cut him off and tackled him. Abe groaned on the floor, unable to move. Dee sat in a full mounted position on Luke's stomach as he squirmed and tried to scream. Dee put his hand over Luke's mouth, and Luke gnashed his teeth into Dee's hand. Dee cried out in pain, but successfully kept Luke pinned down as Bill came over to help.

There was no time to be nice though, and Matt came over and punched Luke's face repeatedly, sending it bouncing off the wood floor. Matt ripped off one of his disgusting, dirt-covered socks and shoved it into Luke's mouth while Bill wrapped the jumper cables around his frail body. Matt searched through drawers and cabinets in the kitchen, leaving them wide open, until finally he found duct tape. Matt secured Abe's legs together around the ankles and followed up by taping his arms together around his wrists behind his back. He finished with a few feet wrapped around Abe's mouth and head. He tossed the roll of tape to Dee, who secured Luke's feet and hands. Bill checked the front yard through a window—no sign of anyone.

Matt retrieved the tire iron from the floor and hustled back to the kitchen to grab the butcher's knife from the rack. "Take some," he implored his friends.

Bill and Dee grabbed steak knives for each hand.

"Let's go," said Matt. He quickly scaled the large wooden staircase to the second level which led to a short hallway and several bedrooms. Matt went into the first bedroom and Bill and Dee checked the second, searching under beds and in closets. They inspected every square inch of the rooms for any sign of Rachel or her friends before meeting back in the hall.

"Anything?" asked Matt.

"No," said Bill.

A search of the remainder of the second floor yielded nothing.

Matt stormed downstairs and began opening every door in the house—first a food pantry and then a closet before he found the basement. Matt trampled down the stairs, followed by Bill and Dee; the idea of keeping the element of surprise never occurred to Matt. All he thought about was finding Rachel. They reached the carpeted basement but found nothing but two bunk beds, a couch, and a table with four chairs. The closets only contained clothes.

"Where is she?" yelled Matt, pacing back and forth. "Where else could she be?"

Then it came to Bill. "The shed… The cages weren't for any animals. They were for us."

"Oh, shit," said Matt.

"What cages?" said Dee.

"In the shed, there was a bomb shelter underneath with a bunch of rooms. One of the rooms had cages. Jacobs said they were for animals, but they're for us. That's where they're bringing everyone… Tom and Rob. That's where they're doing this. She has to be there."

Matt flew back up the stairs. Abe still lay in the same spot as before, but Luke was gone. Matt found him squirming his way to the door and pulled him back to the center of the living room by his feet as he grunted and choked on the sock.

Mark's voice suddenly came in through the walkie-talkie on the table. "Abe, there's no sign of them in the buildings. We're going to begin searching the woods."

The words made the boys pause. The voice came in again. "Abe? Do you read me?"

The boys moved to the table with the walkie-talkie, littered with the contents of three purses: phones, wallets, cash, makeup, all strewn about the rectangular table.

"What's all this stuff?" said Dee. "There's phones!"

"That's Rachel's phone." Matt grabbed it and repeatedly tapped the screen, but it wouldn't turn on. Dee tried the other phones, but they were also blank and unresponsive.

Mark's voice came over the walkie-talkie. "Delilah, do you copy?"

The boys paused and listened.

"Yes," Delilah responded.

"Switch to channel four."

"Roger," said Delilah, and the walkie-talkie went quiet.

"I don't like that," said Bill, moving to the front window to watch the empty trail to the house.

Matt switched the walkie-talkie to four.

"We'll take care of it," said Delilah.

"Are these the keys to Rachel's car?" Dee held them out in his hand, and Matt inspected them.

"I think so," said Matt.

"Then we can get out of here!" said Dee.

"I'm not leaving without Rachel," Matt said. "We have to get to the shed."

"Guys," said Bill. "We got company." Bill joined the boys at the table.

"Who is it?" said Matt.

"Delilah, with about ten students." There was clear panic in Bill's voice. "What do we do?"

The boys armed themselves with their knives and tried to come up with a plan.

Dee spoke up. "I'll distract them. I'll get them going in the other direction. Then you guys go to the shed. Maybe I can get to the car and try to get help somewhere."

"No heroes," said Bill. "We have to stick together."

"Do you have any other ideas?" said Dee.

Bill had nothing, and they were out of time. They could see the students approaching the front of the house.

"Let's do it," said Matt. "You get the car, go get help and we'll get the girls.

The other two agreed.

"Come on," said Matt. "Out back."

The boys left the warmth of the house through the back door into the cool night and paused to ready themselves.

"You guys go to the front of the house that way." Dee pointed to his left. "I'll go around this way," Dee pointed in the other direction, "and get them to follow me. When they leave the front, you guys run to the shed, okay?"

"All right," said Matt. "Good luck."

The boys separated, Dee to the right and Matt and Bill to the left. Dee kept the keys in his left hand and a steak knife in his right as he hugged the side of the house while Matt and Bill made it to the front corner. Half of the students went into the house. Four others remained outside.

Dee hopped out from behind the house and began waving his arms and shouting at his classmates. "Hey, guys, you want me?! I'm right here. Come and get me!"

The four students turned their heads to Delilah but remained still as Dee continued to yell at them.

"Go get him," said Delilah sharply.

Dee charged toward the back of the house, and his classmates followed. Bill and Matt watched the students clear out, then they sprinted toward the path for the shed. Over Bill's shoulder he saw Delilah raise the walkie-talkie to her mouth, but he couldn't hear what she said. The boys ran down the trail and into the woods while Dee led the students around the back of the house to the front again.

Dee had a straight line to Rachel's car. He passed within five feet of Delilah on his final sprint. She only stood there and calmly said, "You can't get away."

"We'll see," said Dee in a huff. He opened the door, jumped into the car, and turned on the engine as the group bore down on him. The car skidded and kicked up a cloud of dirt as he jammed the accelerator, raising the four automatic windows with his left hand and steering with his right. Bodies thudded against the back door and trunk, and the car shot forward down the trail. The car curved around the trees, and Dee saw a mass of people in front of the main buildings. He slowed down, looking for a clear route to the road, but students blocked every direction. He had no choice but to drive forward and hope his classmates would get out of the way. Dee pressed down hard on the accelerator, and the car jumped to thirty miles per hour. He swerved back and forth, shouting at the students, "Get out of the way!" Students dove left and right to avoid the deadly battering ram. Ahead there was only one person left. Dee pointed the car directly at him and drove forward. The student didn't move. Instead, he jumped and sprawled onto the windshield and hood of the car—it was Pete.

Dee's vision was blocked as Pete slid down the windshield and clung to the hood of the car. Dee veered hard left and right, trying to throw Pete off, but he still held on, without a worry on his blank face. Dee was so focused on getting Pete off he never saw the fence until it was too late. The car broke though, partially collapsing the fence, and came to a sudden halt on the basketball court, throwing Pete ten feet in front of it.

"Shit!" said Dee, terrified he'd just killed Pete. He watched Pete's lifeless body in the glow of the headlights. "Please get up." Pete's arms moved, and then his legs before he slowly rose to his feet. "Thank God," said Dee.

Dee put the car in reverse, but the wheels were stuck on the fence and only spun. In the rearview mirror, Dee saw the horde of students coming right at him. He put the car in drive and circled the court as the rest of the fence collapsed. He had a clear path now. He gunned it over the downed fence back onto the field and then lined up the road for his escape. Dee pressed the pedal to the ground, leaving a trail of dust behind him as he sped off into the forest.

Matt and Bill ran toward the shed, completely exhausted, gasping for air. Bill's lungs were on fire, and his legs felt like they were a thousand pounds each. At any moment, he thought he would collapse and that would be it. He'd either be dead or he'd wake up as some sort of fanatical zealot, his real self possibly lost forever. He wondered if his mom would notice. Would anyone notice when the class returned and were completely different people? Was the entire school in on it?

"Come on," said Matt, as he huffed and puffed. "Almost there. We can make it."

Matt picked up his pace, and the words gave Bill the strength to keep up. Finally, the shed and the monstrous dish towering above it came into view. Their pace slowed to a jog.

"Delilah called someone... on the walkie." Bill could barely talk. He gulped for oxygen. "I don't know what she said, but it's a good bet they know we're coming."

"Let 'em know," said Matt. He reached the stairs first. He held the butcher's knife in his left hand, extended in front of him, and he kept the tire iron in his right hand raised by his ear, ready to strike. "Get the door."

Bill clamped down on one of his steak knives with his teeth and kept the other in his right hand. They scaled the stairs together, and Bill opened the door to the small room. Inside the light on the keypad lock was green on the steel door. This troubled Bill—both doors had been left unlocked. Did someone forget to lock them, or was it an invitation—a trap? Matt nodded to the door, and Bill opened it up. Matt went down first, slowly, step by step on the metal-grated stairs, and Bill closed the door behind him. Matt paused at the bottom and wiped the sweat pouring down from his forehead with his sleeve. His face itched from the stubble that had grown unkempt after three days without shaving. The next door's keypad also coaxed them through with a green light, and Bill pushed it open it to the hallway.

Dee sped down the dirt road to the highway, high beams blaring so he could see everything on the pitch-black road. What had taken the bus fifteen minutes to traverse took Dee three in Rachel's car. The car bounced up and down and sent Dee's head bumping into the ceiling. Only then did he remember to put on his seatbelt. He reached the highway, turned the wheel hard to the right, and skidded out onto the asphalt, leaving two tire marks imprinted on the surface. He straightened the car and zoomed down the two-lane road faster than he had ever driven before.

At that moment, he felt the cool breeze and heard the air whooshing by the speeding car through the back driver side window; it was wide open. He thought he had closed them all, but he must have missed that button. He pulled the button back to close the window, but nothing happened. And then he felt arms wrap around his neck from the backseat. In the rear-view mirror, he saw Evan, newly born child of God, trying to choke him. Dee's foot pressed down on the accelerator, pushing the car past eighty miles per hour on the dark winding road.

Officer Reagor sat in his squad car, in the same spot he did every night—a small nook in the woods—and unwrapped the foil on his double-cheeseburger. He had been on the force for almost ten years, and this had become his favorite spot. His car sat at the back of a curve, hidden by trees. No car passing him could see him until it was too late. It was the perfect speed trap. Not that it mattered all that much; at this time of night, he rarely saw cars, and he hadn't pulled anyone over on this shift in weeks. Just as he dove in and took a quarter chunk out of the burger, a white sedan flew by the curve, tires screeching and smoking. The officer's radar gun read sixty-seven miles per hour—far too fast for the posted forty-mile-per-hour limit on the curve. He crinkled the foil around the burger and tossed it to the passenger seat.

Dee was finally able to separate Evan's hands from his neck, and he landed several weak punches to his head, which held Evan off long enough for Dee to slow the car down just before he hit another wicked curve. The hard turn sent Evan sliding across the back seat against the door as the tires screeched on the pavement. Dee started to pull the car over when Evan attacked him again. The car swerved on the road, crossing back and forth over the yellow-dotted center line, and Dee sent right elbows at Evan's head. Evan pulled himself into the passenger seat, and Dee fought him off with his right hand and steered with his left. The car jerked around the road, decelerating to fifty and then forty and then thirty miles per hour. Behind him, Dee saw the flash of red and blue lights. *The cops!*

At that moment, Dee lost control of the car and it went off the road, flying across a small ditch and crashing head-on into an embankment. The noise was awful and loud. Both airbags exploded from the dashboard. The front half of the car was crinkled like an accordion, and smoke billowed from beneath the hood. Dee groaned in pain as the shock slowly wore off. Evan was unconscious; his head rested against the passenger door. Dee could only open the mangled driver's door halfway. His foot was stuck at the bottom near the pedals. He wrenched and pulled until it finally came loose, then squeezed his way through the door and landed face first on the long grass.

Officer Reagor tailed the out-of-control car, quickly making up ground. The vehicle crossed the shoulder and leapt the ditch, coming to a sudden and brutal halt. He slowed to a stop next to the smoking car, jumped out of his cruiser, and pulled his flashlight. He crept forward with his flashlight pointed to the car as he kept his other hand on his holstered sidearm. He came upon the embankment and saw Dee lying in the ditch. "Hey, are you all right?"

Dee lifted his head and saw the officer walking to him. "Oh, thank you." Dee pushed his body off the ground and rested on his knees. "Officer, please help me. There—"

Evan lunged from the car and jumped onto Dee's back.

"Hey," said Officer Reagor. "Get off him!" The officer pulled his sidearm.

Dee swung back and forth, trying to shake Evan off, but he held tight. Officer Reagor lowered his gun, unsure of who was the correct target, and watched as Dee backpedaled and rammed Evan into the car several times until he released his grip. Dee backed away, but again Evan charged. Dee punched him square in the jaw. Evan's knees buckled, and he collapsed to the ground.

Now the cop raised his gun and pointed at Dee, completely bewildered by the situation. "Put your hands up!"

Dee breathed heavily and put his hands back up in the air before his body gave out and he fell to his knees.

"What the hell is going on?" asked Officer Reagor.

"You're probably not going to believe this, but here goes…"

The hallway underneath the shed was bright and empty. Bill and Matt both knew someone had to be down there somewhere. Getting inside had been far too easy. It was just a matter of when they would come out, and the boys would be ready. They didn't bother trying the first few doors; they didn't want to waste any time, and they knew they had to get to the room with the cages. Slowly they moved forward, Bill trailing behind Matt. Bill hoped he wouldn't have to use a knife again, but he was sure at this point Matt would have no problem doing whatever he had to do to rescue Rachel.

And then they came upon the room at the end of the corridor filled with cages. It was empty. Matt scanned the first row of cages. He saw only one body—male—lying unmoving. His eyes moved to the next row, and he saw the body of a girl with long brown hair sitting directly against the front gate, head pressed against the grates.

"Rachel!"

She looked up with wide eyes. "Matt!"

He dropped his weapons and slid across the floor, stumbling over his own feet to get to her. They held hands through the grates.

"Get me out of here," Rachel cried in scared relief.

Matt pulled on the cage as hard as he could. Bill found Maddie in the cage next to Rachel and another female body in the next cage over; both were unconscious.

"How do I open it?" Matt's biceps bulged as he tore at the cage door.

"I think there's a control on the wall," said Rachel.

Bill searched the walls and found a black keypad with numerical buttons one through nine and buttons labeled 'open,' 'close,' and 'enter.' "Is there a number on the cage?" he called.

Matt's head danced around. "Thirteen."

Bill punched in thirteen and open, but nothing happened.

"Come on, Bill," Matt frantically called. They were so close.

Bill's hand shook. "I'm sorry. I don't know what to do." He hit open, and the button turned green. He punched in one and three, but nothing happened, and the green light went off.

"Hurry," cried Rachel. She leaned her head against the cage, and Matt did the same as they continued to hold fingers through the grates.

Bill breathed deep. "Okay." He hit the 'open' button, and it lit green. He punched in one and three and then hit the 'enter' button. The lock sprang, and the mechanical cage door slowly swung open. Matt pulled Rachel out of the cage, and they embraced, sitting on the floor. Bill unlocked Maddie's cage next and hustled over to her. Her feet were positioned at the front of the cage and her torso and head at the back. Bill struggled to pull her out, his strength entirely depleted.

"I'm gonna need some help," he called as he climbed fully into the cage.

"Matt, grab her legs." He grabbed Maddie around the shoulders and lifted. "Matt?"

Suddenly the cage door shut and locked him inside. "Matt!" Bill frantically shouted. He couldn't see anything from the back of the cage, his vision blocked by the black plastic separating the cages. "The gate closed! Open it!" There was no response. Fear permeated Bill to his core. "Matt! Open the god damn gate!"

Bill climbed over Maddie's body to the front of cage, and his mouth dropped open. Near the cage control, standing with Rachel, was Jacobs, holding a syringe. Matt's unconscious body lay face down on the floor in the doorway. A sinister smile slowly crossed Jacobs' face as Bill's heart sank into his stomach.

Bill wrapped his hands around the grates of the cage. "You son of a bitch." His grip tightened and he violently shook the cage. "You son of a bitch!"

Jacobs sauntered over to the cage, waving his finger in Bill's direction. "Now, I thought I told you to stay out of here."

"Let me out of here, you sick fuck!" Bill tried to rip the cage door off.

Jacobs crouched down in front of the cage, a foot away from Bill. A silver gun dangled in his hand between his legs. "That's not very nice... but don't worry, we'll fix those manners soon enough."

Jacobs lifted the gun to the cage and stuck the barrel between the grates. Bill backed away from the door and tried to crawl over Maddie's body.

"Are you finally ready to join us and be welcomed into salvation?"

Bill still didn't give in. "I swear to God, you're not getting away with this."

"This is all His plan." Jacobs pointed the gun at him and fired, hitting Bill in the chest with a dart. Bill pulled it out as quickly as he could, but it made no difference. He began to feel woozy. His head felt light, and his vision blurred as the room faded away.

The dark highway was lit in blue and red flashing lights from two police cars and an ambulance. Medics were tending to Evan, who had a broken arm that hung awkwardly to his side; his wrist and palm faced the opposite direction of what they normally would. After coming to, Evan had once again tried to attack anyone that came near him, so he'd been sedated and readied for his trip to the hospital.

Dee was trying to explain the ludicrous story to the two police officers before him. Somehow, someway, the staff at Eternal Springs had successfully brainwashed the students of St. Zeno. They were turning all of the students into religious fanatics and were possibly using them as some sort of an army to take over the world. Or at least the general area to start. He was the only one to escape the grounds unchanged, and they needed to hurry back before the final few students were brainwashed as well. It only elicited eye rolls and snorts from the unbelieving cops.

"It just isn't possible," said Officer Reagor. "What you're saying is insane."

"I know," agreed Dee. "But it's true. We have to go back."

Officer Danault, younger and slimmer than Reagor, lowered his cell phone from his ear. "Still no answer."

"Right," said Dee. "Because they're out there trying to capture students. Or maybe they're trying to escape."

The younger officer looked to his superior. "There's only one way to find out," he said with a one-shoulder shrug. He had only been on the job for a year, and this was certainly the most interesting thing to happen to him while on the force.

"All right," said Reagor. "Let's have a look."

CHAPTER 20:
Revelation

BILL THOUGHT HE WAS FLYING UNTIL THE SENSATIONS RETURNED TO his limbs and he felt his bare feet dragging along the cold floor. He peeled his eyes open, and the bunker hallway came into focus. His right side thudded hard to the concrete ground when the person carrying him let go.

"I'll get the door," Jacobs' voice called and pierced Bill's brain like it did every morning through the speaker in his room. It brought him to full attention, and he remembered he was in grave danger. Bill lifted his head and saw that it was Mark holding up the other side of his body. He then felt the steak knife in his waistband pricking him in the lower back—they hadn't found it… He still had a chance!

Jacobs took the keys from his pocket and unlocked one of the mysterious dark rooms as Mark continued to hold the left side of Bill's body. Bill casually wrapped his arm behind his back and pulled the knife from his waist band. He stabbed the three-inch blade down to the handle into Mark's thigh.

Mark yelped like a wounded dog and tried to pull the knife out, but it was wedged in too deep. Jacobs turned back to Bill and received a straight right to his nose that sent him forcefully through the doorway. Mark tried to grab Bill, but Bill countered, kneeing him in the groin and shoving him to the ground. Rage pumped through Bill's veins, and he followed up with a few kicks to Mark's midsection borne from pure wrath. Mark cried with each kick, and the keys on his waistband jingled from the impact. Bill unclipped the keys as Mark lay curled in the fetal position, no fight left.

Bill barged through the half-closed door, and Jacobs immediately attacked him. They grappled with one another, exchanging blows to each other's shoulders and heads before Bill gained the upper hand. He grabbed Jacobs by the collar of his polo and used his face like a punching bag. Blood gushed from Jacobs' nose; it ran into his mouth and sprayed out with each breath. The final punch knocked Jacobs back into a chair in the center of the room. Even with his entire face covered in blood, Jacobs tried to get up. Bill's front kick to his stomach knocked the wind out of him. He fell back into the chair, gasping for breath.

Bill noticed restraints on each side of the blue padded chair's armrests. The apparatus reminded him of a dentist's chair. He tightened the restraints around Jacobs, who faintly fought as he tried to recover his breath.

"Let me out of here! *Right now!*" Blood spurted out of his mouth with every word, and one of his front teeth was missing.

Bill locked the door and looked around the unfamiliar room. Attached to the top of the chair directly above Jacobs's head was a large grey helmet contraption, and a bundle of wires led from it across the ceiling to a large console against the wall. The console hummed gently and was filled with several built-in screens and all sorts of buttons, knobs, and levers.

"What is this thing?" said Bill, inspecting the control panel. "Is this how you've been changing everyone?" Only the left side of the console was powered on. On the screen, a number labeled 'range' flickered from 179 miles to 189 to 173. *Range for what?*

Jacobs calmed himself as his face slowly swelled. "Bill, this is just a big misunderstanding. We're trying to help people."

"Help people? By brainwashing them? Controlling everything they do?"

"Not at all. We want everyone to find salvation. We want everyone to be at peace. This is just a tool… like the Bible… to help people see the light."

"So much for free will, huh?"

"We're no different than the apostles spreading the word of God, Bill."

Bill scanned the console. "You're a *little* different."

"Think about it, Bill, everyone—all the people of the earth—living in peace and harmony together, as one family… brothers and sisters of Jesus Christ and sons and daughters of God Almighty. No more wars, no more hate, no more apathy or suffering… the perfect Eden. Heaven on Earth! And we have the means to make it happen!"

Bill pondered what Jacobs was saying, and he hated himself for believing there was some truth to it. Hell, he had said the exact same thing to

Mark a couple of days ago. Mankind had had millions of years to prove their worth and failed repeatedly. Maybe mankind's only hope was to have their free will taken away, to be forced to be good and righteous.

"Bill, join us. We can be your family. You can finally have the father you've been searching for… God, above. He can take away all of your anger and fear and anxieties. He will love you unconditionally. We all will. You just need to join us."

The idea may have seemed compelling to Bill had it not come from a religious nutjob trying to take over the world. Bill shook his head. "You're out of your mind. I'll never join you."

Boom! A huge thud hit the outside of the door.

Bill returned to the chair, pulled the helmet down onto Jacobs' head, and pulled the strap tight across his chin.

"What are you doing?" Jacobs wrenched his body in the chair. "Bill, let me out of here!"

Bill returned to the panel and searched through the knobs and buttons on the right side of the console.

"Now, Bill, you need to let me go. This is crazy. You don't know how to use that. You need to undo these restraints right now. Bill… you will be in *so* much trouble."

Bill located a switch labeled 'on/off.' "Thanks for labeling it. This seems easy enough to use."

Bill slid the switch to 'on,' and the machine awoke as the console screens and buttons lit up. He heard more footsteps in the hallway, and the thuds on the door grew in frequency and power. He gazed around the console to see several heads through the frosted glass window on the door. Time was almost up; this was his last chance. Bill saw a knob labeled 'power' set to '0.' He twisted it clockwise to '1,'" and Jacobs began to shake as power flowed through the wires, first into the helmet and then into Jacobs' head. Bill watched in amazement as Jacobs' entire body convulsed and spit dribbled from his mouth.

"Stop!" gurgled Jacobs.

Bill turned the knob back to '0.' "Interesting."

The squad car bumped up and down along the dirt road to Eternal Springs, much slower than Dee would like. "Can't you go any faster?" he whined from behind the partition in the back seat.

"No," Reagor said bluntly. He kept his eyes fixed on the road and his speed at fifteen miles per hour. He was exceptionally annoyed at Officer Danault, who was tailgating his bumper in the car behind him.

"What about backup?" said Dee. "There's too many of them. You need more people."

"More officers are on the way," assured Reagor. "Besides, I think we can handle a few religious high-schoolers."

The cruisers exited the woods onto the grounds and continued along the dirt road while the red and blue lights reflected off the lake and the windows of the buildings. They then saw something in the bright headlights which they never would have expected to see in the middle of the night: handfuls of high school students, sitting cross-legged on the grass with their hands folded in their laps.

The cruisers stopped in front of the seated students.

"Wait here a minute," said Reagor.

Dee leaned forward and pleaded, "No, don't go out there. They're crazy. You need—"

The door shut, and Dee watched as Delilah approached the two officers. Abe stood with Luke next to the students. He had a white bandage—doused in blood near his temple—wrapped around his head.

"Good evening, ma'am," said Reagor.

"Officers, thank God," said Delilah in a calm and collected tone. "We have a serious problem. A few of the students who are staying with us have gone crazy. They assaulted several of their classmates and then they broke into our house over there and assaulted and tied up two of our leaders. Now they've gone into the woods to a supply shed where other people are working. I haven't heard from my coworkers in a while." Delilah held up the walkie-talkie in her hand. "I don't know what's happened to them."

Reagor looked at the thirteen students sitting in two horizontal single-file lines—a slight smile on each of their faces, as if nothing at all was happening. "You're saying some students attacked other students and the workers here?"

"Yes!" Delilah eagerly confirmed. "You have to go to the shed and help them!"

Reagor pointed to Abe. "You were attacked by students?"

"Yes, Officer." Abe pointed to his head. "They broke into the house, hit me in the head, and then tied me and him up."

Luke nodded along to the story.

"How many were there?" asked Reagor.

"Three," said Abe.

"Did you see them?"

"Yes. I know who they are."

Reagor took a deep breath. "Well, we were told by a student that left here that the workers were... assaulting the students here."

Delilah's head quickly shook back and forth as her face contorted in disgust. "Assaulting the students? Absolutely not. Look!" She pointed to the two rows of well-behaved students. "Does it look like we're assaulting any students?"

Reagor and Danault looked at the quiet students.

"What are they all doing out here?" asked Reagor.

"We weren't sure who or where the offenders were. We were worried they were still in the building, and we wanted to get a headcount and see who was missing."

Reagor cleared his throat. "Do you mind if we ask them some questions?"

"We don't have time for that!" Delilah said, raising her voice. "We need your help! Our friends are in danger."

Officer Danault walked over to Freddie sitting in the grass. "Good evening, son."

"Good evening, Officer," said Freddie with a smile and a nod.

Danault watched his tranquil face as it flashed red and blue. "Everything okay tonight?"

"Well, Officer," started Freddie, "we were having a great time here at this retreat until some of our secular classmates started acting like sinners. They broke out of the dorm building and assaulted some of the students and the staff. We just want them to be caught. Will you help?"

Freddie looked up to the officer with puppy-dog eyes. Behind Freddie, Danault noticed Pete, covered in dirt from head to toe, slumped over to his left side.

"Excuse me, son, are you all right?" Danault crouched down next to Pete at the end of the line students.

Pete gradually turned his head towards the young cop. "No, Officer. I was run over by one of my classmates for my beliefs. And I think there's something wrong with my shoulder. I'm hurt both emotionally and physically. Will you please help catch these sinners who have ruined our retreat?"

Danault couldn't process all of the information. "You were run over?

197

With a car?"

"Yes, sir." Pete nodded. "It was Dee. I thought he was my friend, but he ran me down in a car."

Danault turned to Reagor with a baffled look. "What the hell?"

"Why didn't you call the cops?" said Reagor.

"We thought we could handle it at first," said Delilah. "But we didn't know just how bad it was, and then everyone was running around trying to get control of the situation."

"Who's in charge here?" said Reagor.

"Mr. Jacobs runs the retreat facility," said Delilah.

"And where's he?"

"As I said, I can't reach him," said Delilah. She held up her walkie-talkie again. "He's at the shed and he *needs help!*"

Danault returned to Reagor and whispered in his ear, "Looks like the kid's got a separated shoulder. Do you think our friend in the back seat is the one that ran him over?"

Reagor whispered back, "Could be. Everything about this is strange."

From the car, Dee shouted, "Don't trust them!" at the top of his lungs.

Reagor thought for a moment. "Check with the kid in back."

Danault opened the door but blocked the exit. "Everyone seems fine. They're saying it was you and some other students that were attacking them. You ran someone over with a car?"

Dee's heart sank. At this point, it was just his word versus their word, and they had a lot more people on their side. "I had to. Like I said, they were trying to kidnap us. We were just trying to get away from them."

"How are we supposed to believe you?" said Danault. "Everything seems fine."

Dee pointed back to the students. "They seem fine to you? This isn't how they normally act. What the hell are they even doing out here?"

Dee barged past Danault out of the car, and Abe's eyes lit up in rage. "That's him," he said, pointing at Dee. "That's one of the students that assaulted me." Abe lunged forward toward Dee, but Officer Reagor caught him.

"Hold on there, big fella." Reagor kept Abe in a bearhug.

Dee shouted, "Don't believe them! They're lying! You have to help my friends!"

Officer Danault pulled Dee closer to the squad car as Abe continued to push through Reagor. Reagor used all of his strength to shove Abe backward a few feet.

"I said take it easy, son." Reagor held his hands in front of him to dissuade Abe from moving.

Abe again charged, and with a swift motion, Officer Reagor tripped him, took him to the ground, and pinned his arm behind him. "Now hold still."

At once, all of the students rose to their feet and jumped on top of Officer Reagor. Reagor flailed wildly, shedding students in every direction.

Danault pulled his gun from the holster as he shut the door on Dee.

"Don't shoot them!" Dee shouted behind the glass. "They don't know what they're doing!"

Danault thought twice and holstered his sidearm. He entered the fracas, pulling students off his partner. More red and blue lights filled the campus as two squad cars approached the melee.

The door to the control room began to splinter. Jacobs groaned as the pain dissipated. "Do not turn that knob again!" Jacobs' face was bright red, and veins bulged from his forehead. He strained with every muscle to break the restraints. "Do you hear me?!"

With a final crash, the door broke open, and the mob rushed in, leaving Bill with no choice.

"Bill, what are you doing?" said Jacobs.

"Committing blasphemy," said Bill.

Bill turned the knob to the maximum setting, sending a huge surge of energy through the machine. Jacobs screamed as he violently shook. Bill fought the first two students off, but Richie and Gus tackled him to the ground and smothered him, blocking all light from the room and sending Bill into a cocoon of suffocating darkness. The machine began to smoke and spark. The lights flickered, and then the bulbs burst in the ceiling panels. Bill gasped for air and kicked and punched and scratched and gouged any piece of flesh he could. Richie rolled off of Bill, but he was still pinned to the ground under a horde of students, now face to face with Matt.

"Join us, friend," Matt said, his eyes empty and his face pleasant, as if he were meditating in a peaceful field.

The control panel exploded with a huge pop and sent sparks everywhere. All of the lights went out, and the machine finally broke down, leaving the room in total silence.

The mayhem continued on the grounds. Reagor and Danault grappled and fought off the students and Abe as two other officers joined the fray. The retreaters had the numbers advantage, but the officers used their strength, training, and equipment advantages to even the playing field. Punches flew through the air, batons smacked flesh and muscle and bone, and officers deflected students away with their riot shields. Tasers discharged and sent students to the ground in wild convulsions. Amazingly enough, no shots were fired. Students were restrained with handcuffs and zip ties, but even then, the restrained students still charged forward, using their heads and shoulders as battering rams and kicking ferociously.

And just like that, as quickly as the attack had started, it ended. No more students charged. No more students attacked. They just stood exactly where they were in that moment, as reality came back to them, and the officers were no longer in any danger.

"What the hell?" said Reagor in perplexed frustration.

It was quiet in the machine room. No one was fighting. A single emergency light in the corner enveloped the room in a red glow as smoke billowed from the console. All of the students peeled themselves off one another and rose to their feet. Matt came to the realization that he was lying on top of Bill.

"What's going on?" Matt winced from the pressure of the people on top of him.

"I'm not sure," said Bill. "But you better buy me dinner first."

"Where's Rachel?" Matt lifted himself up, dumping two students to the ground. "Rachel!" He searched the room. "Rachel!"

"Matt!" a voice called out. "Matt, I'm here!"

The two found each other and embraced.

Matt pulled back to look her over. "Are you okay?"

"Yes, I'm fine," Rachel said, clutching his arms. "What happened?"

They hugged again, and Rachel rested her head between Matt's neck and shoulder.

"I don't know," said Matt.

"We were changing the flat tire and..."

Matt rubbed her back. "I know. I know. It's over now. You're okay."

Rachel remembered her friends were here too. "Where are Maddie and Sara?"

"I'm not sure." Matt looked around the room at the faces of his classmates. "They're here somewhere."

Bill sat and watched as the students staggered around the room, trying to figure out what had happened. There were gasps of shock and disgust when they noticed Jacobs' corpse sitting in the chair. Blood leaked out of every orifice of his face.

"Where are we?" wondered Gus.

Richie inspected Jacobs' body closer. "Holy shit! Is he dead?"

Gus looked at Jacobs's body and turned to retch into the red darkness.

"What the hell is going on?" said Jerry. "Bill?"

Bill stared at Jacobs in the red light, his face contorted and clenched in hideous pain. His eyes were open, and they looked like they stared right back at Bill. *Thou shalt not kill.*

"Bill?"

Bill snapped out of it and looked at the room full of eager faces waiting for answers. "Guys, I don't know what happened. But the workers here were using this machine to control your mind."

"Piss off," said Jerry. "That's impossible!"

"Yeah, I thought so too, but what do you remember?"

Jerry thought about it. His actions were clear in his mind. "We were told to find you. We chased after you in the dorm and then outside."

"Yeah, exactly!" said Bill. "Did you want to do that?"

Jerry paused, unable to speak. At the time, he wasn't in control of his actions and hadn't been for days. He remembered everything—the masses, the sessions, the talks, the unwavering piety—but somehow it hadn't really been him doing it. He would never want to do it. Something had forced him to do it.

The room was filled with smoke and stank of burnt rubber and metal and something far worse: flesh.

Bill watched as the students tried to comprehend what happened. "Let's go out and get some air, huh?" He lingered and stared at Jacobs' bloody face while the students exited the room. He finally broke his gaze and joined his classmates in the hallway, which was now only lit by small bulbs near the ground like the center aisle of an airplane. Bill saw the puddle of blood from Mark's wound and the trail down the hallway, but he was gone.

Bill pointed to the lights. "Just follow those lights down the hall and take the stairs up. I'll be right there. I just have to check something. Watch out for the staff though. They could still be dangerous."

The students plodded down the hall to the stairwell, still trying to put together the events that had unfolded at the retreat as Bill went to the kennel room. There he found Rachel huddled with Maddie and Sara while Matt freed the remaining few students from their cages.

"How is everyone?" asked Bill.

No one really knew. After a pause, Matt said, "Everyone seems okay. Bit of a headache, but that's about it. We're all acting like ourselves again."

"Good." Bill glanced at each of the empty cages. "Mark's gone. I stabbed him in the leg and there's a trail of blood leading to the stairs."

Matt clenched his jaw. "He couldn't have gone far. We need to get him."

"Yeah," said Bill. He didn't want to, but he knew they needed to. "You think Dee made it?"

"I don't know." Matt wrapped his arm around Rachel. "You three stay here. We need to go make sure everything is okay outside."

"No," pleaded Rachel. "Let's just stay here."

"We have to see if Dee got help." Matt held Rachel's hands in his. "We have to make sure everyone is okay."

Rachel brought Matt in for a hug. "Just be careful."

"I will." Matt peeled away from her.

Bill and Matt dipped into the medical room across from the kennel and performed a quick search. "Nothing," said Matt.

"All right, let's try the other rooms," said Bill.

As they exited the medical room, they were met by figures exiting the control room. In the darkness, Reagor shouted, "Get down on the ground!" He moved toward the boys with his gun drawn, followed by another officer. Bill and Matt dropped to the floor.

"Wait!" said Bill from his stomach. "It's okay. We're all okay now."

"How are we supposed to know that?" said Officer Reagor. "We just went through hell out there. Everyone attacked us."

Bill could see the scratches and red marks across the officer's plump face. Reagor kept his firearm pointed. Earlier they had been able to end the situation without guns, but the violence was escalating. They had found one man on the trail with a stab wound to the thigh and now another man was dead—killed in horrific fashion.

"What happened in there?" Reagor nodded toward the control room.

"That's where they were changing people," said Bill.

"Someone's dead in there," said Reagor.

"I had to," said Bill. His voice cracked with panic. "It was self-defense."

"Watch him," said Reagor to the other officer, who kept his gun aimed at the students on the ground. Reagor took a zip-tie from his waist and secured Bill's hands behind his back.

"What are you doing?" said Matt.

"Don't move," said the officer.

"This is a murder investigation now," said Reagor. "And until we get some more answers and find out what in God's name was going on here, we're going to detain you."

Reagor stepped over Bill to Matt and secured his wrists with a zip-tie. It was time to get to the bottom of this completely absurd and inconceivable situation.

Law enforcement from across the state flooded into Eternal Springs in the early morning before sunrise to conduct interviews, search the grounds, and catalogue evidence. All students and faculty were accounted for. There were cuts and scrapes, several broken bones, a separated shoulder, and a concussion. Bill apologized profusely to Scott about the baseball to his head, but Scott only apologized even more profusely back to Bill for trying to attack him before thanking him for turning him back to normal. Parents were notified that an 'incident' had occurred and were assured their sons were unharmed—more or less—but were recommended to drive to the retreat as soon as possible. Scores of reporters were kept at bay by the entrance at the highway, completely unaware of what was going on, only knowing that a huge contingent of law enforcement had rallied at the area.

The entire campus was filled with cars and people going every which way. Bill sat alone, holding a cup of hot cocoa, wrapped in a blanket on the grass next to the lake as the sun began to rise. The air was cool, and he could faintly see his breath as he exhaled. He checked his watch: 5:57. He was no longer restrained or bound, nor did he fear any forthcoming murder charge. His story, when compared and contrasted to every other story, was deemed to be the truth, or, in this case, as close to the truth as could be considered possible.

The students who had been changed remembered every moment of their 'sanctity.' They remembered each of the retreat sessions, the meals and the free time, and the final night—running around the grounds trying to catch their fellow classmates and attacking them and the police officers. They all felt bad about it, but they stressed that they'd had no control over their actions. A voice in their heads had told them to do it, and they absolutely had to. Now, with their free will and their ability to control their actions once again restored, they only complained of slight headaches.

The three St. Zeno chaperones were found to be back to their normal selves as well. Mr. Linderman had only just been turned, and Father Stephen was able to avoid being turned altogether. However, he had multiple broken ribs along with several cuts and bruises to his face. When questioned about 'leaving two boys in harm's way to save himself,' he replied, "I was going to get help. I would never leave any of our boys behind. I sacrificed myself so that they could get away." It was left at that.

Father Leo's last memory of being himself came from his site visit at the retreat in February. He couldn't believe he was the one responsible for bringing his students to this place. The shame and embarrassment of endangering them and failing to protect them overwhelmed him, and he'd broken down in tears. All he could do was repeat over and over that he was sorry.

Dee corroborated Bill's story to a T and Matt was able to add the parts he knew, most notably the kidnapping and imprisonment of his girlfriend and her two friends. Officer Reagor confirmed Dee's story, starting with the car crash and struggle with Evan. He also confirmed the scuffle between him and his fellow officers and students at the retreat, which abruptly ended due to reasons he did not understand.

Bill's only opposition came from Eternal Springs' staff. Mark, before being transported to a hospital, told of how Bill was a crazed blasphemer who stabbed him and murdered Jacobs because he didn't believe in the good that Eternal Springs was trying to do for people. Abe and Luke told of how Bill, Matt and Dee had assaulted and tied them up. Most of this testimony fell apart due to Rachel and her friends' personal belongings being found in the staff house. They had no good explanation for how any of it got there. Abe claimed he'd intercepted the girls who were making an unapproved visit to the retreat and detained them until their parents could get them; however, none of the girls' parents had been contacted prior to the authorities reaching out to them. Delilah had fled with fellow leader Ben in a car during the police-student melee, but they were caught at a checkpoint forty miles away and brought back for questioning. The most damning evidence was recovered from the underground bunker. The room of cages looked bad enough, but scores of heavy sedatives were recovered as well. The technology discovered was far beyond anyone's comprehension.

Authorities were shocked by just how honest the Eternal Springs staff was, and there was one simple ironic reason for it—they couldn't lie. Lying was a sin, and they were forbidden to do it. Each told their own perverted versions of the truth, but it was true to them. They were the pious, trying to help the infidels. Leader after leader stated how they were there with one common goal: to spread the word of Jesus Christ, to cleanse the souls of the wicked unbelievers, and to bring everyone into God's kingdom. When asked if they sedated students and brought them to the bunker against their will, the staff answered with a resounding yes. The students had been unwilling to believe and follow on their own, so the staff had done what was necessary to purify their souls and make them true believers. When asked if they thought it was right to force their beliefs on others and remove any chance of free will, they replied that mankind had had its chance with free will and continuously wasted it on sin and doing the absolute bare minimum to be considered a child of God. The time for half-measures and platitudes was over. It was time for a reckoning, and as many sinners needed to be cleansed as possible before Judgment Day. God called them to do this, and they obliged with all of their hearts. How they accomplished this remained the biggest mystery of all. Everyone kept their mouths shut when it came to the machine, and the authorities still had absolutely no idea of how it worked.

One thing continued to eat at Bill—no one was found with a damaged eyeball. Whoever he had stabbed had not been found, and Bill knew it must have been the doctor... with the cold, icy stare that sent shivers down his spine. It was confirmed to Bill that a full living quarters had indeed been found in the bunker. He felt the doctor was the key to this all and told the authorities as much. Dogs were sent in every direction in the woods and roadblocks were set across the state. There would be no escape for him, especially with one eye, assured the authorities.

Bill waited as the hands clicked down to 6:15 on his watch face, and he imagined Jacobs' voice over the speaker.

"Good morning retreaters!" a voice called from behind him in a poor imitation of the deceased retreat leader.

Bill looked over his shoulder and saw Matt approaching with a big smile on his face, followed by Rachel and her friends and Dee and Pete, all wrapped in blankets. He sighed and rose to his feet. "Don't do that."

"Too soon?" said Matt.

Bill couldn't stop the wry smile. "Definitely too soon."

"How ya doing?" said Matt. He rested a hand on Bill's shoulder.

"I'm okay," Bill nodded. "What about you?"

"Good." Matt nodded with a twinkle in his eye. He fully knew that he owed everything to Bill. "I wanted you to meet somebody." Matt extended his arm to the cute girl with blonde curly hair. "Bill this is Maddie. Maddie this is Bill… our hero."

Bill held his cocoa in his left hand and stuck out his right hand through the blanket as his crush walked toward him. "Nice to meet—" She brushed by his hand and wrapped her arms around his shoulders. Her hair was so soft against his neck.

"Thank you," she said into Bill's ear.

Bill wrapped one arm around her back and said, "You're welcome."

"Hero my ass," chirped Pete. His arm hung in a sling.

Bill and Maddie pulled apart.

"He didn't do anything."

"Are you kidding me?" said Matt. "He's the reason we're fine now. And Dee, don't get me wrong. But mostly Bill. And who are you to talk? You were like the first one changed!"

"Oh, eat me!" said Pete.

"You told me you loved me," said Matt, rocking Pete with a one-armed shove to his healthy shoulder.

"Shut up," said Pete out of the corner of his mouth. He saw Sara next to him. "Now, Sara, you want to hear something heroic?"

Sara backed away. "No," she said solemnly.

Matt burst out laughing, and Bill chuckled as well.

"That's twenty each, Romeo," said Matt, wrapping an arm around Bill's shoulder.

"You guys are such dorks," said Pete before he turned and walked away.

Bill and Matt watched the serene lake.

"Well, they were right about one thing," said Bill.

"What's that?" said Matt.

"It really was a life-changing experience."

Matt grabbed the back of Bill's neck and rocked his head side to side. "It sure was."

Behind them, Rachel rolled her eyes and folded her arms.

CHAPTER 21:
And in the End...

—————

*D*ING. *D*ING. *D*ING. *D*ING. **BILL TURNED OFF THE ALARM, GOT OUT OF** bed, and walked past the collection of newspapers and magazines on his desk featuring pictures of him, Matt, and Dee on the covers with various headlines using terms like 'heroes' and 'saviors.' Bill's life had been completely turned upside down—every day interviews, every day questions, every day, everyone wanted to know what had happened. Every show on every network had tried to contact him while book and movie deals poured in. Bill had thought it might be fun at first, but after an appearance on *Good Morning America*, he'd become overwhelmed. The phone never stopped ringing, resulting in his mother canceling the house's landline and changing both her own and Bill's cell numbers. Even his grandma and aunts and uncles were receiving calls looking for an exclusive. News crews were unavoidable, stationed out front of his house, constantly filming and taking pictures despite the many warnings from police and lawyers to leave him be. It was his worst nightmare. He had never wanted any attention from anyone, but now a literal spotlight followed him wherever he went. He tried to push Dee and Matt into the spotlight, but the media wanted him and only him. Everywhere, eyes watched him.

Beyond the overwhelming chaos of the outside world and the excessive stress and anxiety caused by it, Bill was still tormented with guilt for killing a human being. The image of Jacobs covered in blood staring back at him continued to haunt his dreams. He had killed someone, something he'd never thought would even be a possibility in his life. He had to do it, he often reassured himself, but that didn't help calm his mind. St. Zeno had given him an indefinite leave from school to deal with all of the hysteria, but after two weeks, he was desperate to get back to a normal life.

The investigation into what happened at Eternal Springs continued rather aimlessly. The Eternal Springs staff remained less than helpful when it came to the technology. Authorities were no closer to determining how the machine worked and were incapable of replicating it, leaving them with more questions. Everyone who was affected by the machine complained of frequent headaches, and brain scans showed some abnormalities that would need to be researched further. But as of now, everyone was roughly back to normal. The best theory they could come up with was the machine somehow changed the architecture of the brain via radio waves which controlled the victims, hence the massive antenna that could potentially reach the city over one hundred and fifty miles away... Pretty far-fetched.

The lives of the staff were dissected from their moments of birth until their arrival at Eternal Springs. Jacobs had been a preacher, who lured his followers—the young, those scorned and betrayed by the world—with promises of salvation as he moved from small town to small town across the country. He was an old-school Christian, believing the church had become too lenient over the centuries and its followers too apathetic. The rest of the workers came from all across the country. They joined his ranks, taking on aliases based on religious characters and spread their faith. They formed their tight-knit circle consisting of all of the staff apprehended at Eternal Springs as well as one other person who remained unaccounted for: David. They had spent years trekking across rural America, gaining a small following of fanatics. Finally, it all came together in Hillsborough, Nebraska five years ago, where they built a new church for the 873 town members and surrounding folk.

In a stunning twist of events, the entire town of Hillsborough and the surrounding area had just recently 'awakened' right after the events of Eternal Springs. The townspeople finally felt like they were in control of their lives again. They remembered everything over the years. They'd borne and raised children, sent them to school, gone to work, had parties and celebrated—all of the things normal people would do. But it was a holy town. Everyone attended church daily. New residents with no prior religious affiliations joined the hardcore sect within months of arrival. Upon review of the police reports, crime in Hillsborough was almost nonexistent, and what little crime there was had always been committed by an outsider, someone passing through—never a citizen of the town. There were no homeless people or vagrants; each was lovingly welcomed into a home. Life in Hillsborough was virtually perfect, just as Jacobs and his helpers had promised. Except for the whole being brainwashed and having no free will part.

The town returned to normal, and crime rose, and church attendance dropped significantly. Some gave up religion entirely, while others continued with their faith, saying what had happened to them wasn't their theology, just a false prophet. Everyone questioned named the Eternal Springs members as people who had worked at the church in Hillsborough. They were moving on to another place to continue to spread the word of God, while David remained behind with the Hillsborough residents. No technology that could explain the incident had yet been recovered from the area, and David was never found. No one matching the description of the doctor at Eternal Springs was mentioned in Hillsborough, and none of the staff would speak of him other than to say he was part of their calling. Every investigation into Dr. Knapp had led to a dead-end, and he remained missing as a most-wanted person of interest.

The apprehended staff were charged with a plethora of felonies, including kidnapping, false imprisonment, and several assaults. They were disgusted but not surprised when no charges were brought upon Bill for murder. But in the end, they knew Bill would be judged by God and would 'burn in hell for all eternity.' "You may punish us in this world, but you have no control in the afterlife, where we will be welcomed by our loving Father into heaven," Delilah told authorities. Worried family members, hoping that someday their sons and daughter would return to them, were devasted to learn about what they had been a part of. The people they had known and loved were gone forever. The workers never believed that what they were doing was wrong. They were completely justified in their thoughts. They were clear in their message: they were the chosen ones, and they were doing God's work. How else would they be capable of this power? It was bestowed upon them, and they were creating Eden on Earth, leading everyone to salvation.

St. Zeno had devolved into its own chaos. Father Leo had resigned in shame followed soon thereafter by Father Stephen. Father Andrew was made interim principal. All faculty, staff, and priests were thoroughly questioned by authorities, but no connections were made to the events at Eternal Springs. The campus was overrun daily with more and more reporters. Police had to cut the main entrance off at the street, allowing only students, parents, and faculty through with the proper identification. Media members wised up and ditched the branded vans for regular old cars and snuck through the blockades. Once notified of their unwelcome presence, armed security hired by the school would escort the media members off the campus.

Countless parents, citing legitimate safety concerns, immediately pulled their children from the school. Some scrambled to get their kids transferred to different schools, while others would finish out the year either remotely through St. Zeno or via private home schooling. The rest resigned themselves to waiting out the final few weeks of the school year before transferring over the summer. A small band still outwardly supported the school, believing it was safe and the best place for their children to get an education.

Bill's return to school was no help: priests, crosses, prayers… everything brought him back to the retreat. Bill had gone to the retreat to find God and to renew his faith, to find meaning in his life. But Bill was left with more doubt than ever. *There can't possibly be a God. How could God let that happen? How could he let those psychos abduct of all those children and not intercede? That's proof. If there were an all-powerful being it would be so simple to stop what happened.* However, each time he reached the conclusion there was no God, he would have second thoughts; twelve years of training was tough to erase. Maybe God had helped him. Maybe he was the real chosen one. After all, the stag was sent to him by God to stop him from killing himself and to offer up as a sacrifice. Or was that just purely a coincidence… an incredibly timed and appropriate coincidence? The priests added their own unwanted advice along the same lines. "Perhaps God worked through you and gave you the strength to save everyone. Perhaps you were an instrument of God."

"Does that make me the son of God?" questioned Bill.

"I doubt it," reflected Father Andrew.

Bill struggled to keep his head on straight, and he found himself scrambling to finish an assignment before the morning bell rang. Matt walked into the classroom, and all of the students clapped for him. Someone shouted, "There goes my hero, watch him as he goes!" Matt waved his thanks to the adoring crowd and sat down next to Bill.

"It's been two weeks," said Bill. "How much longer are they gonna keep doing that?"

"Hopefully forever," said Matt. "It's nice to walk into a room and have everyone love you."

"Yeah, sure," said Bill. He turned his attention back to his homework.

"What's that?" said Matt. "Trig?"

"Yeah," said Bill. "I had to do more interviews yesterday. I didn't have time."

"Tell me about it," said Matt. "I can't even keep track of how many I've done."

"That's what we get for being heroes," said Bill.

"That took forever," said Matt, pointing at the homework. "I probably did it all wrong."

"Well," said Bill, "I've got two periods, so I should be able to get it done."

"Bill," the teacher called out.

Bill looked up and saw the teacher holding a note.

"Father Andrew would like to see you."

Bill got up as the class 'oohed.'

Bill dropped his pencil in the seam of the textbook and closed it. "Or not," he said dejectedly as he rose from his desk.

"At least you have a good excuse," said Matt. "You were saving the world."

"I'll probably have to explain how I did it using trig." Bill grabbed the note from the teacher.

"Tuck your shirt in."

Bill clutched the note in his right hand, walking down the empty hall. *What does Father Andrew want with me? I just talked to him a couple of days ago.* Bill's concentration was broken as Keith walked toward him, and Bill braced for a confrontation. Just two days ago, Keith had told him, "You're no hero. You're a zero." A fairly benign and lame comment, but it showed that Keith was his usual self, and Bill did, in fact, enjoy disliking Keith more than he liked being fake friends with him. It was just... normal.

Bill prepared his stink eye as he passed Keith.

Keith smiled and said, "Hi, Bill."

"Hey," Bill said through gritted teeth.

Keith stopped, keeping the kind smile on his face. He looked relaxed and happy. "Do you wanna get a milkshake after school?"

Bill's stomach dropped. *It can't be.* "No thanks," he said, hoping Keith would burst into laughter from his prank. "I have some stuff to do."

"No problem," said Keith, completely unaffected by Bill's rejection of his invite. "Have a blessed day!"

The words pierced Bill's heart like an arrow, and he stood there stunned. What was happening? They couldn't be here. It was over.

Bill continued his walk to Father Andrew, heart racing. He thought about running out of the main entrance doors, running as far as he could to escape. *Keith was just messing with you. That's all that was. Everything is fine.* He turned from the exit and made his way down the hall of staff offices until he arrived at Father Andrew's new office—Father Leo's old office. He found the elderly interim principal sitting at the desk flanked by two priests he didn't recognize in long black cloaks.

"Hello, Father," said Bill, quickly tensing up as six eyes fixated upon him.

"Ah, hello, Bill," said Father Leo. "Come on in. Shut the door. Have a seat."

"Okay," said Bill. He shut the door, keeping his eyes locked on the three priests in front of him and hesitantly sat in the chair across from Father Andrew. "What's going on?"

"Oh, nothing, Bill," said Father Andrew, in his usual calm and welcoming tone. He kept his hands interlocked on the desk. "Just wanted to have a quick chat with you."

"Okay," said Bill. His hands clutched the arm rests. "I'm not in any trouble am I?"

"Oh no, of course not," said Father Andrew. "We just wanted to see how you're doing. It's been a circus around here."

"Yeah... I'm all right," said Bill. "It's been pretty crazy with all of the reporters and news stuff. But it's been starting to slow down a bit now. I think everyone's getting sick of me."

Father Andrew laughed. "Well, you are the big hero."

"Yeah, that's what they tell me," said Bill. "I'm just ready to get back to my normal life."

"I don't blame you," said Father Andrew. He unclasped his hands and sat back in the chair. "Unfortunately, I can't let you."

Father Andrew nodded to the two priests, and they came towards Bill on either side of him.

"What?" said Bill. He pushed back in his chair at the advancing priests, nearly toppling over. "What's going on?"

The two priests each grabbed Bill by an arm and restrained him. When he tried to scream, one of them clamped his hand over Bill's mouth, and only a muffled cry came out.

Father Andrew remained seated. "Everything was proceeding as planned, but you had to ruin it. You had to be the hero. We failed the first time. We won't fail again."

Father Andrew nodded toward Bill. Bill's head was pulled to the side by his hair, and above him Dr. Knapp came into view. Bill had no idea where he had been hiding. His cold stare was even more frightening now due to the bandage covering one eye socket. His lip curled as he held a syringe, ready to exact revenge. Bill fought as hard as he could, to no avail. The doctor plunged the needle into Bill's neck and everything went black.

Bill woke up standing, but not under his own power. He was strapped into some sort of device with each of his arms extended to his sides, like Jesus nailed to the cross. His vision was blurry, but he could make out other people in the room—he wasn't alone.

"Good. I wanted you to be awake for this."

The doctor lightly slapped Bill on the face until Bill fully awoke.

"You bastard," said Bill. "You won't get away with this."

"Bill," said the doctor, "I already have." A small smile formed on the side of his face with the working eye, and he pointed across the room to Bill's mom and Matt watching him with happy vacant expressions.

"No!" Bill tried to break free. "Noooo! Help me! Mom! Matt! Wake up! Help me!"

"It's not worth the struggle," said the doctor. "They won't be helping you. But don't worry, soon you will be with them. And you will finally be at peace."

Doctor Knapp strapped the helmet on Bill's head and walked over to the controls.

"No!" pleaded Bill. "Please."

The doctor turned the machine on, and power surged through the wires into Bill as he screamed.

Bill's eyes snapped open, and he jumped to his feet, knocking his books to the floor. He frantically searched the room while his classmates stared at him in amazement. He finally realized he was in school.

"Are you okay, Bill?" asked Mr. North.

"Yeah," said Bill. "Yeah, I'm fine."

"Let me talk to you outside for a second," Mr. North said, motioning for Bill to follow him. They went into the hallway.

"I think maybe you should go home," said the teacher. "Why don't you

213

go down to the dean?"

"I'm fine," said Bill.

The teacher rested his hand on Bill's shoulder. "Bill, it's okay. Just go home and get some rest."

Bill took a deep breath. "Okay."

"Tuck your shirt in."

The words jogged Bill's memory of the dream. He hurried down the hall toward the main entrance, afraid to run into Keith. He looked through the wide bay of glass doors to the outside. Part of him still wanted to run. *It was just dream.* He turned to the hallway which led to the dean's office when a familiar voice called from behind him, "Hey, Billdo."

Bill looked over his shoulder to see Keith. He didn't enjoy the sophomoric insult, but at least Keith wasn't asking him out on a milkshake date.

"Picking up another medal of honor?" Keith said with a scowl.

"Don't be jealous," said Bill.

"There is absolutely no reason for me to be jealous of you," said Keith. "I can't wait to get out here so I never have to see you or hear about you ever again."

"The feeling's quite mutual."

"Fuck off," said Keith as he turned down the hall to the classrooms.

Bill relaxed and chuckled as he realized everything was still normal. He continued to the dean's office, but he first had to pass Father Leo's old office. A pang of queasiness returned as he thought about the priests and doctor lurking within the room, and he tried to hurry by the doorway.

"Bill?" Father Andrew called from inside the office.

Bill froze.

"Bill, come here, please."

Bill walked back to the doorway, heart racing.

"Yes, Father?"

Father Andrew was alone, sitting at his desk. "I wanted to talk to you; see how you're doing with everything."

"Well…" started Bill. He took a quick peek behind the door which made the old priest raise an eyebrow… No one was there. "I just got sent home. So, I guess not too great." He was still too scared to step through the doorway. He kept his escape route open.

"Oh, I see," said Father Andrew. He walked over to Bill and rested his shaking, bony hand on his shoulder. "Well, you should take some time off. I can't imagine what you're going through; everything you saw, everything you did, having to take a life. It's unbelievable."

"Yeah." Bill nodded and relaxed.

Father Andrew brought his other hand up and rested it on Bill's other shoulder and looked him directly in the eyes. "I'm sorry, truly. I'm sorry you had to go through that. It's our fault: choosing that place, not stopping it, not protecting you. We failed you terribly."

Bill believed all of that to be true, but he could see the pain in Father Andrew's eyes. He was sincere, and there was no reason to pile on. Bill said, "No one could have known that's what was going to happen. Even after living it, it doesn't seem real."

The priest removed his hands from Bill's shoulders and sighed. "No, it doesn't. It's hard to process. And it's hard to move on. But in time we will. And you will. I'm surprised you came back as soon as you did. Take some more time off and come back when you are ready. And not a second before, okay?"

"Okay," said Bill.

"Things will slow down soon, and you will be able to get back to your normal life."

"Yeah, I hope so," said Bill.

"If you need anything, just ask," said Father Andrew. "We are all here for you."

"Thank you, Father. Bye."

"Bye, Bill."

Bill's mom urged him to talk to someone about the problems he was having. His dream at school hadn't been the first, and they both knew it wouldn't be the last. The images of the bleeding stag, Jacobs' corpse, jamming the knife into the eye—all were burned into his memory. He wondered if he would ever see the doctor again or if his time in that nightmare had truly come to an end. Bill realized pretending that everything was fine wasn't going to work. Staying hidden in his shell wasn't going to protect him or make him feel better. Bill needed help, and he finally admitted it.

Perhaps the only positive that came from the trauma of Eternal Springs was Bill's decision to see a therapist. After talking about the incident and the killing of Jacobs and the stabbings of two others, the floodgates opened and everything poured out of Bill: his sadness and loneliness, his embarrassment and hatred of himself, his crippling anxiety and fear of life. It all came out, and it felt like the world's weight was off his back, if just for a fleeting moment. He still had so much more work to do, but the first step, the hardest one, was done.

While Bill made progress emotionally, spiritually he had reached his final conclusion—he would never lead a religious life. It just wasn't for him. There was no fate, or destiny, and God certainly didn't have a plan. The world was chaos, and he would just do his best to navigate through it. He wasn't interested in leading any crusades against believers, and if following and praising God added to your life and made you happy, Bill was happy for you. His faith in humanity ebbed and flowed as the world did its usual things, and he was able to trust and believe more in those close to him. At the very least, he had found a renewed faith in himself and a strength he didn't know he possessed.

In the following weeks and months before college, Bill learned to not blame himself for what was out of his control and for the failures of his father, and began to gain the ability to accept himself for who he was while not focusing on the person he wasn't. Bill didn't consider himself a hero, but he at least accepted that what he had done was good and important, and it gave him a long-needed sliver of self-confidence. He was still quiet and mostly kept to himself, but he had a newfound feeling of happiness and peace. He became a bit more social, hanging out with friends on a regular basis, and he even went on a couple of dates with Maddie. The bad memories would fade in time, and he was determined to replace them with good ones. While the events of the retreat would always be a part of him, for the first time in a long time, Bill looked to the future with hope.

Made in the USA
Coppell, TX
02 May 2022